The Haunting at Morsley Manor

GEORGE MORRIS DE'ATH

This book is a work of fiction. Any references to historical events, real people, or real places are used fictitiously. Other names, characters, places, and events are products of the author's imagination, and any resemblance to actual events, places, names, or persons, is entirely coincidental.

Text copyright © 2025 by George Morris De'Ath

All rights reserved. For information regarding reproduction in total or in part, contact Rising Action Publishing Co. at http://www.risingactionpublishingco.com

Cover Illustration © Nat Mack

Distributed by Simon & Schuster

ISBN: 978-1-998076-66-6
Ebook: 978-1-998672-00-4

FIC015040   FICTION / Horror / Occult & Supernatural
FIC015060   FICTION / Horror / Slasher
FIC015000   FICTION / Horror / General

#TheHauntingofMorsleyManor

Follow Rising Action on our socials!
Twitter: @RAPubCollective
Instagram: @risingactionpublishingco
TikTok: @risingactionpublishingco

The Haunting at Morsley Manor

Prologue

England, Trewnway – 2015

*D*eath is easy, it's the living that have it hard, the ones left behind, Shannon thought as she knelt with her camera, taking many shots of the festering, fly-covered cadaver of a squirrel. Dead, drained, and rotting, it was perfect for what she needed. Reviewing her last shot, she puckered her lips at the way the sunlight hit the crusted slime of blood that had congealed darkly down the mammal's chin. A college student, Shannon had managed to build quite the collection of deathly things in the woods of the village of Trenway, England, for her photography course. She sighed with relief, knowing she had finally sponged enough horror to take back home with her to edit and compile. About time too, as the day had stretched into a gaping void of a yawn.

Shannon didn't quite understand what all the fuss was about with the area supposedly being haunted. The nearby Morsley house had so many horror stories connected to it. The Google images she had looked up certainly made the dank, yet pointed, dark features of the house seem foreboding, the home of all manner of horrors. But that house she saw was just on a flat piece of paper and, more importantly, ghosts weren't real. Twisted tales appealed to Shannon, the types that made her stay up all night long when she was a child, the ones she couldn't help but listen to or watch on the horror channels far past her bedtime. Yes, the appeal of Morsley's tales scratched a certain itch for people, scratched it so hard it seemed to draw blood. Surely that's all Morsley was, a load of scary stories, and embellished ones at that.

Assessing the angle and lighting at which she captured the last shot on her digital camera, Shannon rotated through images to see more dead, furry rodents. She wasn't sure if they were squirrels, rats, or other creatures. They were so bloodied and mangled. Parts were missing, and they seemed ... drained of fluids with fang indents as proof. *What could do such a thing? A wolf? A stray dog?* Shannon blinked in the dim light. She shouldn't be out for too long; she didn't want to end up as a husk, like the small prey on the leaf-covered ground.

A snap from behind caused Shannon to jerk her head around. Tremors of a chill crept up her nape. Then, a loud gulp issued from the seventeen-year-old as she turned to leave the forest. She looked this way and that, but the thin trails looked the same. *Shit, I'm lost.*

Her camera shutter went off without being triggered, causing Shannon to jump. She gazed down at the small screen, which revealed dense trees with a shadowy figure lurking behind one. Shannon's eyes widened, and a cold sweat broke out, beading down her forehead.

Shannon lifted her camera and took another shot. The silhouette stood closer this time. When she looked up from the viewfinder, there was nothing in front of her.

She took another shot. Shannon's thumping heart skipped a beat as multiple spectres—void of matter—swallowed the entire frame. She froze, gazing at the nothingness.

A whisper crept into her left ear, "You shouldn't be here."

Shannon ran faster than she ever had, heading in the first direction she saw, straight and forward.

After sprinting until she couldn't any longer, Shannon found the notorious house she'd heard so much about: MORSLEY MANOR. It looked exactly as it had in articles and books, only more intimidating. Tall, ominous, and engulfing all the landscape, the manor snuffed out the last remaining sunlight. Being the only shelter or possibility of help she saw, Shannon stumbled to the front door. Pounding upon it, the wooden entrance creaked open, unlocked.

She pushed the door open, revealing a foyer with a grand set of stairs beyond.

"Hello! Hello? Is there anyone here?"

No one answered. Her voice bounced off the walls. She passed what appeared to be a museum set with photos, which she believed to be of the previous owners. Their eyes followed her. *This place is a museum now? Maybe it's not public knowledge yet?*

Reaching into her pocket for her phone, Shannon turned down, and looked to see the screen glitching violently. Pixels and static attacked the device. She tapped hard. She had never seen anything like it. Giving up, Shannon placed the phone in her pocket and walked to another vacant room. A small doll, redheaded with a sinister grin, sat on a chair in its finest dingy, stained white dress. Shannon didn't like dolls. She never had. Turning to nose around the dining room, she eyed a large mirror that hung on a wall. As she inspected the mirror, a ghastly, white-dressed figure walked past, from behind. Shannon shuddered and broke into a cold sweat; she swore it'd been a doctor or surgeon wearing bloodstained attire.

Shannon hastily, and as cautiously as she could, made her way to the door. The dirt road ahead went on for miles. Her car was parked in a small field about a mile or so away.

What to do? Shannon inhaled and exhaled at a rapid rate, her brain scrambling. Which way to go? Perhaps there was someone or something that could help her around the rear of the house? The idea that anyone else would be there was a stretch, but a hope she clung to. Sneaking to the back of the building, she breathed in relief to see nothing, her gaze then turned to every corner, uncertain if anything would or could pop out next. She froze in place and the hairs on every inch of her skin stood to high end—a presence was watching her from above. Shannon spun and slowly lifted her head.

A circular window in the attic housed a black figure: a woman, rigid and firm, looking down. The woman's face was blurred by the fading light of the sky, but Shannon knew the stories and the history of the estate well enough to know it was Lady Morsley.

It's true. All the stories. If Shannon wanted to avoid becoming a meal for the hungry land, she had to get the hell out of there—fast.

As she fled, Shannon spied a rickety old shack beside the house that sported two large chipped away doors, one of which creaked open. Her hands seized, but she forced her legs to keep moving. Pale balloons on frayed strings floated outward, held by a dirty hand. Something crept past the corner of the other door, wearing a sinister smile which was bloodied, yellow, toothy, raw, and stapled high up on pale cheeks. Wisps of faded, blue-dyed hair glinted in the shadows. The creeper's pus oozing, button eyes twinkled in the fading light, and a long, brown-coated finger beckoned her closer.

Shannon spun round and sped off. Running deep into the woods once more, she bet her odds were increased there, rather than near the cursed house. She tripped over a thick tree root jutting out of the soil.

Stumbling down a steep hill, Shannon felt her body collide with rocks and trees. Finally, her broken form fell flat, her face in a heap of dirt which tasted of iron.

A crunch emitted below her chest when she lifted her weight off the ground, relieving herself from the digging sensation deep within. *Was it a rib?* No, it was her camera, smashed to pieces. A weary sigh escaped her as she tried to bat away tears. She leaned against the trunk of an old tree. *All this, and for what?* Blood seeped through her clothes.

The adrenaline coursing through her waned, thickening like cement. She felt numb, as if her body wasn't hers, like it belonged to the place. Maybe the house was only tenderizing her for what was to come.

No. She could get out of this. She just needed to sit for a while and gather her strength. *There has to be a way out,* she pounded into her consciousness.

Twigs snapped, though Shannon could not place from which direction. Her muscles stiffened as growls and howls sounded. Vicious creatures of torment. She hoped the dry vines, strangling thorns, and shrubbery would help cover her up, and whatever it was would move on. She waited a good, long minute before the noises lessened. At last, she exhaled. Her lips trembled and her hands jittered as she sat at the base of the withered tree trunk. Shannon would never get the chance to exhibit her work if she died. She might never be able to get married, or have children, or see the world. The realization stabbed her heart; right here and now was most likely it for her. The awareness broke her spirit and soul in two. Her energy seeped into the veins of the land before a slithering, mud-covered, clawed hand reached around the base of the tree. Shannon's story ended before it had ever even had the chance to begin. For the darkest of creatures are so often the hungriest.

1

Firebird

North Carolina, Asheville – 2013

Clouds loomed over the derelict Travers Orphanage. Drizzle increased the chill as cold wind blew through loose window joints. Whispers travelled through the abandoned corridors. A wanderer had arrived, a man. With light, scruffy honeycomb-coloured hair and hazel eyes. He wore a white shirt and a blue fitted blazer. He had draped a navy and white ombré trench coat around himself, and a stopwatch chain dangled from one of his many pockets. His boots clamped to the creaky, termite-infested floorboards. In his hands, he brandished a device. The EMF detected electromagnetic fields, a known attribute of the supernatural—his line of work. He was, of course, the world's most infamous and controversial paranormal researcher, Eric Thompson.

This case proved to be even more spine-chilling than most. Mr. and Mrs. Hickford hired Eric a few days earlier to find their missing daughter. *Stupid kids and their dares*, Eric thought. Alice Hickford and her friends broke into the orphanage, and now, she was lost within its walls. *Was she still alive? How could she survive alone here? Just a girl, a child of twelve years old.* Eric recalled her face from the picture provided by her parents on the case file: a lovely girl with curly brown hair, sky-blue eyes, and dimples.

The grief-stricken and frantic Hickfords searched the orphanage themselves, but the only trace of their child was the word "firebird" written on a wall in rat's blood. Someone left the animal's corpse behind as evidence.

In the early hours of the second day, the police searched for Alice, finding no one at the abandoned orphanage.

Scratching sounds had been heard above, and the police had seen moving shadows which they'd attributed both to a stray dog or some kind of animal, but decided not to pursue it in case it had rabies or posed some other danger. The police continued their search for the schoolgirl, though they questioned whether the orphanage was an actual lead.

Eric knew better.

His ability—the gift he possessed since he was a child—told him all he needed to know. His intuition buzzed, tingling with his every breath of the damp air. He sensed the energy draining, the chill in the air climbing his spine toward his cortex. Sweat glistened from his forehead despite the cold. Oh, there was something cooking in this place. The squalor had held something cruel and twisted for a long while, dormant until disturbed. Unfinished business, perhaps? Or something else? Who or what had caused Alice to disappear?

Eric sensed he was getting closer. His intuition called him in the right direction, guiding him. He suspected that somewhere down the dark, endless tunnels and within the maze, Alice was being held hostage, not by a person but by something otherworldly. Eric would enjoy solving the case, yet he hoped for some extra, peculiar detail to make the challenge even greater.

He worked upstairs, which had its advantages, such as a better vantage point of the door and banisters. Eric could track the location of his newest companion in the supernatural, Megan Strong, stationed on the floor below him. This was her first real case. Megan was a young, overly keen, naive newbie who had been his research assistant for all of three weeks. Up until this point, she had remained in the office but was now out in the field investigating and learning about different phenomena from the man himself. From his position, Eric heard the house groan every time Megan moved around. Most investigators would stick together in a similar scenario: a *Scooby Doo Spooktacular*! However, Eric had learned during his time ghost hunting that splitting up was more likely to provoke the spirits into revealing themselves. With such a large building, they had a lot of ground to cover. Besides, being alone added to the adrenaline rush in which Eric revelled when on a hunt.

As he sneaked through the broken walls, roaches scurried in and out of the plasterwork. If he'd been in a horror movie, he imagined an arm would lash out and grab him. Nothing did. There was only silence. Broken picture frames dangled from the walls, pictures of the orphans now hanging like nooses.

The Carolina Orphanage closed twenty years ago due to abusive staff and accommodation problems. Megan had informed him during the ride. She carried out her research thoroughly. She'd found countless reported cases of neglect—so different from the New York orphanage Eric started out in. His home. His childhood. His beginning. It was possibly the happiest time of his life. *A cheerful place, unlike this orphanage.* It had been the place he'd met the only family he ever knew. His friend, and, in many ways, his brother.

The eyes in the photos on the walls seemed to follow him, as if appealing to Eric to leave the orphanage. He choked on the dust, which rattled his lungs and made him wheeze.

"You alright?" Megan called from below, her New Jersey accent apparent.

"I'm fine, Megs. You find anything?" Eric asked as he entered the dark room and switched his flashlight on. He turned off his EMF device and put it into one of his large pockets, relying on his flashlight and senses as he moved forward.

Megan's voice echoed through the floorboards. "Nothing yet. You?"

Eric paused at finding the windows of the room boarded up. A dirty mattress lay on the floor, heavy with decay and stains. Dead rats surrounded the mattress, all of which seemed to have been sucked of blood for sustenance. Broken toys gazed up when he passed, their eyes and plastic skin reflecting off his flashlight.

"Almost." He'd found the epicentre. Surely his presence would trigger something. Hair, nails, and teeth carpeted the floor, crunching like snow beneath his boots. Eric knelt down to utilize a part of his gift. Gently, he touched some of the leftover DNA. In doing so, a flash of images of the past, of a long-haired creature in that room on the mattress, pulling its hair out, gnawing its fingers and ripping out its teeth as it rocked itself, hunched over. The image of the monster misted away as Eric was brought back to the here and now. *What the hell was that thing?*

It looked human, he realized upon reflection with a loud gulp, winching himself up to stand, to find something, a message on the wall. The word written in blood: firebird. *What does it mean? Is it a message from Alice or from the thing keeping her here?*

A prickly sensation climbed up the base of his neck. He knew what it meant. Someone was watching him. Eric turned swiftly, reflexes prepared for anything. Something scuttled past the doorway—a blur in his flashlight. Eric could handle it, whatever it was.

He approached the door with caution, treading upon the dead matter covering the floor. Taking a deep breath, Eric stepped back into the grey, barely lit corridor. And found nothing.

A creak came from the right. Eric jerked his head to see, but the hallway was empty. A viscous snarl emitted from the left. From the corner of his eye, the blurry form of a creature climbed upward, disappearing through a hole in the wall. Eric rushed toward the crack, shining his flashlight inside. Nothing but moths. Stuck between relief and disappointment, Eric sighed. Above him, dust fell, and the ceiling rumbled.

Eric tracked the creature's crazed journey around the never-ending corridors. It moved fast. Eric ran, tripping over debris on the floor.

Without warning, the creature's movements stopped. As did Eric. He held still.

Megan's voice broke the silence. "What's happening? Have you found her?" The young woman's voice shook with uncertainty.

"Not yet!" Eric shouted back, angry and frustrated. He couldn't blame Megan for her lack of experience, but it still aggravated him that she'd chosen to call out given the circumstances. Worse? It threw him off the creature's path. Something scurried from behind. The mysterious being crawled away at the end of the corridor, escaping him. It resembled a hairless spider, but with larger and thinner limbs. Eric *hated* spiders. He ran after the arachnid monstrosity. "Megan! I need you!" he yelled.

He ran too fast to catch her reply, dodging broken furniture as he went. Each time he turned a corner, he caught up with the large-limbed monstrosity. Eric's heart raced. *This is what I live for.* While scuttling away, the creature used its back legs to shove things off tables and walls to slow Eric down. Its efforts did not work. The creature rotated around the twisted terrain, clinging to every available surface, hopping around like a deranged, demented, jumping spider.

Eric arrived back at the banister and realized he'd gone in a circle. No sign of Megan. *No doubt she tried to follow me and got lost in the maze.* The specimen scampered back inside its darkened room. It was trapped.

He jogged toward the half-shut door and pushed it gently. A bewildering array of animalistic, unnatural growls and cries surged. The door creaked open, revealing the critter, which, when he shined his flashlight upon it, was more humanoid than Eric expected. Bloodied and short, ripped nails, with large hands shrouding the being's face, it retreated to a secure position, its glowing eyes peering through its fingers. Its feet were large, and its ribs showed through its skin. It was pale and bore hardly any hair. The fiend wore ripped clothing: dirty trousers and a purple T-shirt.

The being had adapted to its habitat. Much like the orphanage, the specimen was damaged, stuck in its own sick history of pain. Only after the demon's hands dropped down did it become clear what the thing was.

"Alice?" Eric said.

His torchlight repelled the deformed girl into the corner of the room. A feral animal of madness and despair, her pupils expanded to the point they eroded all the blue. The creature gnashed at the blinding light. Between missing teeth, he noticed brown, infected gums and dried blood crusted all the way down to her chin—the rats' blood, no doubt. Her lips were dark and cracked. What little hair was left on her scabbing scalp fell thin and grey—dead—and dangled over her skeletal shoulders. Her face was gaunt and skull-like, her ash white skin peeled in parts, as if shedding her former self. Seeing the once-pretty, innocent, young girl corrupted and twisted into a hellish monster turned and stiffened Eric's stomach. He knew he could fix her. There were ways. Whatever she suffered from could be reversed or repaired. He had to save Alice.

Eric heard a clambering of feet enter the room, as well as heavy panting from running through the tunnels.

"Thank God!" It was Megan. She winced in disgust when her head turned towards the abomination. "What is that?"

Still focusing the beam from his flashlight at the girl, Eric turned his head to face Megan. "It's Alice," he said. Megan's expression turned sour. "Are you okay?"

Megan composed herself. "I'm fine," she said, but could not hide her disgust as she gazed at the girl's new form.

"Good." Eric nodded calmly, trying to reassure her. She clearly struggled, given the pained look in her eyes.

Eric turned back to the growling, possessed Alice. Her cheekbones jutted out, tears trickling from her red-rimmed eyes. Eric licked his lips, preparing himself for the hard questions he knew he had to press. "Alice, do you understand me? Do you know who I am?"

The mutated girl wailed at his statement like a toddler having a tantrum.

"Your parents have sent me to bring you home." Eric stepped forward, leaning in.

Alice retreated further back, relying on her weak, stick-like legs for support. "No! No!" she cried, her voice a rasping croak. She lashed out at his hand and tried to creep past him along the wall, her eyes unblinking as she watched him.

Eric followed Alice's every move, mirroring her to block any chance of her escape. He forced a smile. "Yes, yes. Please. I'm not going to hurt you. I just want to talk. Take my hand. I can take you home." He reached out like they were old friends.

Her jaws snapped. "No! No! You don't know!" Alice cried, whimpering. "You don't know anything. No! Never!" She jerked away, her bones cracking. Shrouding and cradling herself in the opposite corner, Alice fidgeted and twitched.

Eric paused and adjusted his tone. "Who am I talking to?" he asked.

The girl stopped juddering. Time stopped. All was completely and abnormally still.

"What's your name?" Eric asked. He bent and gathered his courage.

Huddling in the corner, the creature appeared to think for a moment, likely blending both its minds into one. She whispered, "My name? My name?" Tears then began to fall from her bat-like eyes. The voice remembered. "Jennifer Langdon." A painful grin splayed across her distorted face.

"Is this how you've been living the past few days, Jennifer?" Eric asked, glancing around the dank room.

"For years and years," she wheezed, her neck cracking. "These walls are my home; it's up here that I'm not welcome." Jennifer pointed to her head with a short, ripped nail. Then she wept.

Eric turned to Megan and indicated for her to film the awful interaction for proof. Megan took out her phone.

"Do you remember who you are?" Eric continued. "I can help you leave this place and get some peace." He reached his arm out to comfort the sad abomination before him.

"Lies. All lies!" the girl screamed, pushing him away while moving swiftly past him and back to her filthy mattress. Her frail legs shook as she attempted to stand, which explained her crawling movement. They soon gave out, and she sank back down, her desiccated, twig arms seeming to fracture on impact with the dirty, flea-infested bed.

"Your body?"

A thin voice snapped back. "That brute, he broke me! He broke me!" Jennifer pulled at her ears.

"Who? Who broke you?" Eric asked.

She whispered the truth angrily, and it echoed throughout the house. "Daddy!" The being paused, then spoke in a harsher, louder whisper of remembered torment. "Daddy!"

Eric leaned over. "You remember?"

The creature known as Jennifer, housing poor Alice, covered her ears and spoke in anger and frustration, blanking out the rest of the world. "This place is a lie, a trick ..." She murmured nonsense that Eric couldn't comprehend.

He squinted at the girl through tired eyes. "Jennifer? What are you saying?"

She howled and winced. "He said he'd come back, but he never came back! Daddy!" Suddenly, she sprang at Eric, attacking him with all her weakened, dying might. Long fingers reached for the investigator's eyes. Without flinching, Eric unleashed a large, black onyx stone with an engraved symbol from his coat. It repelled Jennifer like garlic repels a vampire. Eric backed her into the corner as she wailed and hissed at the sight of his stone of protection.

Megan's eyes had grown large at the sudden turn of events. "Eric? How are you doing that?" she said, still holding out her phone. "What are you doing?"

"Something smart. Just keep recording." Eric's jaw tensed.

The beast clawed its way into the dusty corner using its flailing limbs to cradle itself. "Far above, far above, we don't know where we'll fall. Far above, far above, what once was great is now so small."

"Leave her. Leave, Alice. Now!" Eric ordered.

The creature's lips twisted into a bloodied smile. "She is mine." Jennifer gurgled a sadistic laugh of victory.

"Leave her!" Eric stepped forward, pressing the stone closer, inflicting more pain upon the struggling corpse.

"I can't! I won't!"

Eric's patience ran out. "You will."

The beast's neck cracked; it bit back in agony. "Oh, you're going to die," she said.

"We all die."

"Oh, no. You're going to die." She chuckled with deep satisfaction, gums salivating. "She waits for you." She pointed a twisted finger at him. "As *she* always has."

Eric moved away. "What do you mean?" His throat dried.

Jennifer Langdon unleashed a cackle of dark pleasure which carried through the orphanage. Eric's jaw tightened from the taunts. He sprang closer to her, the stone hovering inches away.

"Speak!" Eric ordered.

Tormented and damaged by the onyx's proximity, she morphed into the worst shape imaginable, snapping all the joints in her doll-like body. She writhed upon her stained mattress. Jennifer's back arched, her arms spasming like a drowning spider.

The house shuddered and shook. Wind blew through with the force of a hurricane. Three wooden panels fell from the windows, hitting the floor hard enough to send gusts of dead leaves flying. Light cut through the broken glass and against the girl, making her thrash even more. The walls cracked, and dust fell from the ceiling.

Eric wanted answers.

"That's enough!" Megan shouted.

He stopped, frozen in the moment.

"Enough!" Megan repeated, stepping forward, still recording.

"Stay back!" he snapped.

The creature ascended in mid-air as the wind in the room slowed. Dust floated down as the monster rose, limbs hanging limply.

"Oh, my God!" Megan said, her lips quivering.

Eric shuddered. The creature grinned, her skin cracking like clay. Her eyes sank inwards, the pupils rolling back into her head, showing only yellow whites. Eric retreated with his stone, but it was too late. The apparition continued to climb in tormented glory before, suddenly, the bottom of her spine snapped like a pencil. The crunch sounded like a thousand tree trunks breaking. Her wilted, broken body fell back down onto the mattress.

Megan dropped her arms, letting go of her phone, which was still recording. She left the room without saying a word.

Eric persisted, his blood like ice. He faced many things—and usually won. Of those he hadn't, none would stick with him the same as this.

None was as horrific. *That poor girl. Her parents.* How would he tell them what happened? They called him to save her. Did he kill her? Or had the thing inside her done so? Eric glanced down at the onyx in his hand and placed it in his coat pocket, his hands shaking. Looking back, he saw only Alice's mangled form, and with no trace of the pretty young girl with lovely hair and blue eyes he'd remembered from the case file. Only an empty vessel remained, used for whatever nefarious purpose, either deliberate or by mistake. Who was Jennifer Langdon? What did the place have to do with her? And why Alice? *At least now Alice is free and at peace. No one can hurt her any longer.*

2

Dark Past

Wrapped in a foil survival blanket, Eric sat brooding in the rear of an ambulance as Megan was giving a statement to police. Rain spat down on his forehead through the open door. *If only I had ... but* he knew deep down nothing would have changed the outcome. The Carolina Orphanage ended up being a case unlike most others he'd experienced. Only one previous case, many years prior, had also ended in tragedy. *Carolina Orphanage is nothing compared to that*, Eric thought. Still, images of this current dreadful day flashed inside his mind. Needing a distraction, Eric took out his phone and searched the internet for Jennifer Langdon. He found a news report:

3 June 1998

BREAKING NEWS: ORPHAN GIRL STRANGLED TO DEATH BY RAPIST GUARDIAN

GEORGE MORRIS DE'ATH

A child was found dead last week in North Carolina, Ashville, allegedly murdered by her adopted father for supposedly running away. The victim spent twelve years of her life in Travers Orphanage before its closure in August 1997. The victim was then adopted by the accused ahead of the closure. Police reports state the girl fled her new home several times and returned to the derelict orphanage. The accused broke several bones in the victim's body and strangled her to death. Police arrived on the scene after a distressed neighbour phoned having heard screams. They arrested the murderer as he was attempting to bury the body. A schoolmate claimed that the victim had told her the accused would, "Touch her and do weird things to her."

Eric had read enough. It explained everything. *That poor soul. Those* poor souls—both Jennifer and Alice. The sadness bellowed then dropped to a hum as Eric's mind flickered to the scene itself. What had she meant by, "She is waiting for you?" *She must have been confused.* What was the significance of the "firebird" message? *So many questions and not enough answers.* He could only hope Alice and Jennifer had moved on to a better place. Hopefully, they were at peace. Eric wished so for Alice. He wasn't as optimistic about Jennifer. *Some just can't let go ... they just can't quite seem to move on, no matter their state.*

He watched the mangled corpse get taken away in a black body bag, its disjointed bones making jagged mountain shapes. *Those poor parents.* Guilt cascaded over him for letting them down.

Eric wondered what would happen to him. A girl was now dead as a result of his intervention; that would no doubt have blowback on him. In the past, others had been charged with murder for performing exorcisms, but Eric had positioned himself in the media that he'd never been one to do them himself. Though he had been charged before, he was unsure if it was pure dumb luck, fate, or his witchy friends having his back that led to none of the charges sticking. Yet, it ate away at his core, his failure to save the girl and how this would have to affect his career. What would the media make of the situation? What would they say about him? His job wasn't what it used to be—not since the incident with his first partner. The press would love an opportunity to humiliate him again.

He possessed the video evidence Megan shot on her phone. Eric spotted her silhouette in the distance; she was speaking to a police officer, giving her report. She turned and made eye contact. As soon as she finished, she made her way over to where Eric sat, still in his foil blanket. Both remained silent as she slumped down beside him, exhausted. Megan gulped from a plastic bottle of water.

"You okay?" Megan asked.

Eric turned toward her. "Yeah. I'm loving my tin foil blanket." He gestured with his hand, causing the foil to rustle, reflecting light like a disco ball.

"Suits you," she mocked.

He stared at her, his smile dropping. "But really: are you okay?"

"I will be," Megan said.

"Course. Look at you. You can survive anything." Eric nudged at her with his elbow.

"Well, I don't know about that."

Eric knew he'd have to be careful how he responded and remained reassuringly calm. "Nah, you're Megan Strong, untouchable." He faked a smile.

"Yes. Well, I watched a little girl die today. I'm going to have to live with that for the rest of my life."

Eric's face scrunched up tight. "I couldn't have saved her ... she was too far gone. You know that, right?"

Wiping tears from one of her eyes, Megan sniffed. "It is what it is."

"Right."

Eric sighed in relief. He lowered his head to stare at his dusty boots.

"That thing you did in there, with the stone ..." she began.

"Yeah," he said in his muffled New York accent, trying to hide his shame.

"What was that?"

Eric stretched his neck, kicking his feet together, wishing he were away from the mess. "Just a little parlour trick I learned from a friend. Nothing more."

Megan turned. "Of course. Nothing more."

The pair watched Alice's parents, Mr. and Mrs. Hickford. Both were coping with the news in their own way. Mr. Hickford appeared to soak in his grief like a sponge while cradling his distraught wife; she'd been sobbing uncontrollably for the last twenty minutes.

Eric deduced what they were thinking—nothing could distract them from their raw pain. The joy that had begun at Alice's birth had been cruelly snatched away. With their child dead, nothing would ever be the same. Their hearts must be aching with longing to snatch away time from the past, time with their daughter, time they knew had run out.

Eric worked to process his part in the death. True, Alice had been too far gone to save, but there was usually hope. He remembered a detail. "Jennifer Langdon." He brought the article back up on his mobile. "I looked her up. She was one of the orphans. She got adopted by ..."

"No offence, Eric? But right now? I really don't care," Megan interrupted.

Eric scratched his wrist, unsure of what to say. "So, are you coming back to work?" he asked, hating the question because he already knew her answer.

"No." "That's fine," he said, trying to mask his feelings of cringing regret.

"I just can't."

Eric's hand rose to stop her from replying. "No. It's fine. I understand—"

"I really can't. I'm sorry. I mean, I've learned so much. But what we did? You live your life that way?" Her deep brown gaze watered.

Eric swallowed hard. "Not all the time."

Tears rolled down Megan's cheeks. "Well, you do. I know you do, and ... I can't."

Eric's expression fell as his heartbeat paused. His nerves twitched, not wanting to be left yet again by another companion. "You know, there's so much out there. So many beautiful answers to find," he said, trying to convince her to stay, despite her grating and sometimes clumsy inexperience.

"Yeah, so many beautiful answers with so many horrible nightmares to follow," she added. "That girl was screaming and dying, and you? You just stood there like it was an everyday thing. I don't want that. I can't become that person. I mean, you're terrifying. One moment you're cracking jokes, and the next you're chasing demons. I'm sorry, but I'm not cut out for this." She shook her head.

Eric shrugged. "Well then, I guess that's that," he said. "What will you do now?"

Megan processed the question. "Who knows? Travel. Get a proper job? I don't know. Just go out there, make it up as I go along, and live my life the best I can."

Eric removed his foil blanket, placing it as quietly as he could behind him in the back of the ambulance. "I think you're going to be great," he whispered, leaning toward her.

Megan stood awkwardly, her jacket shining in the lights. "Just do one thing for me and find that person who can stop you from going too far. Because I think sometimes you need to be told to stop."

Eric nodded and stood.

He evaluated his now former assistant; she'd grown so much in so short a time. "And, oh yeah. Here's your phone." He retrieved the mobile from his expansive pockets. "I have already sent the video to myself."

"Thanks," she said, taking the mobile, seemingly surprised to realize she'd forgotten about it. "Guess I'll have to ring someone for a lift." Megan walked away with a confident stride. "See you around, Eric Thompson," she said over her shoulder.

"See you around, Megan Strong." Eric saluted the young woman, accepting her resignation. He watched her leave through the rickety metal gate, gone to live her life away from the madness. Away from him.

Alone again, Eric believed life enjoyed punishing him. Might he ever fill the hole in his life? So many people had come and gone. He couldn't stop people from leaving. The game seemed rigged. He knew that he presented that of a very confident and self-assured person, but in truth, all he wanted was someone to share his adventures—and his troubles. Someone to help fill the void left by his one true friend—the one who'd disappeared many years ago. Every time someone else came to replace them, Eric was swollen with hopes of joy, though those feelings would always soon deflate upon realizing that they could never quite replace his one true equal in this crazy life. It was never the person's fault, Eric knew; he was the problem.

There, his legs swung, clutching his tin foil blanket with a crinkle. Swinging his legs triggered a memory, one itching below his thin skin that caused a faint grin to form on his face.

Five-year-old Eric sat alone by the side of the wet playground just outside the orphanage. Beside the plants, he plonked alone, swaying his legs in his tiny grey shorts. He watched the others, wondering why it was so easy for fellow orphanage children to make friends. He knew they didn't possess his gift, his power. They all called him a freak for it. Or, they called him a liar. Every day, Eric sat playing happily by himself until, one afternoon, he felt a thud beside him. A dark-haired boy with bright blue eyes held out a mutilated Barbie doll. He called himself Michael. Eric had always seen Michael from across the room but had never interacted with him. They were like the South and North Pole: connected in their loneliness but never able to bask in it together, the ability to meet was always there, they both just chose never to act upon it, not until now.

Bonding over juice boxes and snacks, and how small their hands were. This triggered their signature move, pressing their open palms against each other to compare size. They were both the same.

Michael went to collect a giant red ball for them to play with, which left Eric prey to one of the larger children, Steven. The boy who had the head of a hippo and the arms of a gorilla and knew how to use them, even at such a young age of seven. The boy grunted as he pushed Eric down to the ground, causing him to whimper. As Steven stood tall over the quivering Eric, a large ball bounced off his head, causing him to topple over into a rose bush.

Rushing over, Michael asked if his friend was okay before pulling him up and wiping his tears away. Eric felt seen for the first time ever, and smiled before running away from the scene.

New York, Eric's Home – Evening

That night, it started again. The familiar beginning of an old dream. The only dream Eric knew. One he had relived over and over again.

It always began the same. He was awake, his judgment clouded, shrouded in mist. His eyes focused through the fog. Wearing a clinical, white lab coat, he felt it and gazed down to see that he was wearing no shoes. His feet slid along the clean, white floor. A shimmering white light revealed a door of cut crystal. Nothing else—just a door surrounded by bright white. The entrance of this impossible place gleamed. Its majesty hypnotized him and pulsated pure energy through Eric's veins.

As ever, he approached the door, cautious of what may lie ahead despite having replayed the vision many times before. His palm clenched as he turned the handle. A rush of cooling static travelled along his arm, tunnelling around his spine to the stem of his brain. It electrified Eric's senses. In a rush of deliberation, he pushed through the entrance.

Nothing lay ahead—merely brighter, white light. He travelled slowly through the portal, walking a few feet ahead and turning to find that the entrance had disappeared. As he faced forward, he saw two humanlike figures, dressed in white and black leather, reclining on chairs. They appeared to be non-binary.

One of them had a huge black spider on top of their bald head, like a wig or a hat. Long black legs gripped their scalp. The spider's fangs rested atop the person's pale skin. Were the humanoids alive? Were they the arachnid's victims or pets?

The eyes of the two were shut, resting in a forever sleep. They had fingers but no nails. Their pallid faces had no eyebrows, but their eyelashes were as long and dark as the legs of the beast on one of their heads. Their lashes began to move. Spiders clambered out from within. Parasites. Their eggshell lips cracked open to unleash a gurgling fountain of black blood that trickled downwards. Small, dark, furry spiders scurried from the gaping jaw down to the floor in a long line, dotting the way like a treasure map.

Someone or something banged on the door. The sound pulsed like Eric's veins, accelerating with his heartbeat. He opened the door to find a stark contrast ... black. Darkness. Eric stepped forward, not knowing why, and fell. It was as if he were being pulled into the void's gravity. He should know this by now, having relived this punishment time after time.

He hit the ground softly. His eyes told him that he was in a grey woodland during a dim night. Yellow moonlight beckoned him. Something called to him with a gentle whistle—a sapphire blue owl with white feathers. It had golden talons, and the owl itself appeared to gleam in the moon's rays. They saw into each other momentarily. Then, angel wings spread outward from Eric's back and began to guide him through this decaying woodland after the owl. He struggled to keep his legs up, and twigs snapped underneath him as he moved.

Within seconds, his feathered friend vanished. Eric halted and scanned his surroundings. Nothing but twisted, dead trees reaching up tall into the starless sky. Objects began to jerk toward him: branches and twigs, like reaching arms. A trap?

Eric's bare feet sank into the ground. Panic controlled him as his weak knees began to be swallowed up by the earth. His ears tingled at the sound of drums with a perfect single beat. A shadow ahead of him called his attention. He looked up. Everything around him began to disintegrate.

A cloaked figure appeared in his peripheral vision. He caught a flash of a crazed grin below a heavy hood. A hand bearing long, yellow, dirt-encrusted nails reached out to him.

"Come to me, my lost one." The shrill voice carried on the blowing wind. Leaves swirled around Eric. He shut his eyes, begging this nightmare to end.

"No more!" he screamed. "No more!"

Eric woke from the dream, as he always did at that point. For that second after awaking, he was always relieved, only to realize seconds after that he would have to relive that never-ending hell once again, like the curse it was.

Eric rubbed his eyes, knowing no cure was ever a possibility, having seen many therapists and doctors about this curious nightmare. He didn't know what he would be without this dream. It was a part of him now. Perhaps one day, the truth might reveal itself.

3

Memory Lane

Two Years Later, GMD Studio fest, New York City, October 2015

Spotlights shone down upon a middle-aged man with receding grey hair. Large black glasses adorned his nose. He gripped his cue cards. He wore a fitted mic which picked up everything.

This is my stage, he thought. *Very close to Halloween.* The screen projector panel displayed: "Eric Thompson's Horror Nightmares" in tacky gothic white font against a black background.

Cedric Marion was a presenter, a regular at such fan event festivals. He sweated from excitement and fear. Things could go very wrong for him—or very right. Cedric was known for being overly camp and a seemingly nice interviewer, a softy. It was his gimmick in the business. He took a deep plunge, as he did every time, and spoke to his eager audience. They dressed for the occasion in Halloween costumes: ghosts, monsters, vampires, mummies, zombies, and there were even a few dressed as Eric and Michael.

Eric peered past the stage curtains at the gleaming, bright faces in the dark,
 seeing all manner of past cases glaring back at him in costume. The rabies case of the wolfman in the woods. The incestuous, hillbilly, bigfoot brothers. A few skeletal-looking mer-people from his deep-sea special. Eric itched his tight neck, recalling being in the submarine as he gazed briefly into that creature's glowing eyes. Someone even came as the megalodon. None triggered so much of a response more than the Michaels in the audience. Seeing them dressed in his usual leather bomber jacket and holding his swagger made flashes of his friend's face dart before him and cause him to step back slightly. Eric breathed deeply, concentrating on the echoing cheers from the audience. Clutching at his chest, he focused on the spotlights that blanketed out the crowd and his past. He was ready to tell his tales. He had never been the storyteller—that had always been Michael. The bright stage lights brought forth memories of when Eric and Michael would stay up late in the orphanage as kids. They used to shine a flashlight under their makeshift tent, competing with one another to tell the scariest story. Michael almost always won. Eric knew that Michael had a twisted mind, a deliciously twisted mind. No matter how much Michael's stories scared him, Eric would be settled enough to sleep as they ended the night with their signature move of pressing their palms together with a smile. That washed away all possibilities of nightmares invading his dreams, and

Michael promised to beat any demons or monsters that would pick on his best friend. Yes, Michael had been the natural storyteller, but these days, Eric was left to tell the masses of their adventures and scary stories, with no hand left to feel for comfort.

"His horrors were our delight!" Cedric announced, embracing the crowd's cheer. "Giving us years of mystery and wonder, award-winning and world famous, Ladies and Gentlemen, are you ready to welcome to the stage, paranormal investigator, Eric Thompson?" Cedric beckoned to Eric. "Let's give him a big hand!" As he clapped, the interview cards were clamped in his moist armpit.

A spotlight followed Eric onto the stage as he pushed back a lock of his hair, rolled up his white shirt sleeve and waved to all. The crowd roared, hollering as Eric blinked, momentarily taken aback by the sheer number of people there for him. He was expecting a decent number of people, but not the amount he was faced with then and there. Blood swelled his head.

"That's a lot more people than I expected!" Eric felt his cheeks flush hot, shaking Cedric's clammy hand, who then escorted him to the centre of the stage where two metal-framed, black leather chairs waited.

"Oh, it's a good turnout, right?" Cedric said.

"It's fantastic. I just wasn't expecting it." Eric stated, lifting his shoulders, giddy.

They sat on the squeaky leather chairs. Cedric's eyes lit up as he waited for the crescendo to die down, ready to begin the interview.

"So, first question of the day. How are you?" Cedric leaned in; his voice soft.

Eric crossed his legs, sitting back casually, and adjusted his position. "I'm having a ball," he said. "I mean, I'm here with all of you, aren't I?" He spread his arms, encouraging further applause. "I really do love it. Talking to all of you is just amazing, and I know that sounds pretentious, but it's so true. You guys really make my day." He grinned and clapped for his own fans, thanking them for their support.

"That's great!" said Cedric. "Now, we have to bring up immediately how good you're looking. I mean, you're twenty-eight now, right?"

Eric cringed a little with a forced smile and replied. "Yeah. It's quite scary saying it like that. But yeah!" He chuckled. The sound echoed and bounced off the walls.

"And for someone so young, we have to talk about what an amazing career you've had in that short time." Cedric barrelled on, using hand gestures to accentuate words. "Starting out at the age of twenty-one with your partner, Michael Goode, on YouTube with *Mysteries Explained* and well, let's be frank, it took off fairly quickly, didn't it, with over two million subscribers within nine months?"

"Yeah. It did. It's funny. We never expected that or planned it, or anything. We were really surprised by its success." Eric's eyebrows rose. "I mean, Mikey and I were best friends and grew up together in a New York orphanage. At that point, we were still together, working at a bar near Central Park called Fuzzy's." Eric grimaced, and he chuckled at the memory.

Everyone laughed at his reaction as he recalled the place, including Cedric.

Eric's tone turned casual. "I know, it was funny at the time. We started the channel as nothing more than a bit of fun because we didn't know what we wanted to do with our lives." He pressed his hands together. "But, as if overnight, people began to stop us in the street to ask us about the channel and our cases. It was really weird at the time, but so cool."

"Yes, it's amazing how it happened, but understandable, really—when you look back at those old videos. Take your first case at the Prestige Hotel and the ghosts there," Cedric said. "Can you talk a little about that, and the other cases that followed?" Cedric moistened his lips with some bottled water by his side.

Eric twiddled his thumbs, musing, before replying, "So, at the start, we barely had any money and were living together in a small apartment above a sandwich shop in Queens. We couldn't afford to travel far, so we would just go to places known for being haunted around New York and started filming and investigating. We only made six or eight videos and never expected to get what we got." He chuffed.

Cedric went on. "So, your first case at the Prestige." He pointed his cards toward the projector, and the title faded into a rough photograph of a dingy, darkly lit hotel room. A shadowy figure at the end of the room appeared against the yellow and brown flowered wallpaper. It stared at the camera, the spectre eerie.

Eric glanced up at the photo as he recalled the encounter. "Yeah. A lot of people thought we were faking it at first. Then, when 'experts' came in to debunk us, people realized it was genuine. What scares me is that people now choose to go to the Prestige Hotel and stay in rooms like number sixty-two, which is where we captured that image. And that's both scary and thrilling to me."

"Thrilling? Why?" Cedric asked, laughing a little.

"Well, because it shows just how curious we are despite the risks, doesn't it?" Eric's tongue pierced his cheek as he grinned. "Michael and I pushed our luck on a number of occasions, but this became our career. Some people ghost hunt just to see what will happen, and I love that." Eric ruffled his sun-bleached hair.

"Yes, well, we don't have the footage of it, but there's a moment where you called out to the spirits and we saw a hand grip your sleeve," Cedric said, re-enacting the moment using his own arm. "Right there," he said, pointing to a new slide. This one featured an arm clenched by an invisible force, the handprint clear as day, despite the picture's fogginess.

"In that moment, I was really thinking to myself: what the hell am I doing with my life?" Eric laughed. The audience joined in, falling silent again when Eric spoke up. "It was terrifying but strangely fun, which sums up what I do, really. It's what keeps me going." Eric itched his wrist, regretting his choice of words when it was known he had seen a girl die in front of him. "It's not always fun, as some stuff will haunt me until the day I die. A lot of stuff I regret seeing and experiencing, but I ... er ..." He stalled, biting his lip. "It's all for the greater good, right? To push the limits and learn more about the unknown, for all of us, for everyone."

'Yes." Cedric nodded and turned to his cards. "Now, after the initial success of that first year of ghost hunting, you two were offered your own show by GMD in order to expand, travel, and investigate."

"That's right," Eric replied.

"Can you tell us a little about some of those cases, like the one based around voodoo and zombies, which, might I add, was one of my personal favourites."

Eric uncrossed his legs, drawing one leg up to sit on his foot, swinging the free leg. "Oh boy. That was one of the best, I agree. There was so much there. The two specials focused on the witch doctors and priests of Haiti, who have moved all across the globe now, zombies, and voodoo were so interesting. Voodoo in our western culture gets stereotyped as being a form of dark magic—an evil thing—but it's primarily used for well-being and good fortune. We were very lucky to experience that. Michael was fascinated by it. And it does work," Eric continued, "As for the zombies, we didn't uncover any confirmed sightings, just the one moment when we thought we had found ..."

Suddenly, the screen transitioned to a blurred image of a ghastly creature on a dusty road between two walls. It possessed long, thin limbs, tattered clothes, and ribs you could play like a xylophone. From a distance, his eyes appeared milky white. He dragged a barrel of stones like a mule. Even though the image was poor, Eric recalled seeing it from afar, in person.

"There it is," Eric said, as if playing a game of spot the difference. "We saw some decades-old photos of these zombies from Haiti, where this originated, and heard some mountain walled in an isolated village in Europe, near Spain, called Valdelobos, was resurrecting the art or rather, punishment to create a workforce. Michael was really sceptical, but a priest, who originated from Haiti, came to the village, explained how it's done, and it's very clever." He nodded as if in approval of the method. "It's a kind of mix of science and spirituality. It was hard to find that picture because, as you can imagine, it's not practiced often now." Eric scratched his chin.

"So, how is it done?" Cedric's eyes narrowed.

"I can't remember everything specifically. It's all in the actual programme, but it's mainly drug-induced slavery," Eric said. "The priests of this village use powerful poisons to make their victims appear to be dead, then bury them, depriving the brain of oxygen for a time until they adapt to the change. Then the priests exhume the bodies and keep their victims in a drug-induced stupor to perform hard labour as slaves. It was often revenge-driven." He swallowed. "A kind of karma, as they see it. What I found interesting was that the enslaved would serve only them due to their limited brain capacity and that they felt no pain, no fear, nothing, and so would do anything asked of them. And they could exist on very little food and water, surviving injuries until the bodies could not take any more and would fall apart from decay or worse." Eric shuddered, then poorly masked a laugh. "It was quite interesting. The night we were told all of this, we kept checking that our food and drink hadn't been spiked, in case we had insulted them in any way and ended up as zombies."

"Oh, sounds like you wouldn't want to stay in that village forever," Cedric replied.

Eric shook his head. "No. Holiday? Yes. Zombie slave for eternity? No. But there were lovely people there. Very hospitable, and they treated us well. It was a very peaceful place, away from the rest of the world. Zombies or no zombies."

Cedric flipped his cards. "What about the sea monster special you both did?"

Eric stiffened at the memory. "Now that was scary. Not only because we didn't know what the hell we were dealing with—which is the case most of the time—but also because we had to be careful of storms. We almost died on the boat. It was awful because there was nothing we could do. There was no help, but we got lucky and managed to slip away in time."

Cedric gestured a flat sea with his hand. "You spotted a silhouette beneath the water, didn't you? And you believed it to be a megalodon."

Megalodon triggered the on-screen image to change for all to see. It showed a small fraction of the white boat's side, the rest open blue expansive water, and a cloudless sky. A large, grey, blade-like fin pierced the water. Beneath the surface moved a huge, dark shark shadow, three times the size of the boat.

"Yeah, I mean, that was horrific. A prehistoric shark could have devoured our boat in a moment, but didn't," Eric said, his tone surprisingly disappointed. "It was quite a surreal moment. It just swam calmly by. We all sat there watching it. No one uttered a word while what we believed to be an extinct giant shark swam underneath us."

Cedric lowered his head. "Obviously, some people have questioned whether or not it was just a giant blue whale but, as you said to me earlier, people came in and ..."

Eric jumped in, eager to explain. "Experts confirmed the shape of the fin and the way it swam, and all the comparisons made by the marine biologists suggested it was the best proof of existing megalodons. Of course, many people have reported sightings in that same location near the Mariana Trench, so ..." Eric shrugged.

"Of course, in that special, you also went into a submarine and found footage of what some believed to be merfolk and a large tentacle, which you stated was the kraken?" Cedric sneered.

Eric nodded. "That's right."

Cedric's hand hurried. "Fascinating also, but I know we have limited time, so let's talk about Hell's Gate."

"Yes. Hell's Gate." The foot that Eric wasn't sitting on wiggled like a dog's tail.

He coughed and took a sip from his bottle of water before resuming. "Well, Hell's Gate is a cave in the Amazon used for tribal sacrifices. It has this large pool of deep, blue water where you can't see the bottom. It's just black down there, and the water is completely still, which is really unsettling, along with the silence and scale of it." He shuddered at the recollection.

"We do have a picture taken on set." Cedric looked at the screen. A hollow city of bones, the cave seemed armoured with rocky floors and walls. The walls displayed cave paintings of ancient expression. The sapphire pool looked more like a layer of solid crystal than it did water.

"As you can see," Eric began, "some of the floor is made up of ancient remains from the people who were sacrificed." The skulls on display seemed to have sharper teeth, were not even human, it seemed. "There was lots of writing on the walls. It's off limits—for reasons I'll go into in a moment—as it's the most dangerous place in the world. You can't go there now, well, you're not meant to anyway. I hear people still break in, but in any case, the military issued an official warning."

A new picture of one of the cave paintings was projected onto the screen, showing the finer details. The rocky surface displayed a goddess, bowed to by ant-like subjects. There were two images of her. She was naked. A large, beautiful deity. She had baleful eyes. Below her central line and knees, there stood an old, shrouded hag. The crone appeared larger than the worshippers. Eric always felt there was something familiar about that detail of the drawing. The hag reminded him of the one in his dreams. Eric paused as he recalled the image.

He stuttered. "She ... she was believed by the people of this civilization to be like Mother Nature, a creator. She taught them how to build, how to make fire and other things, such as their extraordinary temples. Some believe that she ties into other ancient societies like the Egyptians and their pyramids, but that's just a wild theory. From what we could tell by the drawings and writing on the walls of the cave and scattered around the temples nearby was she ruled over them, but eventually left. For some reason, they started a ritual of blood sacrifice in what we assume was an attempt to bring her back. A bit like children crying for their mother." Eric paused and took a breath.

"They would slit their own people's throats and let them bleed into the water. It's believed that they were all willing sacrifices. In the early days, they would push them into the water where they'd sink to the bottomless pool. Later, however, the tribe began to starve and started to eat their sacrifices, hence the bones on the cave floor. They became feral. As you can see from the images, it was a large population, and they killed each other." His voice quivered at the mention of cannibalism, a topic which always made Eric shudder.

"The backstory alone is amazing, but what happened on the day was frightening, was it not?" Cedric said.

"Very!" Eric replied. "There'd been cases reported of people suffering from strokes and heart attacks upon entering the sacred cave, which is no coincidence. I remember walking in and my heart stopping for a moment—it does that to you. But later on, Mikey was kitted out in a scuba suit with a camera and radio mic. He swam in the water, which previously contained only dead bodies and blood. Armed with a torch, he saw what was down there. At first, he found only blackness. Then his camera and mic went dead and when he reached a certain depth, he felt like something crushed him. We waited ten seconds before we pulled him up with his safety line." Eric mimicked the action with his arms. "For a moment, something pulled back, but thankfully, we got him out. God knows what was down there; we didn't dare risk going back in again. Mikey was unconscious, and his equipment stopped working for no apparent reason, which was beyond odd. He couldn't remember what happened and didn't like to talk about it. Not even to me." Eric looked around. "The cave was closed to everyone after that." His voice went dry, and he reached for the bottle of water beside his chair.

"No surprise." Cedric's brow furrowed.

"No. The weirdest thing was we didn't see anything alive in the cave: no bugs, no fish, nothing. It was a dead place," Eric stated.

"From those pictures, it looks strangely alluring and frightening, with that blue, glowing water and bones everywhere." Cedric's white hair lifted with his breath as his cheeks bloated like a pufferfish.

Eric nodded in agreement.

"You've had some other great cases, too. The Chupacabra case, Bigfoot, and the Loch Ness monster, to name a few," Cedric continued, reading from his cue cards. "The unsolved mysteries like Roanoke and the Bermuda Triangle." He breathed deeply before carrying on. "You've made the *Explained* series by investigating some of history's biggest unsolved legends, creatures, and lore. They examined the evidence for each one and came up with an explanation as to what you and Michael believed they were." Cedric grinned at Eric, as though inviting him to say something.

"Oh, you mean the vampires, werewolves, and witches Halloween Special we did? Yeah, that was fun, wasn't a huge fan of the title or the way it was marketed. That was our producer's idea, great guy, but yeah, I felt it was a-a little tacky to tell you the truth." Eric said, scratching his chest and causing his mic to buzz.

Cedric smiled. "Yes, it was really interesting to hear your reasoning about how, over time, these iconic monsters have come into our consciousness. A game of Chinese Whispers was the way I think you explained it?"

"Well, throughout history, people have added their own spin on things, their own unique interpretations about these mysterious figures, to try to make sense of them. Adding layers of nonsense, basically, and losing sight of the reality." Eric laughed along with his audience. "But we discovered that the truth of something is often much more straightforward than the way in which culture and movies portray it for their audiences." He clasped his hands, having finished his sentence, but the interviewer gestured for him to continue. To milk it, as Mikey would say.

Eric took the hint with a loud gulp, buffering, then spoke. "W-well, the best example I can give is a brief description of our findings and theories about the creatures you mentioned. Like how werewolves were simply people who caught rabies from dogs during the Middle Ages, and were forced into the wild to fend for themselves. Or how vampires were simply anemic people with an iron deficiency who needed more red meat and were very pale. What can I say? They like their steak bloody," he joked. "Yeah, I mean, for them, and most anemic people even today, they feel the subconscious need to eat red meat because it's what their bodies tell them they need. And culture and movies have just blown it out of proportion with fictional characters like Dracula. Being fair, literal vampires do exist; they take it to the extreme and drink blood as a way of life, safely, I should add, but there are those people out there. But they don't sleep upside down or turn into bats or burn in the sun. They're not evil, they're just different."

"Oh, and we like 'different.'" Cedric chuckled.

"Yes, we do. The world would be a boring place if we were all normal. Then there are witches. Witches are real. I can't go into too much detail because it's very technical, but as humans, we only use a certain percentage of our brains. We concluded that some people can find ways to use more than the average person, and that's how some people can do extraordinary things. And this dates to the Middle Ages. Again, not evil. They can't set things on fire or move things about with their minds but can do very limited 'magic.'"

The presenter chuckled. "A very technical term that."

"Yeah. Limited magic. Sounds like fun." Eric threw his head back, laughing.

"It's really the mystery of it all that keeps us coming back for more. That's why Mikey and I loved this career. As humans, it is in our nature. We're a curious species, it's both a good thing and a bad thing," Eric stated.

Cedric stiffened as if he were a doctor about to deliver bad news. "Now, Eric, I know you're happy to talk about this because you told me backstage, but would you mind if we spoke about what happened at Aokigahara?"

Eric paused, knowing the question would come. "No. By all means. To be honest, I think it's good to talk about what happened that day, no matter how difficult it is."

The audience ceased ruffling wrappers and slurping their drinks.

"Please let me know if there is anything you don't want to answer. First? Can you explain Aokigahara and what happened there?" Cedric asked.

"Of course," Eric replied. He cleared his throat as if he were about to roll out a pre-planned speech. Perhaps, from being asked about it so many times, he'd created an instinctive response. "Well, Aokigahara is the Sea of Trees, better known as Suicide Forest, based in Japan. Most people know it from the large number of suicides that have happened there. No one knows why, but everyone who goes into those woods usually ends up dead, namely by suicide. Michael and I got permission to film what was meant to be our last ever special there with our crew." He lowered his head.

"We never foresaw the events of that day, didn't expect what happened—even though we should have. As most of you know, some of the crew turned on one another. They killed themselves and each other while the rest of us were lucky to escape with our lives." Eric felt the oxygen leave his lungs after saying the words out loud. "I only just got away. Why I was spared, I don't know." He clutched his chest. "Only a few of us survived, including our director and manager, Liam Galavan. He's a great guy, but we haven't worked together since Aokigahara."

Eric felt himself shrink within his seat. "At that time, when we returned to the States and told GMD what happened and showed them the footage, they were adamant about using it in the special. With a disclaimer, of course. Even to this day, I'm not sure it was a good idea. It told the world what really happened there that day, but it still doesn't sit right with me that it was used as a form of entertainment. I didn't want the videos to be used out of respect for the deceased's loved ones, but it was out of my hands, no matter how much I fought for it." Eric's lips trembled, and he struggled to compose himself.

"It must have been very hard to watch crewmembers, friends you had developed a bond with, attack and murder each other. What do you think happened?" Cedric asked.

Eric blinked away tears. "I can, without a doubt, tell you it was the place itself. One thing that we've realized over several cases is that there is a correlation between haunted locations and the number of suicides and murders within that place. You know, I've always felt that emotions can stain places and people." He stretched out his fingers. "The history of a place, its pain and grief, can seep into people, change them even. Although that may sound darkly poetic to some, I believe that's what happened." He paused, then added, "Who knows what took place in that forest before we came along? Who knows why it calls people to kill themselves and others? Obviously, nothing good."

Cedric nodded solemnly. "It was horrible. I remember hearing about it on the news. The world was mortified, and everyone was talking about it. Now, I hope you don't mind us showing the famous clip of the Aokigahara massacre?"

Eric froze. *I can't cause any trouble for the producers or Cedric.* He gulped and answered, "I-I'll just look away. Eric said, his voice a hoarse whisper as he turned to look at the floor.

Cedric nodded sympathetically. He addressed the audience. "Full disclaimer to members of our audience who would rather not watch the clip, it does contain difficult scenes. There are graphic images that may disturb some, so we will give those of you who don't want to watch a few moments to leave or turn away, if you wish."

He waited a mere ten seconds before giving the go-ahead from his bosses, allowing barely enough time for a small number of people to leave or cover their eyes before the horrific event played on screen. "Okay. Let's take a look." The lights dimmed, and the screen lit up with a full disclaimer:

"THE FOLLOWING CONTAINS STRONG LANGUAGE AND VIOLENCE FROM THE OUTSET WHICH SOME VIEWERS MAY FIND DISTRESSING. ALL RIGHTS BELONG TO GMD PRODUCTIONS."

Static hissing, the picture cleared as a scene of woods appeared. Everything appeared dead or dying—from the leaves blanketing the floor to the sparse, dry shrubs.

The filmmakers edited the footage for maximum effect—designed to shock. The first scene showed a man, a set technician, lying dead with his throat slit. A river of blood gushed from his wound. Eric and Michael walked into the shot. A younger Michael and a brunette with short, cropped hair, fine features, and striking blue eyes stood appalled and enthralled at the sight.

"F-fuck, Frank?" Michael's voice rose to a shrill pitch. "Liam, what do we do?"

Before anyone could decide, a sound engineer came into frame. He brandished a knife and stabbed another team member, striking him down instantly. Irrational rage was etched on the engineer's face. Dropping the knife, he pulled out a pistol. Team members jumped on him, bludgeoning him with rocks before turning on each other to fight for the gun.

"Run!" Eric screamed as he turned and fled.

The camera zoomed in as another man hanged himself from a tree, his neck snapping like a branch upon impact.

"Oh my God!" Eric shrieked, looking over his shoulder.

Michael caught up to Eric. "Keep going and don't stop. It's too late," he said, pushing Eric in front of him.

Michael's ankle wobbled, causing him to lose balance and fall. The cameraman, Eric, and the remainder of the fleeing crew watched him get up, not realizing a crazed technician lurked close behind, holding a knife.

"Mikey!" Eric bellowed, running back to help his friend.

Fear gave Eric superhuman speed. He pushed Michael out of the way and launched himself at the technician. In the confusion of bodies, the technician rolled onto the knife. Eric quickly pushed him off and grabbed hold of Michael's hand, pulling him from the scene.

"Come on, we need to leave!" Eric yanked Michael's arm.

The audience jumped as a gunshot rang out. Another member of the production team, the shooter, fired randomly at the retreating figures, fatally wounding the cameraman. He dropped the camera, which captured random images of carnage, finally focusing on the bloodied body of the cameraman lying dead in front of the lens.

The final clip, just a few seconds long, showed a shocked Michael hugging Eric. Aware of the camera, Eric held up his hand to block the lens, and the scene faded to fuzzy static. The room remained silent.

"It's still hard to watch, and that was three years ago," Cedric said. "What was going through your head when this was happening?"

Eric choked on his words. "Well, when you're in a situation like that, your instincts just kick in. My instinct was to run and not look back, except I did go back for Michael, but then I ran like hell with him. I had to save Mikey." He blinked and looked down at his fake snakeskin belt. "I would have saved the others if I could have."

"I think we can all say that you showed incredible bravery by putting your own life at risk to help your friend," Cedric said with a warm smile.

"Still ... the guilt ... I couldn't save the others." Eric paused to regain control of his emotions. "I'm sorry."

"It's fine. Take your time," said Cedric. "So, what happened afterwards?"

Swallowing his self-loathing, Eric continued, "Michael took off. We returned home, and I guess Mikey couldn't cope with what happened. He just left."

"You have no idea where he might have gone? You haven't heard from him in all this time?"

"No, nothing. I looked for him, of course I did. I tried to find him, but in spite of numerous supposed sightings, he just vanished."

"That must have hurt."

"Yeah."

"Why do you think he left?"

"I've asked myself that so many times, but I don't have an answer. Michael wanted Aokigahara to be our last special to, as he put it: 'go out with a bang.' Well, we certainly did that. Michael wanted to use the money we had earned over the years to see more of the world. All he ever really wanted was to travel. Mikey wasn't really interested in the show business part of it all. That was always me. He just enjoyed the adventure. From the day I met him."

"I hear that you've started looking for a new partner?" Cedric said, jokingly pointing at himself.

"Yeah!" Eric chuckled. "I've had to accept that Michael isn't coming back. I've worked with quite a few people now, but it's never the same without Mikey. We were brothers."

"His disappearance must have been a blow and, of course, the tragic death of so many crewmembers. Made worse, no doubt, by the fact that no bodies were recovered."

"I couldn't sleep properly for weeks. We were accused by police of murdering them, or worse, that the whole thing was a hoax, but we were never charged. In a way, I wished it had been a prank on me, but it wasn't. And the reality of it was horrible."

"Hmm ... we will always remember those who died that day."

Eric tightened his grip on the arms of the chair. "Always, they were all truly wonderful people."

The room fell silent, flat, still just for a moment before Cedric's beak started flapping once more.

"Would you ever consider doing more specials by yourself?" Cedric asked.

Eric considered his response. "I don't know. I'm not sure it would work as a full sixty-minute show. Not without Mikey. People enjoyed the friendship and our chemistry as much as the content itself. It gelled the programme together. I just can't see it working without Michael."

Cedric nodded and glanced down at his notes. "So, can you tell me what happened two years ago at the Carolina Orphanage and your failed comeback?"

"I began working with a new partner, a young woman named Megan." Eric recalled her welcoming face, grinned, then sighed.

"The case involved a possessed girl named Alice. She died, and her death was caught on tape, which, of course, the story sent people into a frenzy against me on social media about how wrong it was. In the end, I decided not to upload the footage on YouTube because, although it was compelling supernatural evidence, it was too much, honestly. Even more so than Suicide Forest. I was arrested soon after, but cleared of all charges after the post-mortem and a thorough review of the footage." A muscle twitched in his leg.

"People don't seem to realize how much that also affected you," Cedric prompted.

"I suffered a breakdown. Seeing that girl die broke me." Eric repositioned himself. "I'd rather not talk about what I went through because it's not about me, it's about Alice Hickford. Her poor parents. I just hope they've managed to find peace." His voice calmed, and his stomach unclenched a little.

Cedric leaned in. "I know I'm not alone in thinking you are an amazing person who has been through a lot." The audience cheered louder.

Eric felt himself become flooded with emotion. He lifted his hand. "That's very kind, but I'm really not. I'm just a guy who's had bad things happen around him. I'm not special. That's not me trying to get sympathy, because I don't want it. I'm just a normal guy who does what he does. I chose this life, along with its ups and downs. But I thank you all for your support." Eric bowed his head gratefully, inspiring a rallying uproar.

"Wherever your path takes you, we will always be grateful for the work you've done to help us understand the unknown. Now, we're coming to the end of our panel, but there is just time for a few questions from the audience."

A spotlight lit a small stand with a microphone where a woman wearing glasses stood ready. She wore orange, which blended with her short, bushy, ginger hair.

Cedric gestured at the woman. "Yes, hello, what's your name?"

Her voice trembled. "Hi, my name is Sarah. Just wondering if you would ever consider writing a book about your life. You're such an inspiration to me and a lot of other people, and I know we'd love to know your full story."

Eric stroked the hairs on his left arm. "I have thought about it, but I don't think I'm that interesting, really. It's something I may consider if you all really wanted it."

The floor shook with the sound of cheering.

"I'm not that great at writing, but I know people who are writers, friends of mine, so maybe one of them could help. I don't know ... maybe is my answer to that." He accepted more claps.

"Thank you," Sarah said.

Eric nodded. "Thanks, Sarah."

"Right. Last one," Cedric said. "Yes, the lady in the green. Come up to the mic." The woman had long, messy hair. "What's your name?"

"I'm Maribel, and I just wanted to say you're my hero, Eric." She spoke with a strong Spanish accent and clutched a gift. "You really helped me at a dark point in my life when everything seemed to be falling apart. I just wanted to say thank you for everything. Also, I have something for you and would love to give it to you." Maribel indicated her basket.

Eric smiled and nodded, gesturing for her to bring it to him. Security escorted her on stage. Maribel shook as she carried the large, carefully wrapped basket containing chocolates, drawings, candles, and letters. Eric approached her, accepted the gift, and placed it carefully on the floor beside them. A guard immediately carried it off stage for Eric to pick up later.

Eric hugged his dedicated fan and kissed her on the cheek. Maribel whipped out her phone for a selfie, and Eric complied.

A guard escorted her from the stage as Cedric checked his watch. "That's all, folks. Please give a big hand to Eric Thompson. Thank you for being so amazing today."

"Thank you," Eric replied, soaking up the cheers.

"Eric Thompson, everyone!" Cedric bellowed above the noise of the crowd.

Eric exited into the wings to find solace away from the noise. He relaxed his brow, relieved to be out from under the hot spotlights. He heard Cedric continuing in the background, an echo as he walked to his dressing room.

Eric slumped in the chair and gazed at Maribel's gift. Alone and without purpose after what happened in Aokigahara, even though it happened years before. Stuck in purgatory, Eric feared it'd be his fate forever.

He stayed in and watched television that night, like he had every night.

4

Netherworld

New York, Eric's House – Night

With the curtains drawn back in the realm of dreaming, the veil dropped to reveal grey wooden panels. The floor was coated with dead flies, somehow still buzzing when he grew closer to each. Eric hadn't wandered the netherworld for some time. The place appeared different from within his recurring nightmares. Everything was now all white. Why the sudden change? Dust-coated stairs loomed before him. He felt naked due to his loose grey robe wafting open as he ascended.

At the top, Eric opened a frosted glass door to discover the first floor empty. Sapphire moonlight shone through the tall, rectangular windows, displaying nothing outside other than dead tree stumps extending as far as Eric could see. He glided across the floorboards to look out. Even the stars appeared different. Dots beamed down like spotlights shining straight lines toward the ground.

Humming came from behind Eric, bouncing off the hollow halls. He turned. *A hag?* She looked old, sagging, pale, and withered, with barely any hair. Her eyes appeared shut, her skin wrinkled like raisins. She sat in an aged, rusted wheelchair wearing a dirty gown. Her skin displayed hollowed-out holes like a hive. Her upturned wrists on her lap revealed slits. Two centipedes crawled out of each limb, scuttling through the hag's fingers and down her legs, only to fall to the floor. Running like veins, they possessed armoured, flexible, never-ending bodies. The brittle-sounding rhythm of the humming of what seemed to be an old lullaby sent an arctic tingle down his nape. Other small bugs crawled in and out of the old woman's orifices.

Eric felt drawn to her, like a magnet, and he stepped toward her. A lullaby emitted from the old crone's corpse. He took another step. Still, she hummed. Another step. She stopped making any sound. Dead. Quiet. The silence seemed worse. Eric stood still in his tracks, not wanting to move and trigger anything else. He retreated backwards.

A child's laugh echoed from a hallway to his right. He moved slowly toward the sound, sneaking glances at the now-silent older woman in the corner, bleeding out the long-legged arthropods. Eric's vision became distorted. He tiptoed down the narrow hallway. A glow hummed through the door at the end, sandwiched between smooth clay walls. A silver mirror hung on the right side of the wall beside the door. He crept forward, curious to see what would be shown back to him in the mirror, never having seen himself in such dreams before.

Then, the walls moved. Hands clawed through them, as if through cloth, displaying no threat as Eric passed by, seemingly not interested in him. The hands then retracted into the flat walls, housing their trapped souls. The mirror reflected an image of a faceless little girl with long, wavy, brown hair. Her face appeared as blank as a canvas. *What is this trickery?* A vision, or something else, appeared, all beyond Eric's understanding. The blood vessels in Eric's eye sockets thickened the longer he gazed at the image. Cold palms smashed the mirror, breaking it into razor shards which pierced the ground around Eric's feet like arrows. He flinched from the shower of sharp fragments. The frame hung empty and worthless. Heavy breathing sounded; Eric realized it was him. He calmed himself, then turned. A silhouette of the girl seemed to be on the other side of the doors. He made out her profile through the frosted glass. She giggled as if they played a maniacal game of hide and seek. Then she seemed to skip.

Eric turned the doorknob, and the door opened quickly, smacking against the wall. He gazed out into a starlit night, the beams from the stars reaching to the ground. He was confronted by a maze of tree stumps and a forest beyond. The faceless girl was running, faster than should be possible, her little legs sprinting in between the stumps toward the dark forest. Eric proceeded to do the same, running over dry mud. Eric avoided the beams of starlight shining down from the sky, not wanting to risk so much as stroking the slow-moving rays. The girl disappeared into the shadow of the trees. Only a few starry shafts pierced the tall, looming branches reaching toward the full moon.

On the edge of the twisted wilderness, something watched from up high. The blue owl—the same one he always dreamt about. The blue angel looked down at Eric and flew into the twilight. Eric followed, avoiding the light flares. Eric focused on the guardian bird of prey and failed to notice the object he tripped over. He fell to the rough ground, landing on his front. His ribs felt like they'd been stabbed by something hard and crude. He reeled over, clutching his aching chest.

The owl had disappeared. Eric had lost his guide and his only hope of understanding what was happening. A broken, silver, antique picture frame seemed to have tripped him up. Eric flipped the frame to find an old photo of himself and Michael, one he cherished from the start of their success. One just like it sat beside his bed. They smiled in the photo. Chummy. Brotherly. For the briefest of moments, Eric had forgotten his best friend's departure from his life and the pain of what happened. Then he remembered. The cracked glass divided them, unlike the one he kept in the real world. Eric took a moment for the difference to seep in. Something beside him stirred. A trunk he'd fallen beside had uprooted itself from the soil, revealing itself as a being much like a spider but with a tree growing out of its dorsal side. The tree with arachnid roots moved, crawling and planting itself away from Eric, seemingly for peace and comfort. *This place is getting stranger and stranger.* Eric then realized, in growing horror, he was in a forest with weird, twisted things surrounding him—his worst nightmare.

Bells rang. Chimes shook the forest. Eric glanced around in a panic. Nothing was different.

A whisper echoed through the branches, a taunt, "Firebird." Without warning, the sky screamed. An eclipse appeared, painting out the blue moon, bleeding it to crimson. Eric jolted at every noise, seeing only jarring movements of whatever lurked behind trees. The stars and their beams transitioned to an enlightening, bright white that dissolved into dust. Eric stared at the blood moon.

Then, he woke, safe in bed. Same as always.

5

A Witch's Wisdom

Eric made his way along the pavement, crossing New York City, taking routes he knew well. People glanced at him occasionally as he passed.

Walking past the Regal City cinema, Eric chuffed, recalling the time Michael managed to sneak them both in as teens to see an R-rated horror movie, their first. *The Reckoning* had been about a haunted house. A cliché, jump-scare gore fest, one that fifteen-year-old Eric yelped at and hid his eyes away from. Muscles tensing with every scene, he settled every time as Michael nudged him with a grin. Eric always felt safe with Michael by his side, even when they got caught afterward. Michael stated it was Eric's idea, and so he took the brunt of the punishment from the head of the orphanage, Mrs. Meeks. Eric took the fall a lot for Michael; he tended to panic and throw others under the bus, but Eric always forgave him. How could he not? He was his only friend, and his family, and he knew how to keep him calm and at ease, even when he was the one being punished for his friend's crimes.

A small bar on the street named "Fuzzy's" flashed memories of when Eric used to work in one, and around that time, he and Michael were just starting out with their haunting videos. Most of their evenings were reserved for scraping up tips for rent and food. Michael always got more tips, mostly from older women; he knew how to play them and had a pretty face. However, the day they knew they had made it with their YouTube channel was when they served a customer who recognized them both on shift and asked for a picture, the first of many.

Eric journeyed onward down the street to visit an old friend, a woman of immense power and charisma: Tamara Alzin. They first met years prior when Michael was Eric's right-hand man, and he his. They discovered her secret. Throughout history, there was an alliance of people who used what they called 'nature's gifts'—things society never understood or accepted. Witchcraft.

They explained the bare minimum to Eric, which only served to pique his curiosity. These witches united together, being able to weave their will into whatever region of power they wanted, or needed, they blended in seamlessly. They manipulated the world around them to suit their needs. They followed in their leader's footsteps. They represented what she allowed to exist. She kept them on a tight leash. A fair tyrant.

No one knew how much this organization controlled except Tamara, head of the order and CEO of Alzin Enterprise, a billion-dollar company with branches around the globe. Alzin controlled media and research into science and technology, amongst other things. Blackmail, treachery, and lying helped the siren rise to the top, happy to grasp anything she considered rightfully hers through cunning, power, and charm.

Michael and Eric discovered the group, which led them directly to Tamara. They agreed to keep her secret, sparing the witches from the cruelty the world would inflict upon them if revealed. Tamara rewarded their mercy, saying they could go to her for counsel and make use of her own unique brand of 'magic.'

Eric kept their secret—he did not want to test what Tamara had brewing in her pot. But Tamara's gifts proved useful over the years, all except the engraved black runestone Eric used on the possessed Alice Hickford; obviously something he shouldn't have dabbled with without knowing the true extent of its potential outcome for the girl.

For years, Tamara tried persuading Eric to join her coven, especially after she helped hone his ability, his sixth sense, which he realized he possessed at a young age. Eric recalled how Tamara never trusted Michael, so she refused to teach him any degree of witchcraft, stating that he "craved it too much" and had too much unstable darkness swirling within. The last thing Michael needed was a voodoo doll. Yes, Tamara was a strong ally, but Eric didn't believe she was being completely loyal. Ever since Michael left, she kept close tabs on him.

Eric turned the corner and stood in awe of the Alzin Enterprise Tower reaching high above New York. Silver, metallic, shiny, and sharp, Alzin Tower was a pointed blade of modern architecture. The doors slid open as Eric approached, revealing a lobby filled with busy suitcase carriers and coffee drinkers. Luxurious air ruffled Eric's hair. A huge department map was exhibited on a cream marble wall beside the elevators. Tamara's office was at the top, predictably. It hadn't changed since Eric last visited. If she paid for her tower, naturally, she'd want the best office view. Eric entered the metal elevator and pressed the top button, smiling at his travelling companions in the confined space. Some sniggered and raised their brows.

The higher they rose, the more people got out, until only Eric remained to venture to the top by himself. Eventually, the doors opened, revealing a large, wide room full of extraordinary abstract art. They'd added more since Eric's last visit.

Eric approached reception. A new person sat behind the desk from the last time. Her hair appeared brittle and frizzy. Bags drooped under her eyes, and her skin seemed dry and coarse. Eric read the personal assistant's name badge: Clara. Eric steadily approached and cleared his throat.

"H-hi. I'm here to see Miss Alzin," he smiled, trying to be friendly.

"Oh, okay. Do you have an appointment?" Clara asked, mirroring a smile, still clicking away at her computer.

Eric paused. "N-I don't, but I'm sure if you let her know I'm here, she will ..."

"I'm sorry, sir, but Miss Alzin is very busy today; she has several meetings," Clara winced. "Sorry."

The two large doors guarding Tamara's office opened, revealing a silhouette. A powerful figure stood, surrounded by a bright light. When Eric's eyes adjusted, he made out Tamara, with her long hair draping over her shoulders. She wore a white designer dress. A large circular pendant made of pure starlight rested on her chest. Tamara Alzin had clearly expected him.

"Eric Thompson? It has been a long time," she purred.

"Too long, Tammy. You always liked making an entrance." He shook his head, smiling.

"That's true," Tamara admitted. "It's okay, Clara, dear. I can always make time for one of my oldest friends."

"Shall I cancel your two o'clock meeting, Ms. Alzin?"

"Yes, please. We need to have a little chat, don't we?" Tamara said to Eric.

"We do."

"This way." Tamara gestured with manicured, pale nails.

Eric followed, like a lap dog.

The office smelled of lavender. Black and white motifs highlighted two walls. One housed a bookcase displaying many texts from around the world, as well as treasures and awards, whilst the other was covered in hanging photos of Tamara with powerful people in all manner of differing fields. Two sides of the office were clear glass and overlooked Central Park. From such a height, people looked like ants that Tamara could watch whenever she pleased. A desk, chair, couch, and a table flanked an open area to the right where Tamara might speak to guests in a more relaxed atmosphere.

As Tamara closed the doors and locked them, Eric couldn't help but gaze into her huge, hypnotic, diamond amulet. The chain sported a complex and intricate design of golden feathers and bird claws wrapped around a central gem. A beautiful piece of art. The stone seemed extra luminous compared to other gems, making it as hypnotic as a snake's gaze. It appeared to be a part of her—a seed of her creation. *It's obviously some form of talisman*, Eric thought, as he'd never seen her without the devil's eye.

He lifted his gaze when Tamara approached him, her arms open. "Where have you been?" She kissed his cheek.

"Where haven't I been?" He kissed her back.

Tamara looked him up and down. "I could sense your presence as soon as you entered the lobby downstairs."

"I wouldn't expect anything less." He laughed, though he was unsettled by the thought. Eric never knew anyone able to do such a thing. "You haven't aged."

"But you have," she returned, but not harshly. "How can a man so young have such old eyes? Come, sit down and have a drink." She turned and played with her decanters of different coloured liquids as he sat. "Have this." She placed a glass of clear red liquid on the table before him. "Drink."

Eric peered into the glass.

Tamara seemed to sense his hesitation. "If I wanted to poison you, Eric, I wouldn't do it in my own office now, would I?"

Eric took a sip. It had a bitter taste but was pleasant and refreshing. Replenishing.

"Good?"

"Yeah, really good. What is it?"

"Cranberry juice, it's good for you. Filled with antioxidants—and a little something extra ..." She broke off to take a sip of her own drink. "Have you reconsidered my offer?"

"To join?"

"Yes, of course, to join. You can do a lot with your gift, but you could do so much more as one of us." Tamara smoothed the creases in her dress when she spoke.

Eric's jaw tensed. "It's a very generous offer, but like last time, I have to decline. It's just not for me, but your secret is safe. After all, where would I be without you?"

"True. I am in some ways your fairy godmother." She leaned back, crossing one leg over the other. Tamara's chuckle echoed around the room eerily. "So, tell me. How have you been, old friend?"

Eric took a moment. "I'm doing fine. Yourself?"

"Holding together after my little scrap."

Eric searched his mind. "Oh God, yeah. I read about the car accident in the newspaper a few weeks ago. How are you doing now?"

"Not good enough, it would seem." Tamara lifted her dress, revealing a scar on her thigh. "I managed to heal myself, but it's been a drain. I haven't been my usual self since."

"What happened? A random accident?"

"You know as well as I, Eric, that there are no accidents." Tamara's eyes locked with his.

"One of your rivals?"

"Rivals." She chuckled. "I wouldn't call them that, but probably. Let them try is what I say. I am number one for a reason. The others would fall apart without me, especially in this world we live in. Anyway, I'd haunt the hell out of them and probably scare them to death if they did."

"That's true," Eric agreed, placing his drink on the table.

"They lack imagination when it comes to producing results." Tamara glanced out the window at the ant farm below.

"Even your children?" Eric's voice shook in surprise.

"Especially them. They're too weak; they've never had to fight for anything because of me," Tamara snapped. "An empire doesn't run itself. They're not ready to rise, and I'm not ready to fall." Tamara gulped down the last drops of cranberry juice and placed the empty glass on the table.

All the while they had been talking, Tamara glanced occasionally at a newspaper by her side. She pushed it toward Eric for him to read.

MORE PEOPLE GO MISSING OVERNIGHT.

"Have you seen all these reports? People are going missing. Dozens by the day," said Tamara.

"Yeah. It's weird. Do you know anything about that? Heard any whispers?"

"I've heard a few rumours." Tamara's voice deepened.

"Rumours?" Eric questioned.

"Yes. The world used to be a simpler place, even for my kind. No one makes the time for their own anymore. People go missing. Monsters appear in the night. More so than usual. That's not a coincidence."

"You know something." Eric's eyes twinkled.

"I know nothing. Just spreading idle gossip." Her fingers played nervously with her diamond.

"You do know something, otherwise you wouldn't have said anything."

"But you're not here to ask me about my ramblings. There's another reason. So, why *are* you here?" Tamara asked. "That pesky dream still bothering you or, perhaps, it has developed in some way?"

Eric paused. "It has changed."

"Dreams do change, Eric. Everything changes. It's natural."

"I know, but this was not just a different dream. It felt as if it was the second act, or the second phase. Like it was trying to tell me something." Eric struggled to explain.

"What makes you say so?" Tamara's eyes narrowed.

"My senses. The place was very similar, but there was ... progression. And then the owl."

Tamara leaned in; her brow rose. "The owl was there? The same owl as before—the one with the blue, white and gold?"

"Yes."

"Was everything else the same?" she asked in what seemed to be genuine concern.

"In the woods, the trees moved like spiders." Eric made crawling movements with his hands to demonstrate.

"Hmm ... so what was new. What stood out?"

Eric's mouth grew dry. "Erm ... a faceless little girl, the spider trees and an old woman bleeding centipedes. Weird beams of light."

"That is strange." Tamara pouted her lips.

"Whispers of the word written on the walls of the Carolina Orphanage all those years ago—firebird," he whispered.

"Firebird?" Tamara repeated curiously.

"What does it mean?"

"I don't know, but let's find out, shall we?" Tamara rose from her seat and gestured toward her bookcase.

"From your book?" Eric asked, following her toward the office library.

"Precisely. These symbols must represent something, whether some form of warning, something manipulated to manifest within you, or an internal psychological issue uncovered. We will find out. Don't worry."

Tamara pushed the two central bookcases out like doors, revealing a hidden room. Her sanctum. There were shelves upon shelves of mystical artifacts and paraphernalia. A large, old book was open in the centre of the main table. Elaborate writings, drawings, and languages filled the sacred chapters.

"I'm still surprised no one in this building has managed to find this," Eric remarked.

"You'd be surprised at what I manage to cover up."

Tamara turned the pages with her delicate fingers. "Let's see."

Eric looked around. Bottles of unknown ingredients and potions dotted the room, some dustier than others. "I've got to say, Tammy, there's a lot of dust in here."

"I've been busy," she grunted, still skimming over the pages.

"With anything in particular?"

"Things," Tamara snapped back. "You don't need to concern yourself. Here we are, dream interpretation. The blue owl. Let's see ..."

Eric glanced around the room while Tamara searched for answers amongst the endless texts. In one corner, a large crystal ball glowed hazily from the reflection of a large light above. A circular gold trinket box, encrusted with red crystals and floral patterns, housed ginger powder. A tiny amount had been sprinkled around its base. *Probably left over from recent use.* A small, silver dish glistened with black and gold rune stones. Next to the dish sat a voodoo doll, a variety of different coloured pins sticking out. A gold mirror with runes on its edges hung on the central wall beside a silver broadsword. Unique amongst swords, it possessed a strengthened ridge and lightened blade that narrowed down to its broad steel handguard of jewelled sapphire.

Tamara lifted her finger in declaration. "The blue owl means you're about to receive knowledge and wisdom. Some interpret the blue owl as symbolizing supernatural knowledge. You've always dreamt about the owl, so it may be deeper knowledge, which would make sense."

Tamara took a deep breath before moving on. "The spiders. To see a spider in your dream indicates you're feeling like an outsider. Also, you want to distance yourself and stay away from an alluring and tempting situation. The spider is also symbolic of feminine power." She looked up. "Do you think that means me?"

"What about the other stuff?" Eric asked.

"Let's see ... centipedes are a sign of hidden danger, so look out for that. Seeing an old and sick woman in a dream may mean impotence and weakness. To dream of a faceless person has something to do with a loss of identity or inability to accept a person the way he or she is. Dreaming of a little girl represents prosperity after going through hardship. The beams of light are a little too specific to track. As are the spider trees."

"Great," Eric said.

"And firebird? I can only guess it means a phoenix. An omen of renewal, transformation, or immortality. The dream foretells a new phase in your life. To dream about a phoenix changing shape refers to changes in your life. Is any of this making sense?" Tamara asked.

"Nope. What does it all mean?"

"It could mean a thousand things, but it seems as if your life is about to change, and whether for the better is yet to be seen," Tamara replied, brushing dust from the table.

"Is that the best you can do?" Eric asked.

"I've given you the pieces. You've got to fit them together. It doesn't sound too foreboding, though," Tamara remarked.

Eric mulled it over as he followed Tamara out of the room. "Well, if you're sure."

"Let me see your hand."

"Why?"

"Trust me," Tamara said, reaching out her hand for his.

Eric reluctantly extended his arm, wondering what the witch was up to. Palmistry? Surely, that was a bit outdated. Tamara's eyes lit up from Eric's touch. What could she see? What could she feel that he could not? Energy surged from Eric, draining him and presumably empowering her.

Tamara released her hold and gazed down at her hand as if it were cut or burned, breathing heavily.

"What is it? Am I going mad?"

"Have a look in the ball." Tamara pointed back to the crystal ball housed in her den.

She escorted him over to the large orb.

"How does this work?" Eric asked. "You've never explained. I think about my dream and look into the glass?"

"No. That's not for you." Tamara grasped the sleeve of his arm and placed his hand on the crystal. "Place your hand on it and close your eyes to keep your mind empty. Now, what do you see?"

"I see ... I see ... nothing." Eric ground his teeth, his face tensing up in frustration.

Tamara cupped the sides of his shoulders as she whispered into his ear. "Let go. You can't control it. It will control you. Let it flow."

His muscles loosened. His mind opened, and he felt blank and ready.

"What do you see?" Tamara asked quietly.

Eric gasped as he saw dark shapes and blurred images. "I see ... a house. Trees. A person. I don't know who they are. I can't make them out." The images distorted, and he grew tense again, the vision moulding into the next, returning to the figure.

"Let go," a voice soothed, while his head swirled.

"I see a colour. Blue." Eric smelled charcoal. The lights in his head burned with intensity inside his sockets, making him feel nauseous, and his temples pulsated. He lost his balance, falling into Tamara, who held him steady.

"Are you alright?" she asked, pulling Eric's hands from the orb.

"Yeah. I'm fine. Sorry." He leaned one arm on the table for support, lifting his other hand to massage his aching head.

"What did you see?" Tamara questioned.

"I'm not sure. I never got a clear image."

"It's the way these things work. We never get the full picture, just clues and riddles in mist." Tamara's manner suggested she'd said so many times to others. "We only get shown what we're meant to see—to set us on our path."

"What about the dreams?" Eric asked.

Tamara paused and perched on a table. "Dreams manifest through the netherworld or rather, the astral plane. The space beyond this reality. A place unlike any other, where there are no rules. A conduit through which all of nature flows. A place with no past or future, no time. Just eternity. Another dimension."

"Can it be dangerous?" Eric's jaw tensed. "I mean, I know it's dreaming, but still, is it unsafe?"

"It can be," Tamara replied. "It can act as both a magnet and an amplifier. It's not a physical place. But it's real and can do real harm."

"So, what can I do about it?" Eric asked, following Tamara.

"Keep living and let things happen as they are intended. Danger most likely lies ahead. Accept it openly to move on. In the end, we all wind up where we deserve to be ... in a better or worse place." Tamara said, glancing out of the window.

"That's it?" Eric said, confused. "'Keep living.' That's your advice?"

Tamara turned, her hair whipping round with her. "What else do you expect me to say?"

"I don't know. You're just usually more hands-on."

"Well, not everything requires a definitive answer. You're just going to have to be patient. Let these visions take you to wherever they're meant to take you. Keep an open mind. I thought you, of all people, would know that."

"It's just not much to go on."

"If you're feeling uncertain, I can give you something."

"Uncertain?" He scoffed jokingly. "Me? No, never. But what have you got?"

Tamara strode past him and back to her playroom of toys. Opening a silver box, she gazed down and picked up something small and black from inside and handed it to Eric.

"Here. It will protect you."

"Black onyx. You've given me such a stone before."

"Yes, but this one is portable. Well, *more* portable; you can wear this one." Tamara swung the chain backwards and forwards from her fingers, laughing at Eric's playful attempts to grasp it.

"Wear it always from now on and definitely whenever your senses start tingling."

"Tammy, you're an angel," Eric declared with a smile.

"I know." She chuckled.

He glanced at his watch. "I'd best be on my way. After all, I've got a lot to decipher." "And here I thought you'd come to see how I was for once." Tamara shook her head in mock disappointment.

"One last thing," Tamara called after Eric. "You haven't been thinking about Michael recently, have you?"

Eric stopped and turned. "No. Why?" he lied, not wanting her to know more than she needed and now finding himself more eager to leave than ever.

"Just asking," Tamara said, approaching him.

"Well, no, I haven't."

"Eric!" Tamara's voice cut through him like a shard of glass. She held up a hand to silence him. "It's okay to think about what happened, but just don't get lost in memory. After all, if you keep looking into the past, you'll never find your future."

Eric nodded. "Now, I really must leave." He kissed Tamara on the cheek, then headed out of her office toward the elevator.

"Until we meet again, Mr. Thompson," Tamara called after him.

Tamara watched Eric step into the elevator, press the button, and disappear behind the closed doors, satisfied she'd set him on the path toward his true fate.

6

The Danger of Hope

Eric pondered what Tamara said when he left the Alzin Enterprise building. The encounter had left him with more questions than answers and made him worry about his future.

At twenty-eight, Eric had a lot more living to do, but what that entailed, he was not quite sure. He was tired of taking a back seat, as he had for the past few years. He wanted to get himself out there again, in the world. Eric hoped, in his heart, that Tamara's prophecy would come true. Life would give him something: a new beginning. Maybe that meant him making it for himself and not trusting in fate. *Perhaps YouTube again? A new television show he could pitch?* It was difficult without Michael, and the reason he failed in subsequent attempts, but he'd make it work somehow. What happened at the orphanage had ruined his reputation. Eric needed a comeback.

Walking home, he re-evaluated his options. Every year, Eric set goals: things to do and ways to better himself. He needed to find something lost—something invaluable: hope.

Eric's senses tickled from the back of his neck downward. He stopped as a sleek, black car halted beside him. The dark glass obscured the chauffeur. The backseat window lowered, and a face peered out. Eric regarded the occupant: a young Chinese woman with black hair cut into a sharp bob as straight as a ruler. She had clear skin and a set of dimples. Surprisingly, for a passenger riding inside such a lavish car, she wore casual clothing and looked uncomfortable and out of place, as if unaccustomed to such luxury.

"Eric Thompson?" she asked.

"Yes?" he answered, confused.

The woman's head jolted out of the window with a smile. "I'd like to have a little talk with you."

"I don't know you."

"Well, let me fix that. I'm Popp—Poppy Dearly. So now we know each other, don't we?"

"What do you want, Poppy Dearly?"

"Just a chat, that's all," Poppy replied.

"What about?"

"A case. A good one. One I promise you'll want to take."

"And why is that?"

"Because this case will be your big comeback. That is, if you're interested?"

7

A Meeting of Minds

Eric sat next to Poppy, his muscles tense. The car drove around the same small area of New York City repeatedly, stuck in hellish bumper-to-bumper traffic. The inside of the vehicle's expensive leather seats squeaked when Eric wriggled beside Poppy.

"First, I'm a huge fan of yours, Mr. Thompson. Truly, I am," Poppy stated.

Her cheeks flushed.

"That's very kind of you, but please call me Eric. It's nice to meet you, Poppy." He extended his arm toward her for a handshake. Strong and firm.

"Okay, so, Morsley Mansion, in Essex, in the UK. You must have heard of it?" Poppy asked.

Eric was, indeed, familiar with the place. Morsley had been on his and Michael's list of places to visit, but never had the chance. "Who hasn't?"

he said. "It's one of the most infamous locations for supernatural hauntings. I heard that it has been turned into a museum."

"It has," Poppy replied. "My boss, Michelle Snow, owns it. The museum is haunted. She sent me here to talk to you."

Eric smirked. "To tempt me? So, what's the deal?"

"A documentary." Poppy shrugged. "The usual thing; cameras have been placed in the house to catch any activity or sightings."

Eric's interest bloomed. "That's intriguing. What would I have to do for this particular case, well, job? Anything specific?"

"Whatever you feel needs to be done." Her voice quivered. "Hasn't that always been your way? It's all expenses paid, of course, and you will be paid a sum of five hundred thousand dollars for a one-off special, filming for three days."

"I've never been able to do a TV special on my own. What makes you think this will work?" Eric asked

"Because of who you are and what you've been through." Poppy's pupils dilated. "Who's going to pass up an opportunity to see the infamous Eric Thompson, controversial paranormal investigator? They want to see what's happened to you and what you're doing. People are interested in you."

"I find that unlikely."

"Unlikely or not, they will watch. That much I know." Poppy looked at him in admiration. "I also know that evidence of the supernatural occurrences that have taken place at Morsley over the years will draw in more people to visit the museum, which is Ms. Snow's intention."

Eric chuckled. "So, this is from a business standpoint for this Miss Snow ... clever. Who's commissioned it?"

"GMD studios."

"Not Liam Galavan by any chance?" Eric asked, strongly suspecting the hand of his former manager, whom he hadn't spoken to in months because he was always busy trying to save his many failing projects.

Poppy nodded. "He's one of the producers, yes. The cameras have been set up already, along with mics. It will be like we are filming a reality show."

"We?" Eric questioned.

"Yes. Surprise! I'm going to be your assistant. It's already been decided. You need a sidekick, don't you?" she said excitedly.

"True. But ... yeah. Sure. Fine."

"So, it's settled then. All you have to do is sign here." Poppy produced a contract from a folder at her feet and presented it to Eric on a clipboard with a pen.

"Let me at least read it first," Eric remarked, peering down and knowing full well he would be signing regardless. He was weak when it came to peer pressure, something Michael had programmed into him from a young age. He also had dyslexia, which he didn't wish to disclose.

"Of course," Poppy said.

Eric skimmed, muttering, then skipped to the dotted line.

"Looks good to me," he said, signing his elaborate, looping signature. "When do we start?"

8

Fables of the Past

Marshmallow-like clouds drifted through the clear, blue sky. Eric sat comfortably as the private jet soared through the atmosphere. The plane offered plush, red leather seats, and best of all, isolation—luxury and peace mixed together. Atop the pull-down table sat an assortment of nuts in small dishes. He reached for a few, picking at them one by one, enjoying their woody textures.

Eric sighed contently as his gaze wandered over the case file given to him by Poppy. He opened it. Poppy typed in a stylish, loopy font, not one he'd choose. Eric persevered through the difficult task of reading the notes, struggling through his dyslexia for the sake of intrigue and mystery. He rubbed his eyes, skimming the notes.

The horrors plaguing Morsley Manor were well known. Eric had heard most of the stories at some point in the past, but revisiting them only heightened his excitement. What could he find at this house harbouring such a dark history? A place of witches, ghosts, murderers, monsters, and God knows what else? Something about it all gnawed in the back of Eric's mind, however. Was it suspicion or curiosity? Eric couldn't tell whether it was his senses that tingled or whether it was emotion clouding his judgment. Tamara foresaw a fresh beginning—all Eric could hope for at that stage in his career. *Could this be it? No, something else.* He could feel it, something else was coming, though as to whether it was good or bad, he could not define. He exhaled and let go of the illusion of control, moving on, allowing himself to flow outward with the tide of what he considered to be fate.

Michael would have loved all of this. He saw a glimpse of his friend's face behind his closed eyelids. The last time they saw each other was shortly following their return from the forest in Japan. Michael faced Eric, the suitcase by his side in their apartment, avoiding eye contact, and stated he needed to leave. Eric's lip trembled as he pleaded for Michael to stay and then for Michael to let him accompany him; they had never been apart. Michael wriggled himself away from Eric, saying he needed time away from the world and from him.

Even now, that cut deeply into Eric. He finally begged his best friend to at least keep him updated on wherever he was going, to which Michael merely shrugged and said, "Maybe." Lifting his open palm up, Eric waited for his friend to meet it, to press his against it with a warm, tearful smile, only to be left alone as the door shut. Eric never knew what made Michael want to go, not honestly. Most would say it was what happened back in the suicide forest, but Eric sensed that it wasn't, not just that anyway, perhaps it was Eric himself. All he wished was that one day, he could see his friend and join hands once more.

Poppy stumbled in from a separate cabin, obviously drunk. She wore a flower-patterned, purple silk shirt, a black miniskirt, tights, and boots.

She had straightened her hair and looked somewhat different than at their first meeting. More stylish.

Eric glanced at Poppy as she walked unsteadily to a seat on his other side, exhaling booze-laden breath.

"So, what do you think?" she asked, pointing to the case file. "Can you get anything from it. Any clues?"

"Not yet. It's not exactly like solving a murder mystery. This is going to be a hard one," Eric replied, flashing a smile.

"Most people frown when they don't understand something, but you smile." She paused, regarding him. "Are you familiar with some of the theories surrounding Morsley? Some of them are quite *inventive*."

Eric sighed. "Yes, some of them are very interesting, ranging from aliens to cults. A portal to hell."

"The alien one hooked me the most. Poppy leaned in closer. "The theory that aliens made Morsley does seem to tie in with the strange goings on there. It suggests that experiments by these supposed aliens are behind all the witches, monsters, ghosts, and paranormal activity at Morsley," she slurred.

"Aliens are the ultimate symbolic representation of God," Eric said, using a quote he usually reserved for interviews.

"There's also a theory that there is a crazy cult behind it all, who make blood sacrifices and wear animal heads and skins. All sorts of things have been said about this place. But I guess we will just have to wait and see."

"The killings of women, witches, date back to the beginning and are very interesting. Their power has, no doubt, soaked into the land itself, amplifying the paranormal energies there. That could be why everything has only ever ended sourly there."

"Witches are freaky," hiccupped Poppy. "In a cool way, though. Have you met any real ones?"

"I've met a few," Eric replied, gazing down at the amulet Tamara gave him.

"That's so freaky! Have you seen any magic, like big stuff?"

"Nothing too exciting," Eric lied, not wanting to break his oath to Tamara and her kind. "Mikey was always more intrigued by witches, even going as far as trying to learn some magic. He never could quite get the hang of it, though, let's say."

"I think it's awful that so many women were accused of witchcraft and killed."

Eric steered the conversation in a new direction. "Hmm...sadly, it seems that, throughout history, the unknown has always been feared. People hate what they don't understand."

"What's the creepiest thing you've ever seen?" Poppy asked.

"Oh, jeez. Well, I wouldn't say it's the creepiest, but it kept me up for a few nights when a guy, years ago, emailed me a picture of a message he found in a bottle on a beach. It read something like: 'I am currently flying over the Bermuda Triangle. I have been lost in the same mist for over an hour now, and my navigation equipment isn't working. A light above keeps following me and is getting brighter. If I disappear, and this letter ever reaches anyone, please tell my family that I love them and not to come looking for me.'"

Eric continued. "It was signed by a man who had been reported missing over fifty years ago. Whether it was fake or not, I don't know, but that has always creeped me out a little. Just the thought of being alone, stuck in a mist, high in the sky with fuel running low, and something following you. That's freaky."

Poppy grimaced. "That is pretty bad, especially considering we're on a plane right now." She glanced outside.

"Yeah, but you know the difference between us and him?" asked Eric.

"No, what?"

"We're not in the Bermuda Triangle." Eric chuckled.

"That's true. Not like him and not like those people on that boat in the 80s. The one with—"

"I know the one you're talking about. The boat in 1984. That one, right?"

"Yeah, that one." She gulped, then added, "But it's weird, isn't it, how lots of ancient civilizations have just gone missing, the Roanoke colony for instance. How can people just disappear off the face of the planet?"

Eric shrugged.

Poppy poured a whisky from a crystal decanter sitting alongside other spirits in a small cabinet beside her seat. "So, how come you and your ex-partner, Michael, never went to Morsley?"

"We wanted to, but it just never happened."

"It would have been an amazing case with you two on to it," Poppy said, slurring. "You must miss him a lot."

"Yeah." A muscle twitched in Eric's temple.

"What was he like?"

"He was just ... Mikey."

Poppy swirled the whisky in her glass. "He always seemed very smart—you know."

"That was Mikey." Eric chewed on a peanut. "He had such a wicked sense of humour, so sharp and dark. Some would say cruel, but I guess he was just an acquired taste—even when he was crossing the line. He was always getting himself into trouble."

"Yeah, well, I guess we all like a bad boy, don't we. Most of us anyway." Poppy cleared her throat. "He was handsome."

Is she fishing right now, Eric wondered, trying not to crease his forehead as his stomach tensed. *If that was definitely a hint at her curiosity, don't worry, I'm picking up what you're putting down.*

Poppy shuffled in her seat as her tone adjusted, lower. "Handsome. But he never looked happy, though?"

"I guess."

Poppy paused, as if reflecting on her actions. She leaned forward and placed her drink down. "I'm sorry, I shouldn't say stuff like that. I know it must be a very sensitive thing for you to talk about."

"It's fine, really. Ask away."

"Was he unhappy about something? It felt like he covered up a lot from interviews I saw of him and you."

"Michael was never unhappy; he was just always ... what's the word? Dissatisfied."

"With what?"

"Even I wasn't sure. Life, I suppose. He always was troubled, complicated. He was very unpredictable and inconsistent. Even I couldn't understand his logic all the time."

"It hasn't got anything to do with what the media said years ago, rumours about you two being secret brothers? That you were closer than just friends."

"You watch too much TV."

"What can I say? You've got me."

"We were the only two orphans that arrived with name labels on in the whole orphanage, first names, that is. Isn't that strange? We chose surnames for one another. Mikey chose Thompson for me because he said it sounded very British, and he always made fun of me for being British at heart or always trying to be," Eric joked. "I chose Goode for him."

"Why was that?"

Eric struggled to remember. "It just sounded right at the time." He tapped his finger on the armrest. "It was weird, though, that we arrived within two weeks of one another, me first, and then him."

"Some would call it fate."

"Something like that," Eric mused. "Rest assured we aren't blood related. He was—is—a brother to me, though. We always had each other."

"You must miss him," Poppy said.

"More than you can imagine. That's life. You just have to keep going. Who knows? Maybe one day I will see him again."

"How did you two get started? You know, case-wise? What made you choose this life? What was the spark?"

"We really investigated it when we experienced our first ... encounter. "We must have been around seven or eight or something. We went on a school trip to Massachusetts to see a shoe factory. Michael and I wandered off. Well, Michael did, and I followed, like I always did. I found him in a cave in the woods. The floor was covered in leaves and bones. At first, we were like 'wow, this is awesome,' wondering what the hell lived there. Well, we found out." Eric smirked, his eyes widening as he shuddered.

Poppy licked her lips and leaned in. "What? What did you see?"

"God knows what it was, but it was big and hairy. It had a number tag on its foot. It must have escaped from somewhere, I guess, part of an experiment or something, I don't know. Anyway, it was so dark, all I remember seeing was what looked like a giant, man-sized bat."

"Jesus, what happened?"

"Nothing, it just looked at us. Didn't do anything. Just stared. It looked straight at Michael and didn't blink." He felt his nerves twinge at the memory. "The two just stared at each other; it was so creepy. It was like they were looking into each other, that's the only way I can describe it." Eric paused, then added, "Eventually, whatever it was, it backed away into the dark cave and disappeared. God knows where that thing is now. We went back years later to find it, but it was gone. So, anyway, on that day, Michael and I ran straight back to the class. But we didn't tell anyone, and no one even noticed we'd gone. Great teachers," he added sarcastically, giving her a thumbs up.

"Well, that's not disturbing at all. I'll sleep well tonight knowing there's a man-sized bat flying around out there. Thanks." Poppy scoffed.

"It affected Michael, though, even if he didn't like to show it. Mikey changed that day. We both did. Inspiration was one thing, but looking at that creature made him ..."

"Disturbed?" Poppy suggested.

"Mad." Eric's eyes closed in sadness.

"No great mind has ever existed without a touch of madness," Poppy said, looking up.

"There are a lot people don't know about Michael," Eric stated. "We made a promise, me and him. Every country, every mystery, every idea, dare, and adventure this world had going on it, we were going to do and see it all—together. But nothing was ever enough, it seemed. I don't think he ever truly saw or appreciated anything for what it was. He was never quite happy with the way things were." Eric paused, then smiled. "Anyway, tell me a bit about yourself."

"There's not much to tell," she remarked, gulping down the last drop of whisky in her glass. "Ordinary girl with an ordinary life." Poppy poured herself another drink.

"Maybe eat something," Eric said, pushing the bowl of nuts toward her.

"I'm good, thanks. My mum packed me some sandwiches and cake for the journey."

Eric grinned. "Okay, so you were saying ..."

"My parents originally came from China and moved to New York. They opened a restaurant, had me, and named me Poppy. I went to school, bartended for a while, and tried YouTube and failed. Then I started on the paranormal, and Ms. Snow contacted me about this job. That's it. That's my life."

"If your family is Chinese, how come your name is Dearly?" Eric asked.

"I didn't like my family's surname because, in China, Zhang is just so common."

"So, you're really Poppy Zhang?"

Poppy winced a little. "Poppy Dearly now. I changed it to Dearly because I liked the sound of it. I was called Poppy because it's my mum's favourite flower."

Eric smiled in response.

"Do you ever wonder who your parents were?"

"Not really. Whoever my parents are, they didn't want me, so that makes them irrelevant to my life, to who I am."

"Wouldn't you want to know why they gave you up if you had the chance?"

Eric shook his head. "Nope. I wouldn't want anything to do with them. Nothing good could ever come from knowing that. They are no blood of mine. I've only ever had one family."

"Michael?" Poppy replied.

"Yeah." Eric blinked away some dampness. "So, tell me about this Michelle Snow. What's she like?"

"We've never met in person. I've only talked to her on Skype, but I would say she is quite individual ... unique. She's from the US originally but lives in the UK. Miss Snow is rich ... her money comes from family, but she was very secretive about it all; she always pays me in cash via a third party. But I do know her money didn't pay for any of this." Poppy gestured around her. "The fancy plane and stuff—GMD did. Michelle pitched the idea for the show to the studio and got their funding. She seems nice, though and has been sort of mentoring me. Calls me 'bubbly' all the time and says I look like a 'lost puppy.' I'm not quite sure how to take that, but I guess she means I'm cute. She knows all about you. Big fan!" Poppy looked down at her clothing. "She picked this out for me to wear. It's not my usual style, but Ms. Snow said if I'm gonna be on TV, I need to look the part, and to start dressing for it."

Eric studied Poppy more closely and decided he preferred her dressed more casually. She looked uncomfortable in the outfit, as if she wore someone else's clothes.

Poppy's mobile rang, interrupting their conversation. "It's Ms. Snow. I'd better answer. Sorry," she said.

"That's okay, go ahead."

When Poppy answered, her tone was more sober than before. "Hello. Yes, Mr. Thompson is sitting across from me. Okay, just give me a moment." Poppy covered the phone and talked quietly to Eric. "I've just got to go check some details in the diary. I'll leave you in peace for a while."

"Okay," Eric said.

Poppy winked and stumbled back to her room; the phone clamped to her ear. "I'm just going to check now," she said, shutting the door behind her.

Eric turned to gaze out at the open sky and down to the ocean below in all its terrifying majesty. *What lurks below the waters?* Closing his eyes, he thought about the case and his curious new assistant.

9

Caught in a Web

Colourful, distorted images splashed through the dark. Brightness faded into softness. Fingers tensed, creaking when compressed. Eric's bones stiffened when he rose to his knees. He rubbed the back of his aching neck. He sat in a tunnel of sapphire and violet mystery, enthralled and unsettled by its shimmering beauty. Behind him, a door, and ahead, another door. What was it? Hadn't he just been on a plane?

Eric tried the rear door and found it locked, and his stomach sank. He crawled slowly to the door at the other end. Pulses like the Northern Lights flowed over the skin of the tunnel's surface. The other door was locked too. Eric turned back, heading to the door through which he entered. A sudden bang released a red glow through the frame of the door behind, the locked one. The banging quickened to the beat of Eric's heart. He hastened to the door ahead, the one he had come from, stumbling a few times when whatever lurked approached.

He moved faster and faster as his nerves pumped with adrenaline. His hands almost punched the door as it opened with ready ease. As he fell forward through the frame, the door sealed itself shut behind him. He tumbled down, down, down, but not to the ground. He got stuck at the centre of a dark, sagging web. Jolting and convulsing as he struggled to break free. He floated in an empty void that he'd often visited as a child. The netherworld Tamara had spoken of. Eric's limbs spread akimbo, stuck with a tacky, dark goo covering the vines holding him.

The ceiling was a dark, flat pool of ink. Impossible. The silent, still liquid above formed ripples. Long, hairy legs emerged, followed by bodies. Spiders! Thousands crawled down toward Eric—an arachnid army swarming down to eat their defenceless prey. A man's face that soon morphed into a woman's emerged from the pool's surface. A warning. Simple and clear. His nightmare signalled his doom; oddly familiar.

"Firebird."

Eric felt as if his heart was ripped from his chest when he awoke. Night crept in from his plane window. The interior lights had dimmed. *What on earth could that foreshadow for me?*

Poppy sat next to Eric, texting. She smiled warmly. "Having a nightmare?"

"Yeah, a nightmare," he said, rubbing his temple and sitting upright.

"I read somewhere that dreams are your subconscious trying to tell you something."

Eric frowned. "Where do you read all this stuff?"

"Social media, mainly. Facebook sometimes," Poppy replied. "Here's one for you. Did you know octopi have three hearts, have blue blood, are as smart as dogs, and can fit their whole body through a hole the size of a coin?"

Eric's expression didn't change. "Why do you need to know that?"

"I don't. It's just interesting."

Eric chuckled and gazed out the window into the dark.

10

Wind Chimes

The car rolled through the tree-lined streets of Trewnway, a typically English village in Essex. The song "Sweet Dreams Are Made of This" played on the radio. Poppy sat beside Eric on the backseat, tapping away at her phone, sunglasses on, chewing minty gum. The driver was an older, stocky man with years of apparent hard work built into him. Wisps of white hair and dry skin attested to it.

The village looked quiet and overgrown—a place people never left; they were born, lived, and died here. The residents appeared drained and hollow to Eric, a stark contrast to the appearance of the overly green village itself. They watched the car drive past. One milky-eyed lady sat alone on a bench and turned, staring at Eric. *Something seems not quite right about these people. Not menacing, just blank.* Perhaps it was because Morsley was on their doorstep, a place where many lives were lost. Perhaps they feared more would follow, and the cult theories were true. The buildings looked as if they were once very pretty, but now lacked any signs of life other than the vines that crawled up them. That and every wall was coated in many a missing person poster, the most recent labelling a college student named 'Shannon' as vanished. The trees were dead. Autumn had stripped the life from Trewnway, it seemed.

They took dusty trails off the beaten track through bushes and bends and stopped at a sign: MORSLEY MANOR.

Poppy lowered her phone. "We're here."

The mansion appeared out of nowhere, as though hiding, situated away from the village, in the middle of a forest. Eric knew the mythology. The mansion cast shadows over everyone and everything. Foreboding settled upon all who dared to step on the blood-soaked land. The house possessed something intangible—stuck between heaven and earth in an eternal purgatory. An invisible force emanated with a negative polarity, like a black hole drawing things and people toward it. Distracting and disorienting, it infected Eric at first glance. Tall, wide, and old, the building obstructed the sunlight behind it. The architecture appeared timelessly gothic. Dangling wind chimes rang from a balcony, clacking and chittering in the air like rotten teeth swinging from a string. A black cat with yellow eyes watched from the porch as they approached.

"It certainly is a sight to behold," Eric said, watching men leave the house. "Who are they?"

Poppy peered at them. "Looks like the tech guys are finishing up the cameras, microphones, and equipment. They must be leaving."

The driver stopped, removed the keys from the ignition, got out of the car, and opened Poppy's door. Eric got out from the other side, gazing up at Morsley's dark majesty.

"Here you go," said the driver in a rough-sounding Essex accent, offering his hand to help Poppy out of the car. "Though why you'd want to come here is beyond me."

"Thank you," Poppy said. "The cost should be covered by Ms. Snow."

The driver smiled. "Yes. Let me help you with your bags." Opening the trunk of the car, he huffed, then reached in for the two cases. He picked up Poppy's fashionable case and made toward Eric's tattered brown one.

Eric snatched his own case. "Allow me," he insisted.

"This way, Eric," Poppy directed.

The departing technicians' van started up. They pulled away, escaping off into the wood-lined road, a trail of dust following them. Eric gazed upwards at the manor. He thought he saw a small silhouette watching him from the top left window, but couldn't be sure due to the failing light. His skin itched more with every step he took toward the enormous double doors. The wind chimes grew louder, even with little wind to jangle them. Eric turned to see the furry feline watcher who continued to observe the pair from its position nearby.

Poppy pushed the doors, opening them wide, sending a gust of air through the house. A large double-sided staircase and a balcony with a rear window. Dark brown floorboards creaked as they passed the cream-coated walls. A dusty electric chandelier large enough to crush ten men hung from the ceiling.

Poppy whistled as she did a little dance, eying the spectacle of it all. "Ah, wow, this is cool," she casually stated as she went to reach for the chandelier, then flopped her arm back down, rocking her head. "Damn I vibe with this place, check, it, out!" She smiled, tapping the glass of the displays on the walls. "This place is bigger than it looks in the pictures."

"You can say that again," Eric said, searching for anything creeping in the shadows. The house seemed to breathe as though it were alive, its history bleeding through the cracks and crevices. Eric felt its wheezing pulse pump through his.

"The displays are all on these walls. Why don't you glance over them?" Poppy instructed. "I will go find Ms. Snow. She texted me to say she was here, finalizing everything for us." Poppy drifted off with her phone toward the sitting room. The driver followed and plonked her case down before he departed. He couldn't leave fast enough.

Upon the wall read the beginning of a very long backstory of the house, which Eric struggled with, his dyslexia making the words blur at times.

THE LAND

In 1646, Matthew Hopkins came to Trewnway to hunt witches. Twenty-three women were reported murdered that year through use of a 'swimming test' in the local river, used to determine a witch.

MORSLEY MANSION

The house was built in 1862 by the Morsley family on the outskirts of Trewnway, Essex, in England. The family was wealthy and from London.

A year after moving into the house, Lord William Morsley fell into a depression and would take long walks in the surrounding meadows and woods. His wife, Lady Elizabeth Morsley, began following him into the woods and found him talking to himself. The pair became distant from one another, and in 1863, Lord Morsley slit the throats of his two children in their beds. Lady Morsley witnessed his actions and beat him to death with a fire poker before slitting her own throat. The house remained empty for almost one hundred years.

Eric looked below the text to see a photo in a glass case and found a black and white picture of the Morsleys. They stood side by side, unsmiling, as if forced to be together. He placed their two children in their teens. They wore nineteenth-century clothing. Amelia and Philip Morsley. Both resembled their mother. Eric believed their smiles hid the sorrow of living a life under tyranny. William Morsley was a short, stubby man with a wide moustache. Elizabeth Morsley appeared to be a skeletally thin matriarch with dark hair and striking eyes. For a moment, he believed the image shifted, as if Elizabeth's head had jerked. *Nothing but jetlag,* he reassured himself. He wondered what the place could have done to them. Would anything happen to him and Poppy? The faces lingered a little too long in his gaze. Faces that time had gazed at and Eric knew that time never forgets.

"Do you like it?" a voice asked in a New York accent, similar to his.

Eric gazed at the top of the stairs and spotted a shadowy figure, backlit by a grand window, making her striking silhouette powerful and potently female. *A dramatic introduction if ever there was one.*

Poppy clip-clopped her way across the floor from the other room to greet her boss. "Miss Snow. There you are. I just tried to call you."

The mysterious Ms. Snow moved away from the window, revealing herself as she walked down the staircase toward Eric. She wore a shiny, black pantsuit decorated with excessive lace and ruffles, topped off with a distinctive faux noir, crocodile skin collar. He placed her age at around thirty, like himself. Dark brown hair flowed like waves down her shoulders. She painted her lips rouge and wore false, dark eyelashes like a glamorous Golden Age Hollywood movie star. Her eyes reflected like deep pools of sapphire. Eric found something oddly familiar about her—something dangerously reassuring. Perhaps it was the way she walked down the stairway with such elegant ease, each heel carefully placed on the step. *Her red carpet. Her domain.* It reminded Eric of something, someone, but he went blank like a computer freezing. *Maybe I've met this woman in another life, or maybe she's a witch, part of the coven.*

The tall, elegant figure glided toward Eric with welcoming ease. "Here I am," she gushed. "Can it be *the* Eric Thompson in my web of madness at last? You're even more handsome than in your photos," she said through curled lips. "Michelle Snow. Nice to meet you." She extended a manicured hand.

Eric shifted backward and offered his hand. When their skin touched, he felt a fizzle of energy shock through him, something familiar, something warm. After a moment, it was gone. Frowning, Eric couldn't name the feeling that brewed inside.

"Eric. Eric Thompson," he said eventually, retrieving his hand. He stood, his mind itching away at the feeling burrowing deep within his core. *There's something about this woman.* "It's an honour to meet you, Ms. Snow."

"Please, call me Michelle." Her voice was deeper than he expected, but smooth and controlled. "I'm so glad you're here. I trust my protégée, Poppy, has explained everything to you?"

"Yes, she has," Eric answered. "Very much so."

"Marvellous, then you know about the cameras. They will be filming round the clock to catch everything that ... *occurs.*" She emphasized the last word.

"Yes."

"Wonderful. Then let me show you both around."

Michelle escorted Eric and Poppy into the opposite room. It was dark and dingy, stuffed with large sofas showing signs of excessive wear. A once-grand fireplace stood cold and unused against one wall. A large-scale model of a pirate ship sat beside the window.

"This is the lounge area where, in 1996, the Joy family's boy stabbed his two friends in the eyes with pencil crayons," Michelle stated with strange enjoyment. "The Joys threw the little guy into an asylum. He's still there ... I think. It's hard to track. Same goes for that pesky Berkane family who seem to have moved on to the other side of the world."

"They probably wanted to get as far away from this place as possible," Eric said.

Poppy chewed loudly on her gum as she followed them.

Eric approached a sofa, knowing what might happen. He touched its rough fabric and was transported back to that day. He saw flashes, images of a blonde boy, Thomas Joy, staring blankly at two other boys, each dead on the blood-stained, hard-oak floor. Wax crayons stuck out from their bloodied eyes.

Eric jumped back, snatching his hand away. He gazed down as the blood stains faded away, absorbed into the wood. Michelle watched him as if she understood what had just happened.

"The cameras are in every room?" Eric asked, recovering from what he had witnessed.

Michelle drifted toward the model ship and fiddled with its sails. "All rooms except for your own bedrooms and en-suites. Each room has three to five cameras. We won't miss a thing." She pointed out each of the cameras in the room. "They're fairly obvious." Michelle paused to glance at Eric and Poppy, as if to gauge their reaction, before walking to a connected room. "Right this way."

Eric and Poppy followed Michelle quietly into a large room full of books. A long window-lit wall of ancient texts. Piles of papers were draped over a desk. Strange ornaments adorned some of the shelves between the books. A large, red leather chair sat in one corner. The air was heavy with dust, making it hard to breathe.

"This is the study, so if you get bored, you can always find something to read in here," Michelle said, placing her hands on her hips.

Eric stepped forward and traced the tip of his finger across a line of books, scanning their titles. "Can I ask if you have ever experienced any unusual activity yourself?"

Michelle seemed to mull over the question. "I have. Many times. If you believe in such things. But nothing bad. Nothing harmful. Shadows have flickered past the corners of my eyes, that's all, but people have reported worse. Much worse in fact."

Poppy asked, "Like what?"

"Feelings of being choked. Some claim to have seen the previous inhabitants, ghostly apparitions. But like I said, that's only if you believe in such things."

"Yeah, well, I think it's fair to say that I've seen a thing or two," Eric said solemnly.

"And I'd love to hear all about it sometime," Michelle said before glancing at the books upon the shelves. "The house sold to the Rolfe family in 1973. Their eldest daughter, Bridget, spent a lot of time in here, and she kept a journal recording the supernatural incidents occurring in the house. The typical bog-standard stuff: feelings of strangulation in the night while the family were in bed; sightings of a girl watching them;

radios turning on by themselves in the night; the sound of balloons popping; objects and people being pushed; shadows moving; lights turning on and off."

"What happened to them? The Rolfe's?" Poppy asked.

"Oh, they went missing in 1974, leaving all belongings behind with no clue as to where they went." Michelle casually stated, then added. "Creepy, right?"

"Very," Poppy replied as she rubbed her arms.

"One of my favourite creepy moments here happened in 1994, when two local kids broke in and reported being chased out of the house and through the woods by a man. They claimed to see multiple pale, skeletal creatures. Police searched the house and the land but found no one and nothing suspicious."

"Skeleton creatures? How very ghoulish sounding." He forced a smile.

"What is a ghoul?" Poppy asked Michelle abruptly.

Michelle turned with a slight frown. "What?"

"What is a ghoul, like what is it? I've never understood? Like a ghost is a ghost, a demon is a demon, a monster is whatever. What is a ghoul?"

Eric chuckled internally as he watched Poppy wipe the grin off of Michelle's seemingly always-smug face. Her expression fell flat, like a dropped pie.

The lady's lashes fluttered. "I ... I don't know—"

Eric interjected, "It's a very commercial Halloween term, but I believe it's meant to be the spirit of a supposed monster. Though, that could be argued as being a demon anyway. I know in some cultures the world demon is frowned upon so it may originate from that."

"Thank you!" Poppy nodded with a wide grin. "That was going to itch away at my brain like a maggot until I found that out."

A warm chuckle escaped Eric. 'Don't mention it."

Michelle cleared her throat. "Let's carry on, as we still have the rest of the house to cover."

Michelle led them through the lounge and across the hallway to the dining room, a pale room full of creepy animal paintings and dead plants that hung on some shelves. The only furniture was a table and eight chairs.

"The dining room in all its glory," Michelle remarked, not stopping, but continuing through a door to a connected room. "And here is the kitchen."

Clearly, no one had used the room for cooking in some time. It was more a home to cockroaches than fine cuisine.

"Is there a story connected to every room?" Eric asked.

"Not as such, but history, yes. We like to tell the whole story, not just about the supernatural goings on. After all, a house reflects its owner. This building is a historical landmark."

Poppy nodded. "That's interesting."

Michelle nodded and rewarded the young woman with a patronizing smile. "Now let's get the creepy one out of the way." She moved toward a small door in the wall, revealing a steep staircase descending into darkness. She gestured to them both. "After you."

Eric stepped down first, shining a flashlight retrieved from one of his coat pockets. He pushed past Michelle, who was smiling the whole time. She seemed to be getting pleasure from watching Eric stumble about this sad place with such a horrific history. Each step downward became harder, like they descended into hell. A squalid, dirty room came into view in the torchlight. A surgery with bloodied equipment and towels lay upon a metal trolley and an operating table. A large mirror hung on the wall, reflecting into the cellar. Eric approached, sceptical. "Umm?"

"This looks like a horror movie set," Poppy noted.

"We managed to buy the doctor's old equipment through an auctioneer. He would do all sorts of things down here with his patients, all sorts of experiments. Poor souls, he started killing them down here eventually, or worse," Michelle explained, tinkering with the bloodied equipment. "Fake blood helps with tourist interest. Makes the place seem that much more ... real?"

"But those are the actual tools he used? I didn't even know he killed his patients," Eric said in disgust.

"Me neither," Poppy added.

"Few do." Michelle chuckled sadistically.

Eric's back arched at hearing her cackle at that, and he winced a little.

"Yup." She blabbed on. "Most things are authentic in this place. It's not just window dressing." She set a syringe back on the trolley. "It's crazy to think, isn't it, 1952, the respected Dr. Edward Felstead bought this house and restored it just so he could carry out his twisted work here, alone, in this little dank room. Oof! It gives my quiver a shiver!" Her neck tensed with a slanted sneer.

Eric refrained from approaching the instruments of torture, not wanting to do so in front of Michelle and Poppy, even though he was interested. He picked up echoes of screams.

"I didn't know about the patients. I didn't think this place could get any worse," Poppy said, cringing, as she hugged herself tight.

"Not worse. Just more beautifully tragic." Michelle laughed

Eric peered closer, watching this callous woman. He was intrigued.

Michelle turned to climb the stairs. "This way."

Poppy followed. Eric noted the cameras around the room. Something bothered him, however, and it was neither the cameras nor the vile tools nor Michelle's very dark sense of humour. It was the mirror. Had he really stooped so low as to give in to cheap reality show gimmicks for the sake of his career? *Yes, this was who I am now. Times keep changing.* He would have to change if he wanted to remain a part of the game. He would need to evolve to survive. He straightened his ombré coat and smoothed his hair distractedly.

"Coming, Eric?" Poppy called from the top of the stairs.

Eric turned. "On my way."

The trio continued the tour. To Eric, the house of horror looked decked out for Halloween. He fell behind as they ascended the grand staircase. Michelle resumed the lead. They walked past the grand window that lit the landing; Eric accidentally brushed the banister with his hand, triggering a psychic flashback. The image was fuzzy and grey in his mind. A man in white, who seemed to be entranced by something, placed a noose around his neck and stepped over the banister. The brutal crack of his neck as he jumped caused Eric to snap back to reality.

Michelle seemed to smirk looking at him, then turned to caress the wood as Eric regained his breath. "This banister was where the doctor hanged himself. He was a bit of a lunatic," she said, continuing down the gloomy hallway. "There are three bedrooms with en-suites that have no cameras. There is a bathroom that does have cameras, but you won't be using that." Michelle stopped abruptly and turned to face them, pushing open a door revealing a shabby bedroom. "This was the one where Lord Morsley killed his two children and was beaten to death by his wife. I know, romantic, right?" Michelle giggled.

Is this woman psychotic? Eric wondered as a current passed through him. "Yeah, I can tell this was the place."

"How's that?" Michelle asked, watching him closely.

Eric shrugged, forgetting for a second that very few knew he was gifted in the way that he was. "I can just sense it." He stated.

Michelle's eyes turned reptilian. "Right ... well, there is also the nursery, which was the Berkane girl, Madeline's, room. Follow me."

She led them along the corridor, stopping in front of another door. Her slender hands pushed it open, revealing a brightly coloured room in contrast to the others. It showed signs of neglect and decay despite having been more recently decorated than the others. Eric walked over to the window, the one he swore he had seen someone watching him earlier.

Teddy bears, toys, and music boxes sat in a corner waiting patiently to be played with. A doll sat in a rocking chair, which moved eerily backwards and forwards. The doll looked handmade, with buttons for eyes and stitching that was coming undone. She had crude, blushing cheeks fashioned from scraps of material and a sewn-on smile that reminded Eric of poor Alice Hickford's expression as she died. The memory of that day, the helplessness he had felt, brought forth a wave of melancholy.

Eric moved away from the window and approached as if to touch the doll, but simply placed one finger upon the arm of the chair to cease its rocking. Silence filled the room. He walked away, and it started again. Eric's brow furrowed.

"Oh, that usually happens," said Michelle. "There's quite a draught from the window in this room."

"I hope that's the reason," Poppy said.

"The Berkane's arrived in 2003. After a few incidents, they brought in a local psychic, Jacqueline French, to cleanse the house. French reported never having experienced anything like it before. According to her, the house was alive. Soon, Madeline, the daughter and poor thing jumped from that window one night with that doll she found in the Clown's shed out the back." Michelle said, leaning on a wall. "Her parents said that she was always talking to it— kids and their imaginations, ha? Now, it's all social media and apps."

"What's its name?" Poppy asked.

"Sorry?" her mentor replied.

"The doll?" Poppy pointed toward it. "All creepy dolls have creepy names."

"She doesn't have one, not that I know of anyway."

Poppy sighed. "I can't lie. I'm disappointed. I'm going to name her Rosie."

"Why's that?" asked Eric.

"Because she's got rosy cheeks."

"Can't argue with that," Eric said.

Michelle looked unamused before glancing at her expensive watch. "Right, now to the attic."

The trio climbed more stairs to the top of the mansion. At the peak, a door creaked slowly open, revealing a room full of mirrors and nothing else. A large window lit the way through the maze of reflections.

Michelle walked through the labyrinth. Eric and Poppy followed, seeing themselves reflected a hundred times over. Michelle stopped abruptly by the window. "This was where Lady Morsley killed herself, slit her wrists, right here."

"What a view," Poppy said, peering out.

Eric gazed out of the window. It was somewhat sunny outside, despite the gloom inside the house. It looked misty in the forest, with miles of woodland stretching and obscuring the horizon. The trees were nearly as tall as the house itself.

"Sometimes they say you can hear her cries in the wind up here," Michelle added.

"What's with all the mirrors?" Poppy questioned.

"We put them all up here out of the way. So, they don't show the cameras."

"So, this room doesn't have any cameras, then?" Eric asked.

"No, it doesn't," Michelle snapped. "I don't know why—they tried to set them up here, but something kept interfering with them. The signal or something. Maybe it was the old bat herself wanting some privacy."

"I wouldn't joke about that," Eric said. "You just might be right."

"I usually am," Michelle replied, looking at him like a spider at a fly.

Eric squirmed ever so slightly. The woman's pendulum swings in mood and tone kept him on the edge. He felt as though he was being played with, though for what purpose, he could not tell.

Poppy squinted through the window and pointed. "Is that the river over there?"

Eric and Michelle both looked at the same time.

"Yes. It runs right through the village," Michelle said. "God knows how many women were drowned in those waters back when Witch Hunter Hopkins was around. And the shed belonging to that paedophile Clown is also just down there." Her slim finger tapped on the glass and pointed toward a shack. "It's filled with stuff that we bought from the same auctioneer."

"Well, this place is just a bundle of joy, isn't it?" Poppy sniffed. "And I'm beginning to feel like bait for whatever evil resides here."

"You can catch more flies with honey than vinegar."

Poppy regarded her boss coldly. "You can catch even more flies with manure."

Eric gave Poppy an odd look. His suspicions about the house were growing, along with the show, Ms. Snow, and her true intentions. It was as if she were hiding behind a veil, one he could not quite see through or lift.

They clambered down the staircase to the landing where the large chandelier dangled above.

"I can tell that has whetted your appetite," Michelle stated.

"Got to say this place has a lot more going for it than I expected ... and I expected a lot," Eric said, attempting to flatter Michelle. Wanting to keep her sweet, at least for now.

She smiled as if it were a personal compliment. "That's good to hear. I just knew you'd love it." Michelle looked at her phone. "Gosh, look at the time. I must be off. Poppy, please make sure Eric has everything he needs."

"Will do," Poppy responded.

"And if you should need me, Mr. Thompson," Michelle approached him and stood close, handing him a card with her number, "answers are just a phone call away."

Eric grasped the card in his fingers. "Thank you. Last question: how soon do we start recording?"

"The cameras have already started and will continue to run until we have what we need."

"Right. So, I guess we better get to work then, Poppy," Eric said.

"Wonderful, well, it's probably best if I leave you to it then. Have a look around, take all the time you need," Michelle said. "See you both soon."

Michelle Snow backed out of the double doors like a movie star, all the time observing the duo with a grin.

"Well, I'd better start unpacking," Poppy said, her voice quivering, though Eric didn't know whether from fear or excitement. "God knows how long we will be living in this hellhole."

Poppy picked her case up and began her journey to her room up the staircase closest to her. She stopped midway and turned. "So, what's the plan?"

"I will be unpacking in a second. I just want to have a look at these displays for a moment." He smiled.

"Whatever you say."

Eric went back to the picture of the Morsley family. Then he looked at the others that had been added over time. History. There were drawings of women being drowned and burned as witches. The deranged Doctor Felstead. The Rolfe family with their three daughters. Jonathan Creeda, the psychotic Clown kidnapper, and the missing children were never found. The Joy family and their children of two girls and the one boy who stabbed both of his friends in the eyes with crayons. The Berkanes, the blonde girl, Madeline, with the doll, newly named Rosie.

All the photos had something in common. Their eyes hid dark, devouring secrets Eric recognized all too well.

11

Children of the Forest

Eric's hand cramped from carrying his worn case, as he lifted it up onto his bed, one which hadn't housed a body in years. Luckily, it was not the room where the Morsleys had died. The walls were painted a dingy, pale yellow. The weather wasn't too cold or warm; reason enough for him to wear his coat indoors. His watch chain jingled.

He opened his case to reveal a wealth of untold treasures: his own unique brand of clothing, items, and tools he planned on using in the house ... and a stuffed monkey. The toy rested on top of everything, grinning at him; it made him recall simpler times in his life. When he and Michael were kids, they visited the zoo with the orphanage as a special day out. They both bought their favourite animal. For Eric, a monkey, and for Michael, a dolphin. His palms caressed the small ape's fabric. The memory warmed his heart, though only for a moment.

A tingle ran down him to his very core, like a droplet of cold water. His eyes widened, alert. His body tensed. Something lurked behind him, watching. A lifetime of chasing ghosts had taught Eric to keep calm in such circumstances. He turned. A shadow dressed in white disappeared, running away. Eric leapt after the apparition. Further on, he saw another door wide open as the white figure ran through it. Someone—or something—let out a childish giggle. Eric followed, sprinting down steps, almost tripping. Through the kitchen they went. The apparition ran out the back door, leaving it wide open.

A blonde girl, wearing a white dress, entered Lacey's shed. Eric followed her into the dark shack. Its wood was splintered with decay and grime. The interior was a dark abyss riddled with cockroaches, toys on the floor, hanging chains and hooks, tools, and cages where the smiling psychopath had once kept his young victims.

He recalled the tale of Lacey the clown, what was known. How, in 1990, a man named Jonathan Creeda moved into Morsley. A frustrated performer who kidnapped children from the village to try out new material for his clown act. He kept them hostage in the very shed Eric stood in. One day, villagers found him dead and the children missing, never to be found.

Eric shivered. He couldn't see the young girl he had followed. His senses hummed. , Eric tapped a dangling hook with his ear. He shuddered. A flash image revealed how Lacey would string up pigs on the chains and feed them to his children, as they cried and called out for their mommies. Eric gagged at the sight of the conditions. He imagined Lacey with his long, greasy hair and powdery, pale skin, his eyes filled with madness.

Lacey scared the children for his own amusement. Until, over time, a bolt from the cage came loose, freeing his captives. Collectively, the children attacked the deranged Clown, using a knife to cut into him an eternal smile that they proceeded to stitch together using their shoelaces so he would never again be able to taunt them. Then they stabbed both of his eyes. Blood gushed from the wounds. The feral beasts stitched button eyes into his bloody sockets, leaving him to bleed to death on the hay-covered floor as they stumbled out into the forest.

Eric's vision snapped back to the present. *Those poor kids*. What had come over them to make them act so violently? Had it been Lacey the Clown's cruelty, or the place itself?

Movement in the cages spun him round. He approached, hoping to find the little girl. Eric leaned into the bars. Something sprang out with a hiss. The black cat. Eric's eyes followed the startled animal as it exited the shack. He caught sight of the girl watching him through the crack of the door. She darted off as Eric lurched toward her, giving chase into the dark woods.

Poppy began her ritual in her en-suite, safely away from the prying cameras. She felt a sense of accomplishment she hadn't experienced in quite some time. Things were looking up. Everything went just as Poppy hoped, her new beginning finally coming to fruition. She smiled in the mirror; a glow softened her skin, and her eyes twinkled. Her hands slipped off her clothes, leaving her naked and free. She turned the tap of the shower to a comfortable temperature to help relax her muscles. The steam hit the ceiling above, causing a groan. *It must be the pipes*, Poppy thought as she stepped into the cleansing waterfall. She stood underneath the water, dousing her head under the streams, making her feel alive and refreshed. Her heart pounded harder as the pulses hit her face. She closed her eyes tightly. Her fingers massaged the muscles around the back of her neck.

A creak beckoned from outside the shower. Poppy turned but saw nothing through the misted glass. After wiping the water out of her eyes with the back of her hands, she saw a blurred silhouette, distinctly male, through the misty glass of the shower. He was watching her. Poppy blinked and jumped back, choking on her own air as her muscles clenched. She cursed as she stubbed her heel. "Fuck-fuck!" she yelled angrily. She turned the tap off, which emitted a rusty squeal. Grabbing her towel, Poppy stepped out gingerly. She was alone. The figure had left.

Had it been a ghost? Was that it? Or her imagination? Poppy had always been a very open-minded person, if somewhat naive. She could just make out what seemed to resemble a dripping handprint on the steamed mirror. Her instinct was to find Eric and tell him. No, it was just her mind playing tricks on her. He would dismiss it immediately and think she was easily frightened. *It was nothing, just paranoia, nothing more*, she thought as she wrapped herself in the towel, trying to calm her racing heartbeat. Then her mind flittered and she wondered, *Can you punch a ghost?*

Twigs snapped ahead as Eric moved forwards, pushing shrubs out of his way. Girlish giggles rattled through Eric's head like nails in the tin that was his skull. He was gradually catching up. Something about the woods made Eric lose control, maybe it was the triggering suicide forest or something more primal. Maybe it was something leaking through this land, in the air. Feeling more and more like an animal hunting prey, about to pounce. Feral and wild. Suddenly, he halted, losing any breadcrumb sounds she was leaving, hearing nil in this empty part of the forest. Nothing moved. The girl had vanished.

Eric looked back and saw only trees. He neither had any idea how long he had been tracking the girl nor how deep he had ventured in the woods. The crunching earth seemed familiar to him. *Where have I seen this kind of thing before?*

Wind blew through the thistles and leaves. Whispers crept. A symphony of childish voices called to Eric. Softly, quietly, and then louder, "Firebird."

Again and again. Eric screamed through the growing winds. Confused and alone, he gazed around, looking for the origin of the call. Thousands of young, tormented voices screeched at him. They stopped. A buzz sounded from his pocket. His chest beat hard, and his breathing was fast and heavy. He slipped his hand into his pocket to reach his cell phone. Poppy.

"Hello? Where are you?" Poppy asked, clearly trying to mask a frantic tone.

"I just went for a walk," Eric replied unconvincingly, not wanting to scare her, not this early on anyway.

"Walk where? We're in the middle of nowhere?"

"In the woods. I'm coming back now. I will be there soon."

"Okay. Please hurry," Poppy replied.

Eric disconnected and rubbed his eyes, then began his long trek back through the woods, still feeling eyes watching him through the trees.

12

A Call to the Other Side

Eric burst through the front doors of Morsley Mansion, and a gust of air caught his coat, causing it to flap behind him. His head turned to see Poppy in the dining room finishing preparations for a séance. She swung round.

"There you are, finally," she said. "I've had to set everything up on my own."

"Good, good. I'm sorry," Eric replied, still distracted by thoughts of what had happened.

Poppy peered at him, "Are you sure you're okay?"

Eric walked across the floor to the window. "Yeah, yeah." He lied. Not wanting to risk freaking her out.

"What were you doing out in the woods?"

He ignored her question. "Is everything set just as I said?"

"Exactly like you told me to earlier."

The table was at the centre of the room with five unlit, green candles. Chairs had been arranged around the table. His EMF device was ready and positioned on the side table.

"Well done," Eric congratulated her. "It's always good to start with a séance to contact the other side. To find out what the spirits want and what their intentions are. And make them aware of ours, of course."

"Sounds good to me," Poppy said without conviction, gazing up at the paintings of animals dotted around.

Eric threw off his coat and took out a box of extra-long matches from his pocket. "Do you want to help me start lighting these candles then?" he asked.

"Sure thing."

Eric sparked a match and passed it to Poppy for her to use at one end of the table, while he began at the other.

"So, how did you learn to conduct a séance?" Poppy asked, lighting the first candle.

"Someone taught me a long time ago, along with a few other things," Eric said, feeling his amulet around his neck still.

"Who?"

Eric chuckled. "An old friend."

"Don't want to say while the cameras are rolling, that's fair enough," Poppy remarked.

"Quite." Eric winked at her. "Now, whatever happens, you must remain calm."

Poppy swallowed. "I'll do my best."

Eric ignited the last candle and blew out his matchstick. "Shall we begin?"

"What happens now?"

"You sit there, and film what you can with your phone." He pointed to the chair closest to the door. "I don't trust all these other cameras."

"Sure, sure," Poppy breathed, whipping out her phone. "Just say when."

"Start now, as we can cut out anything unnecessary." Eric sat down on another of the chairs and pulled out a long pin from his trouser pocket. Pricking his finger, he allowed three drops of blood to fall into the central flame of the candle. Eric's voice spoke out loud and powerful. "Come, spirits of this place. Speak to us. We mean you no harm. We want only to talk with you."

A sudden rush of cold air seemed to move through the room, putting out all the candles at once. Both Poppy and Eric jolted. The walls creaked as if in painful mourning. Different noises sounded: a girl's giggle and a Clown's laugh. Louder and louder, together and all at once. They stopped.

"Who dares enter my home?" a harsh female voice came through the walls. The EMF device remained still.

Poppy's hand rushed to cover her mouth. "Fuck! It's Lady Morsley."

"Two humble servants, Ma'am, who wish you no harm. We want to know nothing more than what you and your fellow spirit friends want from us," Eric said.

"I wish for your wretched souls to leave my land for good," the voice replied.

"Eric?" Poppy whispered.

He turned his attention to Poppy, who was pointing to the floor, which was moving. Each floorboard its own way, as if the room were breathing. The creaking became noticeably louder, cracking through the walls and floor beneath.

Eric frowned, having never seen anything quite like this before.

"But, fair Lady, we can help you move on. Bring you peace."

The door behind Poppy swung open and hit the wall, causing her to jump and squeal. The EMF still sat unmoving.

"Leave. I will give you no further warning, sir," the voice warned.

Poppy shivered, still holding her phone up, recording what looked like an earthquake.

"Eric? What's happening?"

"Your veiled threats will not work on us, Elizabeth Morsley," Eric said. "This land does not belong to the dead!"

Suddenly, the three large windowpanes smashed. Poppy screamed. The device remained still, as if switched off. A strong gust blew through the open windows. Eric clutched the amulet beneath his shirt.

Poppy cried, "F-fuck! Eric! Please, I can't! Stop!" She dropped her phone, tears falling down her cheeks. She remained seated, petrified. A frozen spectator.

Eric sprang to her aid, helping her swiftly out of her chair. "Come on and get up. Let's get you out of here." They rushed out together, grabbing their personal effects.

Outside, Eric sat Poppy down on the steps, as she cradled herself, shaking. Eric huffed, both frustrated and sympathetic. The woman was out of her depth. She took on way too much. Eric realized she was all he had and swallowed his disappointment.

He patted her arm reassuringly. "Poppy. Poppy. Listen to me. You're going to be okay."

"I'm sorry, I just couldn't take it."

"No. It's fine. It just spooked you a little. That happens to everyone. Even me, sometimes."

"I'm not sure I can—"

"Hey, listen. You were born to do this. It's your dream, remember? Don't give up because of one bump in the road."

Poppy nodded as she clenched her fist.

She had a fire that fought true and brave; he could feel it simmering, even now. It was a warmth that he was not used to, and he found himself flushed and grinning at her.

"Now, how about we go back in and get what we came for?" said Eric.

"I can't right now. I'm sorry, I just can't. I will later, but not now."

"It's fine," Eric reassured her. He was eager to continue his quest but knew it wouldn't look good if he abandoned his partner to chase ghosts on television. "What do you want to do?"

"I need to eat."

"Let's get some food and come back later."

"Yes, please," Poppy said, blowing her nose noisily.

"Good. Wait here while I go back in. I just need to make sure none of the candles are still burning."

"Okay," Poppy said, drying her tears.

Eric entered the house, swiftly turning to the right. The dining room was completely empty, as quiet and untouched as they had left it. He was disappointed. "You'll need more than some cliché tricks to scare me out of this place," Eric said, hoping to provoke a reaction. This was a technique he often used. He waited a moment before leaving. Nothing happened. The wind whistled through the shards of broken glass still attached to the broken window frame. Eric shut the door and left.

13

Bedtime Stories

Walking always cleared Eric's mind. Made him re-evaluate a situation, no matter what the circumstances. It helped him attain a calm, measured train of thought. Journeying into the village to find refuge from the Morsley estate, however, didn't seem to assist. What he witnessed stopped him in his tracks. *What just happened?* He couldn't process it. Eric spent his life chasing and witnessing the strange, but something was not right. But why? Even the EMF hadn't detected anything. Poppy walked silently beside him, visibly shaken. Eric gazed upward at a sign that read The Stag's Head.

"This will do," Eric said, escorting Poppy with a supportive arm through the door.

The interior of the pub was dark and dank, the air booze ridden. Animal heads hung on the walls. The patrons stopped their conversations and turned to look at the newcomers. Eric and Poppy walked up to an ale-stained bar to order their drinks before moving to a rickety table beside a warm fire.

Poppy read the menu card on the table, clearly distracting herself with the promise of food. Eric continued to consider the strange events. Suspicious eyes watched the pair from all directions.

"What are you having?" Poppy asked Eric.

"I'm not really hungry. You go ahead. I'll get something later."

Poppy went to the bar to order her food. Eric fixed his gaze on the hypnotic flames, trying to work out why he felt so uneasy.

Sitting on mute, time soon passed in the silent flickering of the fire's glow. Poppy's meal arrived, fish and chips, the special of the day. She tucked in hungrily. They didn't speak until Poppy finished, rested, and her plate had been cleared. Eric's brow was still heavy with concern as he obsessed and replayed recent events.

"So, what do you think?" Poppy asked, sipping her drink.

"I'm not sure, Poppy," said Eric.

"Well, did what we just witness actually happen?"

"Of course, it happened," Eric said, uncrossing his legs.

"But was it real?"

Eric stroked his lips. "That's a good question, one I've been pondering myself."

"Do you think it was faked?" Poppy asked, leaning forward.

"By whom? Your boss, Ms. Snow?"

"Our boss," Poppy corrected.

"She wants tourists for her museum of curiosities. So, maybe. There is definitely something going on at the house, though, that much is clear."

"How can you tell?"

"I just can," Eric replied, not wanting to reveal too much. "Can't you feel it when you're in that house? All that pain?"

"Yes!" Poppy yelped.

"Ms. Snow is a tricky one. She has an ulterior motive; I knew that the second I met her. Has she ever said anything to you that has seemed weird or suspicious?"

Poppy's chin lifted. "Not really, she was just very eager for all this to happen."

Eric pondered. "Hmm ... I often find the dead are easier to deal with than the living."

"Who said she was alive?" Poppy joked. "Maybe she was a ghost the whole time?"

Eric felt himself form a smirk as it was soon kissed by the warmth of the fire. "I'm glad you've managed to retain your sense of humour."

"Guess I've always got that to fall back on."

"It's weird. I've dealt with cases before, the good, the bad, and the wild, but nothing like this," Eric explained. "Morsley is definitely haunted. It's a dark nexus with all the death and madness surrounding the place. It's like the Pharaoh's tomb; everyone who enters gets cursed. It's stained by dark energy. Everything that touches it ends up dead. It's a powerful force, triggered by events. The history unleashes a psychic energy. The house is like a battery holding negative energy that feeds on trauma and pain. But there is something else at work there. Why the cameras? Why now? There's something I'm missing, something in plain view."

Poppy shrugged her shoulders in response. "Everyone loves a ghost story, I suppose."

Eric sipped his drink. "Roanoke, the Bermuda Triangle, boogie men. Bedtime stories we tell kids and one another to make us realize the scale of what's out there. The enormity of it all. Stories that, with a bit of belief, become reality."

"You're talking about the power of faith? There's got to be more to it than that," Poppy said.

"There often is, but with this, I'm unsure. It's not just a ghost story; that would be too easy."

"What do you think we should do then?"

"I suggest we play our parts out until we find the right thread to pull on. That's all we can do for now."

"So, we're going back tonight?" Poppy clarified.

"Well, it's a full moon. That means the spirits will be at their most potent tonight. The lunar cycle affects more than just the waters of the sea and our brains. In any case, we are contracted to go back so yes, it's what we have to do."

"Okay," said Poppy, finishing her drink.

"What's wrong? Still scared?"

Poppy nodded.

"It's okay to be scared; it's a survival tactic. You're just being smart, unlike me." He took a sip of his drink.

"Well, you're brave."

"No. Not really. You know what I am? I'm an idiot who just goes blindly into things. I'm a kid poking a plug socket with wet hands." Eric pointed to Poppy. "You, on the other hand, you're a woman trying to survive, to find her chance and come out with her head held high."

"Don't you ever get scared?"

"Yeah, I have done, in the past. But I remember what Mikey told me years ago ..." Eric lowered his voice further. "Do whatever the hell you want to do and whatever you've got to do with no regrets. Worst case scenario is we die, and we've all got to do that at some point anyway. Once I realized that, I never held back."

"Worst case scenario is we die?" Poppy repeated.

"Well, there are worse things to do than haunting people at Morsley; we could be doing something really boring like accounting."

"If I die, Eric, I will haunt the hell out of you. Fly through walls and do all kinds of scary shit." Poppy laughed.

"That's the spirit."

Poppy's grin soon mellowed as her gaze drifted to the fireplace.

She needs a little motivation; I can see the spark in her dying. I need to pour some gasoline on it. Licking his lips, he then spoke. "You know, you shouldn't be trying to be like me, or a replacement for Michael. You're your own person, someone who has a flame burning inside you."

She chuffed. "Corny much?"

"True, but you have something in you, a fighter, you're a protector," he said softly. "I can ... sense it."

Her head bobbed as she rubbed her neck. "My mom has always said I'm fiery, that I'm a fighter."

"Hmm ... something to think about," he said, then added, "Now what do you say, shall we go and investigate, partner?"

Poppy took a deep breath. "Might as well. What's there to lose now?"

"Very true!" He rose, along with Poppy, feeling happy that he had managed to inspire her.

Eric held the door for Poppy as they left the pub, still feeling eyes watching them.

A man beside the door spoke to Eric. He was of an older age, with grey eyes and white hair. "Morsley Mansion, eh? You're gonna die up there." The man seemed to revel in the words he had just spoken; whether he meant them as a warning or a threat, Eric could not tell. Though much like a naughty child being told not to press a button, Eric couldn't help but press it. *I've survived this long,* he thought, lifting his shoulders. *I can survive Morsley, I will survive Morsley,* he beat it into himself like a drum.

14

Child's Play

Every step closer to Morsley made Eric's stomach tighten. The dark sky could not disguise the sheer enormity of the monstrous building. Its hollow form conjured up shapes of nightmarish spikes and figures that Eric knew, in his heart, were simply parts of the exterior. The lights were on inside. The show had sensor lights to come on automatically to catch anything on camera. Still, his heart skipped a beat or two upon seeing a silhouette watching from the attic window, the same watcher from earlier when he arrived. What was it? A shadow, a trick of the night, a lost soul, or something else? He turned to Poppy, walking along beside him.

"You okay?" he asked.

"No, but let's just do this."

"Just remember that whatever is waiting for us in there can't hurt us," he lied. A rustling sound came from the forest, and they both turned. Nothing. Maybe a fox or some other animal. Eric's pendant tingled against his chest. Arriving at the front door, he opened it with careful ease. The chandelier above lit the entire landing, pouring light into every room.

"Stick together, no matter what," Eric said. Usually, he preferred to split up, but with Poppy being so anxious, at least he could keep her safe.

A girl's giggle echoed through the lounge to their left. They both jumped. Poppy followed Eric as he stepped into the room.

"Hello?" he called out. "Is there someone here with us?" Eric glanced at the cameras dotted around the room. Another laugh emanated from the small study that sat through the lounge. It was a small figure. A child.

Eric stepped forward. "Are you lost?"

The being did not move. Just watched as Poppy stepped back, then paused, puffing her chest out.

"I don't want to hurt you. I'm a friend. Can you tell me your name?" He crept slowly forward.

Nothing. Then the door slammed shut. Eric paused for a second. Leaping at the door, he attempted to force it open, but it appeared locked. He peered through the keyhole. "I want to help. Please open the door."

Pale moonlight poured in through the window, picking out dusty books scattered around. "Please!" An object then covered the keyhole. Someone, or something, was hiding in there. The broken old radio that sat on the lounge table began to play "Tonight You Belong to Me." Its eerie tone resonated off the walls. Poppy's fist tightened as she gazed around, evaluating.

"Fucking dumb ghosts." Poppy huffed under her breath.

Eric stormed over to the radio, pulling the plug.

"It's nothing," he insisted to Poppy. It played again, unplugged. Eric turned and pressed the 'off' button with his finger. Nothing happened. Eric smiled to reassure her. The lights flickered. The paintings on the walls flew off, crashing hard on the hard, wooden floor. Poppy jolted back, avoiding a narrow hit from a piece of artwork.

"Fuck y—" Poppy licked her lips and looked around. "You fucking missed, bitch."

Eric ran, grasping her arm.

"Don't give in to it," he said. "It wants to scare you, alright?"

Poppy took a deep breath. "Alright!" Her head nodded, avoiding eye contact. "I ... I'm not scared." She winced a smile.

All the lights in the house went out. Darkness descended. Eric waltzed to the light switch, flicking it to check that it was not working. *The whole house must be out.* Eric shone his flashlight around. Tied to the landing rail at the top of the stairs floated a yellow balloon he hadn't seen before. A large anamorphic shadow appeared against a wall on the landing. It beckoned with its finger. Its shape expanded and abruptly retracted.

Another laugh followed. Older. Male. Amused. Demonic. Strangely infectious. A Clown's calling card. Poppy and Eric traded glances.

Eric moved to the stairs, climbing a few steps before turning to the terrified young woman behind him. "Coming?" he said, reaching out a hand to Poppy.

Poppy grasped his hand and followed Eric up the stairs. The laughter rattled through the wall to their right, vibrating with mischief and madness. Eric's senses prickled, but not as much as they should have, given the circumstances. Something was wrong. As he turned the corner to open the nursery door, he saw the moon leaking in through the window. The shadow of the tendrils of a tree reached across the room toward Eric.

The door creaked open as he approached, inviting them in. Rosie the doll sat in her white wooden chair, as she always had, rocking, only now she faced the window.

Poppy gripped the door frame, leaning on it like a crutch.

The toy's eyes followed Eric as he walked across the rainbow children's rug toward the demonic presence. Poppy gasped as Eric grew closer to the doll. It rocked rhythmically, the movements stronger and heavier the nearer he got. Tension grew in Eric's muscles, and his chest thumped hard as he reached out to stop the chair.

"One, two, three ..." he counted and then acted. He gripped the wooden frame with a sweaty hand. It stopped. Eric stood still. He crept back to the centre of the room. *Hmm. Odd.* He'd expected ... something. *How anticlimactic.*

Softly, "Ring Around the Rosie" played through a music box on the dresser, a ballerina twirling within.

A clapping monkey animated. The children's toys came to life. The sound grew, building to a pulsating cacophony. Eric spun and saw a blurred figure hiding in the bundle of toys in the corner of the room. A face white as death, with a gloss of blood staining its lips and razor-sharp cheekbones. His untamed hair was a vivid shade of orange like a lion's mane. He wore a smile so sinister even the devil would have recoiled.

Poppy turned in the direction Eric was looking. Amongst the stuffed animals and fluffiness, a crazed clown rose to his feet. Johnathan Creeda. Lacey the Clown smiled below his cherry-red nose and yellow, snake-slit eyes.

Poppy stammered. "Yuh ... you ..."

The cruel clown winked and waved, saying nothing. Poppy lifted her fist and punched the smile right off the clown's face, causing the spirit to fall back into shadow. Eric turned at the sound of Poppy's footsteps racing out of the room. It was only a second but when he looked back, the clown had gone. He shuddered. *That's not right! She shouldn't have been able to do that!*

Eric chased after his young companion, skidding around the corner. He yanked Poppy back just as she passed the nursery.

"Hey!" he yelled, growing impatient.

"I can't. No, that fucking clown was the last straw! I'm leaving. Don't try to stop me. I can't do this," she wheezed through panic-stricken breath.

Poppy was shaking. Eric clutched her shoulders, clamping her to him. "Listen, just breathe. It didn't hurt you, did it?" he said as a statement more than an actual question.

"No, but ..." she said, glancing behind him.

Eric spun in the same direction. A small red ball rolled out of the nursery. Eric picked it up, examining a yellow star upon it. As he looked up to see who had rolled the ball, the door slammed shut, and he fell back.

Poppy clutched her chest. "Jesus-fuck!" she spat. "That's it! I'm done!" She rushed down the staircase.

"Poppy!" Eric shouted after her.

Hanging above her was the doctor's body. The corpse wriggled, only for a moment, his heart beating once more.

Eric ignored the vision and focused on bringing back his assistant. "Poppy!" he shouted after her. "What did I say? Never give up, never give in."

"No! No more!" Poppy said in horror as her head turned towards the macabre body swinging above her. "I thought I could do this, but I just can't."

Eric caught up with her as she opened the front door. He slammed it shut. "Listen, you keep getting yourself worked up."

"Well, of course I am! Anyone would. We just saw Chuckles the fucking psycho clown in there!"

"Who you just punched."

Her face twinged, then she asked, "Is-is that normal? Can you usually punch a ghost?"

Eric held her reassuringly as he hesitated before responding, not wanting to freak her out with a truthful answer. "Go and sit in the car," he said, keeping his tone mellow and dangling the keys from his slender fingers. "Listen to some music. Let me handle this one. Okay?"

"Okay." Poppy sniffed, grasping the keys.

Eric opened the door.

"What if I need you?" she asked.

"Phone me," Eric replied, beginning to shut the door. "Or failing that, just yell."

"What if you need help?"

"I won't," Eric said, pushing her out of the door and closing it.

15

Shadows on the Walls

The darkness consumed Eric now. He felt it lingering, still and dormant. Morsley's creaking bones groaned around him. He scanned all angles with his flashlight but found only shadows. *This place must be very powerful to manifest a spirit who was able to be punched.* He had never seen or heard about such a thing happening with a ghost before. *Does that mean they can punch back? Or worse?*

A sudden knock sounded from the right of the dining room door, which was shut. Eric crept toward the old wood, placed his ear against the door, and knocked. Nothing. A reply knocked back, but it came from the walls, floors, ceilings, and steps. Everywhere.

"Get out of here. Get out of here." Whispers accelerated so fast that each sentence collided into the next and mangled into an endless loop.

Eric's head spun. Banging sounds came from the closed dining room door. He ran back and careened hard toward it, not knowing what waited on the other side. Anything would be better than the continuous ringing voices. As the door swung open, the whispering stopped. Inside the dining room, everything remained untouched from Eric's earlier failed attempt at a séance. Broken glass covered the floorboards. Melted candle wax sat upon the rickety table with chairs crowded around.

Eric breathed hard, clutching the black onyx around his neck. His EMF remained unmoving on the side. Eric thought he would prefer the whispers to the unnatural quiet. A sound came from behind the kitchen door. Eric took a deep breath and walked through, adrenaline pumping his veins. His hand pressed against the oak. His flashlight revealed a selection of knives, stabbed into walls and surfaces alike. Eric walked through the blades as if they were giant thorns.

In most cases, Eric chased things he understood—to a certain degree, anyway. He could sense them, sniff them out, and gain some control over the experience. He had no idea what he was dealing with here. He must have missed something obvious. Surely, the situation wasn't a prank from the television studio. No, it couldn't be. All the power was off, so the cameras couldn't be working. Maybe it was revenge from someone? But who? Perhaps it was just some lunatic stalking him. Was it even possible that it was all real? He didn't know. But he had to find out, and the only way for him to figure out the mystery was to move forward and do it alone.

Eric approached the next closed door. Gripping a large knife in one hand from the kitchen, he used the other hand to tap open the door with his torch. Eric stiffened and adopted a defensive stance. Dark stairs awaited him. His flashlight revealed scuttling insects.

Each step Eric took made him feel the gravitational pull of the house. Tightening around his neck. He was sensitive to every creak and groan. Finally, he reached the cellar. The beam from Eric's flashlight lit up the doctor's surgery table and all the horrors left behind. Eric almost jumped at his own reflection in the large, rectangular, oddly placed mirror on the wall. Something glimmered on the floor, and Eric shone his light downwards. It was one of the surgical tools. Eric picked up a small silver scalpel. He examined it and placed it back on the small, dirty table.

Unnatural light emanated from outside. Eric hopped back like a startled cat and dropped his flashlight to the ground. Another flash accompanied thunderous rumbles, causing dust to fall. Eric's heart beat fast. He picked up his torch. A flash of light hit the mirror, revealing the doctor staring right at Eric from the mirror. He wore a white lab coat covered in bloodstains. He had greying hair and burning, rage-filled eyes. He held up a syringe.

Eric gasped. He reached behind. In the next flash, the doctor appeared younger, with dark hair, operating on a fully conscious patient, who cried and writhed in pain. A blood-splattered, rusty saw sat upon the side table. The image disappeared, but a flash of lightning brought it back. For a few seconds, Eric glimpsed the lunatic in the looking glass. It was enough to convince Eric he needed to get out.

He ran up the stairs, each foot landing awkwardly in his haste. He only made it to the third step before a hand reached up from below and pulled Eric back, causing him to fall back down, and his flashlight became a swirling spotlight. He sat uncomfortably at the base of the stairs. Looking behind him, he made out no sign of whoever had pulled him down. The hand had disappeared, as had the lighting and the awful man in the mirror.

Eric's need for thrills abated. He clambered back to his feet and evaluated his surroundings. Nothing had changed. Eric took a moment to calm himself. He shouldn't rush or make a tactical decision without considering his options. He wanted to get out of this hell but didn't know which instinct to employ: fight, flight, freeze, or fawn. His heart felt weak and uneasy.

The stone on his chest tingled as a breeze blew in from the stairs, across the room, and to the mirror. Upon further evaluation and now from a different angle and light, Eric spotted fingerprints on the dirty mirror. The air lightly pressed the mirror inward into the wall. *How is this possible?* Eric tilted his head. He picked up his flashlight and approached the mirror. On inspection, the mirror was concave and covered in fingerprints.

The breeze blew through Eric's trench coat as he felt the cold glass. He looked at his cut and bruised reflection and grimaced. He pushed the mirror, revealing a secret passage behind. His amulet vibrated softly as he investigated the dark tunnel ahead. As he moved forward, a slight give beneath his feet emerged, along with a sudden damp earth smell. Soil. Only uncertainty lay ahead. Eric continued along the tunnel as the mirror shut behind him, sealing his decision—and his fate.

16

Blink

The company's GMD car had been dropped off hours before. Poppy rattled the keys Michelle had gifted her and slammed the car door shut and locked it, disappointed in herself. Now feeling somewhat fired up, she slunk back into the leather seat. Why had she cracked? She should have just gone along with it, handled it, and proved to Eric that she was more than some stupid fan or wannabe. But it was too late now. Poppy couldn't go storming after him in that haunted death trap. No. It was a ridiculous idea. The best thing to do was sit and wait for him, apologize for everything, and try again. Then show everyone—ghosts included— what she was capable of. Yes. Her self-doubt swallowed her whole, drowning her in guilt for what she had done, or for what could happen to Eric now that he was alone. No, he was a professional. He would be fine. Poppy needed a distraction from her thoughts and, acting on Eric's suggestion, turned on the radio, flicking from station to station until the opening of "I Can Feel Your Heartbeat" by The Partridge

Family filtered through the speakers. Its rhythm soothed her nerves and mellowed her thoughts a little.

She gazed at the manor. Something moved in the attic window. A shadow. Poppy tried to focus but couldn't make out any further details. Probably nothing. Just the residual fear. She needed further distraction. Her phone. Yes. She could check her notifications, anything to stop the negative thoughts crowding her brain. Whipping out her mobile, Poppy noted the weak signal. The screen froze when she attempted to check her messages and emails. She tapped, pressed, clicked, and whacked it to stop the phone screen from freezing. She cranked the music up a notch, the sound pulsating through the wheels of the car, down to the solid earth, wanting to drown all outside noise out. Distracting her.

Poppy jumped at a sudden knocking on the back window. She sprang around. Nothing was there. She looked round and toward the back again. All seemed still in the moonlight, even the wind. She positioned herself to watch through the front again, shivering. A rustling came from the bushes to the right. Poppy looked but saw nothing. Then another knock came from the rear window.

"Eric? Is that you?" she called out, her teeth chattering. "This isn't funny." Another knock came, closer, at the front side mirror. Poppy twisted her head forward but saw only the house looming in front of her. She breathed slowly, exhausted from fright. This must be some sort of trick. Wanting to just drive off, she knew she couldn't, not without Eric. Her heart told her to get out of the car and run, but where would she go? Into the woods? Back inside the house? No! She needed to stay put and fight, if necessary, for Eric's sake as well as her own.

Something knocked at the rear of the car, the back window, it seemed. *What would Eric do?* she tried to rationalize. She turned calmly, her mind clear, ready to face her tormenter. *Don't be afraid, it's what they want,* she thought, remembering what Eric said. Her neck stiffened like antique wood as she turned, only to, once again, see nothing. Poppy forced herself to relax, unclenching her muscles. Maybe it was a branch falling from the trees, or a bird, or something. Smiling, she felt more in control of her fear.

Poppy turned back around and, inches from the glass, appeared the cruel, sadistic grin she'd seen in the nursery. Lacey the Clown had come to play. Button eyes gleamed as his crusty lips, stapled high on each side of both cheeks, revealed his receding, bleeding gums. He held up the squeaky ball and laughed maniacally. Poppy's scream blasted over the song on the radio. Lacey's yellow eyes burned into her.

Another knock came, followed by a childish giggle from the left window. A little girl dressed all in white peered at her with big blue eyes and long blonde locks. She smiled and waved. From the back, another knock came from the doctor, blood dripping from his white uniform. He held a syringe in one hand and adjusted his spectacles with the other.

Poppy could no longer scream or make any noise. Frozen in shock, she dropped her phone. The doors were locked, yes, but how long would the glass last? Were they ghosts—and if they were, couldn't they just pass through the doors? Or lunatics dressed up and intent on trying to kill her? It didn't matter, Poppy didn't have the luxury to ponder such details. Instinct kicked in, and she turned the key in the ignition. The car wouldn't start; the engine failed. Its headlights flickered. In her frustrated focus, Poppy failed to notice someone else approaching.

Until the flickering headlights caught her.

The woman stood still every time the car lights came on, moving as fast as lightning when they went dark. A woman wearing a black, Victorian dress and wielding a bloodied knife. Bearing a pale, ghoulish face and eyes of pure madness. She peered out of her wasted face. Closer and closer she came with every flash of light.

Lady Morsley had come for blood.

Poppy finally accepted that the engine was not going to start and there was little she could do. The other three spirits turned to the matriarch with deference, or so it seemed. The lady glared at Poppy. Blood seemed to stop flowing to the petrified young woman's brain, paralyzing her completely. This was the power of fear, and it was a weapon that the Lady of Morsley clearly knew how to wield expertly. The song screamed one final note of "I Can Hear Your Heartbeat" before ending bluntly as Poppy sat frozen, awaiting what would surely come next: her death.

17

A Perfect Illusion

Eric's boots pressed into soggy earth. The tunnel smelled like rot. Or a sewer. Or a bit of both. Eric turned when the entrance behind him clicked shut. He saw straight through it. A two-way mirror. Things were growing more curious by the minute. Why the gimmicky mirror? This had clearly been fitted for the television show, surely? It was not some sort of Sweeney Todd escape route for the doctor to dispose of his bodies. *It has something to do with the show, but what?* The image of the doctor in the mirror wasn't real, either. He would have sensed it. It was just an actor in a costume trying to scare him in an attempt to attract a large audience across the globe. *Yes, that was it.* Cables hung from the ceiling, raising Eric's suspicion.

Something crunched beneath his shoe. Insects crawled and sprouted everywhere. They scuttled around Eric in the mud and muck with armoured legs. The walls moved. The light from the flashlight harried the crawling beasts. Eric's chest thumped as the black stone vibrated. He groaned and readjusted Tamara's gift.

A scurrying sound came from behind him, and Eric spun round, flashlight in hand, aiming the beam toward the spot. He caught only a glimpse of something dark blending into the wall. Eric pressed on. He followed the tunnel through a web of sharp twists and turns until he arrived at a place where a warm lightbulb glowed from above, illuminating metallic stairs leading toward another closed door. Yellow and black hazard tape blocked it. Eric frowned, then climbed up, tucking his flashlight away.

The cold handle turned. Apprehensive about what could be on the other side, Eric was still eager to learn what the hell was going on. The inside of the room was lit by a bright light that made Eric wince. The room looked extraordinary, like something from the set of a sixties sci-fi show—bleeping machines, flashing lights, power generators, and wires hanging high and low. No windows. Warning signs hung over every piece of machinery and wall. If the secret room was generating power, why was the power off in the house? His idea about the show being a huge joke seemed likely. Was Poppy in on the joke? Did she know? Eric thought hard. If she did, she was an Oscar-winning actress for her crocodile tears. Eric mulled it over, nearly tripping over the carpet of endless serpent cables. He reached another door, an exit.

Eric went up the steps leading from the door and staggered outside. Chills of air whirled into his face, cooling the sweat forming on his brow. He came out of the woods. The tall trees cried in the wind. The moon loomed above, filling the forest with a blue haze.

A set of large, thick, joined cables ran from the building along a track further into unknown terrain in the trees. Eric decided to follow this trail. His head stayed low, ignoring anything in the wilderness that could be watching him. He didn't want a reprise of the symphony of whispers he experienced. He continued forward, sensing eyes lingering on him as he passed, as if he were prey. Feeling the necklace humming, Eric stopped.

"Lost, are we?" a familiar voice teased him.

Eric turned around to see Michelle Snow leaning against a tree with her arms folded, one wayward curl of hair dangling against her cheek. Eric sensed her overwhelming self-satisfaction. "My, my, you look like hell. Ready to do things my way now?" Her smile glowed in the darkness.

"What are you doing here?" Eric asked angrily. "What's going on?"

"Not so fast," she said. "All good things come to those who wait." Her eyes twinkled.

"I've had enough games." Eric moved toward her in a threatening manner, although with no intention of harming her.

"You had to go through that damn mirror and spoil everything, didn't you? Typical! Still, we got what we wanted out of it." Michelle grinned.

"What exactly did you get? Please explain," Eric demanded in an icy voice. "Tell me what's going on. What is this show really about?"

Michelle mimed zipping her mouth.

Eric sighed. "Oh, come on. I've travelled very far. This is your chance to tell me your whole plan."

Michelle said, "Oh, believe me, I know and what a long time I have been waiting for this moment."

"Right, so we can cut the bull. You've been making some sort of prank show, right?"

"Not a prank show. More a mockumentary, though not to mock you."

"Then why?" Eric asked.

"Why not?" Michelle shrugged.

"That's not a reason."

"That's my business."

Eric couldn't help feeling that this dance had been performed before between the two of them. The back-and-forth interaction between them had a strange familiarity to it. It confused him. "Is Poppy safe?" Eric asked.

"Oh, she's safe. Don't worry. Isn't that right, boys!"

A wall of spotlights suddenly exploded with light from high above, from the trees. Eric shielded his eyes while he adjusted to the brightness. "Christ."

Other shapes now emerged. People. Two men with cameras were filming them. Michelle circled around Eric playfully like a little girl with her new best friend on the playground. More people revealed themselves from the sidelines: the ghosts, Lady Morsley, the demented Clown, Madeline Berkane, and Dr. Felstead. Followed by a tear-streaked Poppy who seemed bewildered.

"Poppy, are you alright?" Eric asked, somewhat blinded.

"I'm fine," she said.

"See? She's fine," Michelle waved off her charge like a neglectful babysitter.

Eric's face soured. "Who the hell are you?"

"Haven't you figured it out yet? I would have thought a renowned investigator like yourself would have no trouble in working it out...that you'd have felt it ... in your heart?" She clutched her hands to her chest theatrically. "Surely. You must be able to ... sense it?"

Eric stepped back, realizing she had him sussed. "You know about ... *that*?"

"Oh, I've always known." She smiled.

"How? Who told you?" Eric stepped back. "How could you possibly know?"

Michelle smiled seductively, playing to the cameras. "God, you've become stupid over the years. Then again, you always were the slow one, weren't you? You never saw what was right in front of you."

Eric's eyes widened. "Who told you?" he asked again.

"The only person who could, Eric," Michelle said, her tone teasing. "The one person who has always known. You."

"I don't understand," Eric said.

Michelle batted her false eyelashes as she drew closer to him. "Look at my eyes, Eric, look very closely, because they are about the only things they couldn't change."

Eric gazed deep into her striking blue eyes. "No. It can't be," he gasped.

"Oh, it can be."

Eric reeled. "Michelle Snow. You're ..."

She raised a long, painted fingernail to his lips to silence him. "Now you see," she said. "You understand why I couldn't keep calling myself Michael Goode, don't you?"

"You ..." Eric struggled to form words.

Michelle's face froze. "That's right. It's me. Your old Mikey! Surprise!" She extended her arms.

"Impossible."

"You of all people should know that nothing is impossible."

"But how? Why?" Eric's face burned red.

Michelle moved closer, clutched Eric's shoulders, and spun him toward the cameras and spotlights. "There will be plenty of time for explanations later," she said, grinning. "For now? Why not give us a big smile? You're on TV, after all, and the night is young."

18

All is Fair in Love and Madness

Michelle escorted Eric in silence. He had no idea where they were heading and couldn't tell if they had been walking for thirty minutes or three. He caught sight of cables as they went, hanging low down to the woodland floor, disappearing amongst the dead leaves and dirt. He was seeing the veil drop. Mikey had torn away the backdrop, the fake scenery of the night, with one blunt swoop. His world was folding in on itself as he felt his chest tighten. All appeared out of focus to Eric as he contemplated what had just been revealed to him. He didn't quite know what to feel toward his old friend—if he could even call her that. Eric knew she was Mikey. He recognized those Pacific blue eyes. Even small mannerisms seemed to connect. The same dark sense of humour, everything. What her motives were, though, Eric just couldn't fathom.

What a shitty way to reveal something like this to me, Eric thought, *what was he... she... thinking.* Michael—now Michelle—was intelligent but not *emotionally* intelligent. In that department, Mikey was always and still now, apparently, woefully inept in understanding others and their feelings. For that, Eric had picked out his fair share of emotional shrapnel inflicted upon him by his best friend, though the scars lingered from being the pain sponge between the two. Though now, he felt years of stitched-together old wounds had been torn wide open once more, with a dash of salt rubbed in for good measure, tenderizing his already weary mind and aching body.

Eventually, the cable ran to a small portable studio, far from the house and the generators. Michelle swung the door open with black, manicured fingernails and pushed Eric forward. The room shook from their weight as they stepped in, causing it to shake. Inside, various whiteboards bore the results of brainstorming and planning sessions. Control panels above showed different camera angles, recording the action from all angles of Morsley Mansion.

Michelle shoved Eric down in an office chair. She marched over to the door, her black, high-heeled boots clacking, and shut it. She turned to face Eric with her hair up, in her dark blue satin pantsuit complete with pointed shoulders.

"Oh, that was brilliant," she said. "Your face." Michelle twisted up her face into mock terror. "Classic. I mean, I love the crap they show on TV now, but did you see that? And dear Poppy, she was so scared, it was hilarious."

Eric glared.

"We have so much to catch up on. Social media these days is just amazing, which reminds me I need to update my story." She clicked away on her phone.

"Why did you come back?" Eric asked, his jaw tense.

"Oh, come on now. You always knew I wouldn't be gone for good. Go on, admit it; you're glad I'm back."

"But why did you just go off and not tell me where you were? And about ..." Eric gestured to Michelle's appearance. "I was so worried, confused and ... hurt. Why didn't you confide in me?"

Michelle shrugged. "It was something I felt I had to do on my own. I thought you knew. You did, didn't you? You must have known that I wasn't happy—that something was missing. I was unfulfilled."

Eric thought back, shaking his head. "I don't understand. I tried to be a good friend to you. Always." Eric's voice quivered.

"Yes, and you always will be," Michelle said, approaching him.

Eric rubbed his tired, sore eyes. "Now this mad set-up. Why have you done this to me? Let me guess. You went and saw the world, lived your dream, our dream, but it wasn't enough?"

"No. Only because I wasn't a complete person. Now, I'm back and ready to pick up where we left off."

"So, you want your career back? And you thought you could drag me into your little scheme without asking me, like a puppet on your string."

"This will lead us both to a blazing final act. Now, doesn't that sound good?" She pressed against his chair, forcing him to lean back.

"Hmm, you may have changed your face, Mikey, but you're still the same," Eric whispered.

"I'm glad you brought that up. What do you think?" she asked, strutting up and down the pine floor like a model on a catwalk.

"Why do you care?"

"Of course I care what you think. Your opinion is the only one that matters." Her brow twitched with uncertainty.

"Why didn't you tell me? I would have supported you."

"I was born in the wrong body." Michelle peered at Eric closely.

"I had my suspicions over the years, but for you to sneak away without a word. That hurt."

"Oh, come on, I'd never want to hurt you, Eric. You must know how I feel—"

Eric held up his hand for her to stop. "Don't. I can't do this ..."

"You have so many questions. I can see it in your eyes."

"How did this happen? Tell me everything, from the start."

Michelle gestured with her hands, as if she were already prepared. "I wanted a new beginning, a happy one, I thought, after ... the incident."

"Aokigahara?" Eric said dryly. "That time you upped and left me—"

"Yes, that. The only chance I had to escape from it all. To start anew and be the person I knew I was inside." Michelle wandered over to a small window and stared out. "I withdrew from my old life, came out from the public eye. I needed space alone to explore who I really was. Who I wanted to become. Who I have always been, deep down."

"And you did that by shutting me out, your oldest friend. You couldn't tell me? Send a message, make a call, tell me that you were okay?"

"I'm not proud of that, but it was something I felt I had to do on my own. I needed time to myself. I knew you would never give me that," Michelle said, turning to face him again.

"So, what, you just went travelling? And then what?" Eric asked, incredulous.

"Well, I've had adventures. Travelling the world. Oh, the places I've been." She whipped out her phone and held it in front of Eric, flicking through photos of her travels. "I've been everywhere, Rome, Marrakesh, London, Singapore, LA. Everywhere." She leaned in and pouted beside Eric before taking a selfie. "Just wait till this goes viral." She sighed heavily. "But after a time, I got bored with my new life and felt dissatisfied. Sure, I had money from our many specials, but having to live a lie, a life under sunglasses and hats, made me feel … restrained. I knew I needed a complete transformation into the person I was always meant to be … the woman I was meant to be."

"So, what then?" Eric regarded Michelle through weary eyes.

"I travelled to Switzerland under a false name and had … several operations, hormone therapy and stuff. That's it." She shrugged. "When I looked into the mirror afterwards, once Michelle was born, I felt a sense of freedom. Of completion."

"Then what happened?"

"Eventually, I realized that wasn't enough. So, I came up with a plan to get what I really wanted. I bought Morsley Mansion for a bargain price and turned it into a profitable museum. Then I contacted Liam with my idea. You know, of course, he's in on this."

"Liam Galavan? I bet he couldn't resist."

"He couldn't, and neither could you. I knew you'd jump at the opportunity to come to Morsley with the possibility of jumpstarting your career again. And hiring Poppy to be your plus one was just the icing on the cake. I know what you like, after all." Michelle winked.

Eric shuddered. "Wait, you used Poppy to persuade me to come here and to do all this?"

"Yup. You've always had a soft spot for the ditzy types, eh?" She laughed.

"Don't talk about Poppy like that!" Eric fumed.

Michelle's jaw locked, and she peered at him through long lashes.

"Why do this dumb, cheap prank show?" Eric threw his arms up.

"Because this is just the first phase," Michelle said. "The big reveal will be unveiled to the world when this goes on air. Imagine the publicity. We will trend," Michelle exclaimed, so wrapped up in her fantasy that she failed to notice a sudden unscripted blur appear on one of the screens.

"You'll be shunned and shamed for leaving me alone, or, better yet, sectioned," Eric said.

"Maybe, or perhaps I could bend the story in my favour."

"What?"

"I can say that the shock of what happened in the forest that day made me realize what I truly wanted out of life, to be my truest self. My story is one of transformation! People will love it! The truth!"

"It'll never work."

Michelle's cheeks glowed. "Listen to me. Liam's connections with GMD studios and their influence over media and news coverage will be in my favour. Our favour."

"And then what?"

"Then we make more specials together. I always planned to come back. I would never leave you on your own forever."

Eric paused. He leaned forward, the chair creaking under him. "Together? So, what you're telling me is that after all this time of reflecting on your life, of journeying by yourself, you've just come full circle to where you started and put me through hell to get here?"

"I made mistakes I can't deny, but I wouldn't change any of it. We are where we are meant to be."

Eric glared. "What you did. The decision you made ended your career, and mine in the process. You ... you left me, alone." He held back a whimper.

"I was stupid, I admit it. Can't we just put it behind us and start again?" Michelle asked. "Go on, you know you want to. "This place could be our Switzerland. The place to put all that behind us. Call a truce. Could be like the old days, work and play."

"No, you were selfish," Eric snapped. "Do you know how many people I've spoken to, interviews I've given, talking about you and your disappearance. Now everyone will think I've known where you were all this time. That I knew about your transition. People will believe that I was a part of the plan. You'll throw us both under the bus for the sake of what, maybe having some sort of short-term comeback?"

Michelle rolled her eyes. "Oh, for God's sake, you're not listening to me. You never listened! This is why we're in this mess."

"We lost our chance the day you chose to disappear. You've never understood that your choices have consequences," Eric said.

"But don't you see? We have a chance to wow the world again. Start up with a bit of a bang. If anything goes badly you can blame it all on me. You can say you never knew anything about it, and I will confirm it to the press. We will find a way. We always have. Please do this with me. We can have everything we've ever wanted." She knelt down in front of Eric.

He shook his head. "We had that once. I had all that, and because of you, I had to throw it all away."

"And I want to get it back for you. Let me do that. Let me do that for you, my ... friend." Michelle took Eric's hand in hers, then lifted them both. Palm to palm, as they always did. "I promise the best is yet to come."

Eric snatched his hand away. "I don't believe you, but I guess I have no choice."

"What do you mean?" Michelle asked.

"I signed a contract, so no doubt I am bound to it."

"It binds you to doing Morsley and nothing else after that. So, yes, this will be out there for the world to see, for sure."

"You're unbelievable," Eric said, scratching his head. "You knew I wouldn't read that contract properly."

"Well, yes. Your dyslexia did help in that regard. That and I worded it very slyly."

Eric stiffened, trying to hold back his raw emotions. "I don't know what you expect me to say?"

"Say you'll think about it, please?" she begged.

"You just had to come back, didn't you?"

"Like a bad penny."

A voice broke in from outside. "Go check on the actors, Marian, see if they need anything." The door sprang open, and a short, redheaded man, wearing black glasses, entered. His clothes were dishevelled, and he was clearly low on money and pride. Liam Galavan, their old manager and director, was now working for Michelle and against it, Eric could tell.

"Hey, Eric. It's been a long time," Liam said, lifting his hand to wave. "So, has he said yes?"

"No, I haven't," Eric hissed.

"Why not? We've got this in the barrel."

"Have you, though? Have you really thought this through?" Eric asked. He believed everyone else had lost their senses. "You haven't had a success since everything ended in Aokigahara. You're desperate like ... her. You're both blind. Michael disappeared years ago and now is back as ... Michelle, and you think no one is going to think it's a little odd that we are suddenly reunited for a comeback."

"We spin the headlines to suit us," Liam said.

"That's what I told him," Michelle pitched in. "You can peddle any old shit these days, just by saying its organic or plastering a sticker of a tree on it."

Liam bared his teeth slightly as he waved a finger at Eric. "Speaking of making things seem more ... organic, natural for this little *reality* show of ours, Michelle ..." He rubbed his hands together as he hesitated before he spoke. "Perhaps you should try not ... performing so much for the cameras? You know, just tone it down a little?"

Michelle's dark eyes widened. "No! My whole life is built upon toning it up! To snatching the time I have left in life, the time that has been stolen from me being my former self. I will not tone it down. I will only ever settle for more. More love, more money, more power! More! More! More! That's the only life that's ever worth living. A life that is always reaching for more. A life that is worth *more*!" she yelled as the men sat in silence. She stepped toward Liam and loomed over him. "Do we understand each other?"

The small man cleared his throat and spoke. "Yes, I ... I see your point now. That and I do suppose the camera does love your ... expressiveness," he replied, forcing a strained laugh.

"I thought you always said faked and staged reality shows were cheap and trashy, Liam?" Eric asked, chipping in.

"I lied," Liam stated. "Listen, the world's changed since then. People want to see this stuff now, bud. They want to see celebrities suffering, cheating couples, and petty dramas. This special is a two-parter. The first half is done, which is the prank and reveal, and the second is you two investigating Morsley Mansion. There is a real story there. We will only use the actors if we need to spice things up."

"So, the cameras were on this whole time? Even during the power outage?" Eric questioned.

"Yup. We got some good stuff. Want to see? Look here …" Liam sat beside Eric on another chair and clicked away at a keyboard, rewinding footage. "Just rewind back a bit and here…" He ceased rewinding to when the cameras filmed in the nursery, the Clown incident. The footage showed both Poppy and Eric investigating. "That's one of our actors, Todd," Liam stated, pointing at the figure hiding in the pile of toys.

"I figured," Eric said, his forehead wrinkling. "How did he manage to shut the door without being seen?"

"We shut the door from here. The whole house is rigged and operated from this room. We have secret hideaways and passages we made during production." Liam smiled, gazing at the screens of the monster house he helped to create.

"Like that tunnel behind the mirror that led me to the generator?"

"Precisely. Speaking of which … here it is." Liam presented the scene on another screen, revealing the light flashes and Eric jumping back in fright at the appearance of the doctor's reflection in the mirror. Liam laughed.

"Two-way glass. Very clever." Eric noticed a blurry image flicker across one of the screens. And something else ...

"It shows the other side when triggered by the light," Liam said.

"Yeah, hence the lightning," Eric mused, still thinking about the unexplained shadow on-screen.

"Everything was us. Those falling paintings ... us. The voices you heard ... us. What happened at the séance? The knives in the kitchen ..." His ginger hair gleamed in the light.

"What about that little girl that lured me into the shack and the voices in the woods?" Eric asked.

"When was that?" Michelle asked from the corner of the room.

"This afternoon?"

"About two o'clock?" Liam asked.

"Yes," Eric said quickly.

The producer paused. "Ah, that's when our generators developed a fault for some reason. We fixed them soon after."

"So that wasn't you?"

Liam shrugged. "So what? It must have been a glitch. It all adds to the spookiness."

"Still an idiot, I see," Eric added.

"Oh no, Eric. I'm a genius. Everything that has been done here today has been executed with impeccable planning. Everything ..." Liam's eyes shone with confidence. He appeared not to notice the treacherous glares from Michelle.

"You sure about that?" Eric asked, knowing the answer.

"What do you mean?"

"You know very well what I mean." Eric glanced past Liam to Michelle.

Michelle obviously knew what Eric's expression implied but remained silent, acknowledging but not acting upon Eric's inference.

"It's going to revive your career, your life, Eric," Liam said, rolling his sleeves up. "We start shooting part two tomorrow with Michelle. This will be going out in a few months' time, so you better start getting used to it."

"And do put a smile on your face," Michelle chipped in.

"I'll cooperate ... for now," Eric said.

Liam punched the air in victory.

"I'm not promising anything, particularly about future specials. Let's just see what happens here."

"Marvellous! I'll take that for the time being," Michelle said. "Now, let's get to work."

"First things first," Eric said. "What the hell happened to Poppy?"

19

The Ensemble

The actors and Poppy laughed, exchanging stories and jokes. Wigs were cast aside, make-up washed off, and costumes were loosened. A Victorian woman, a colourful clown, an innocent girl, and a doctor wearing a blood-drenched coat made an odd group. Poppy quizzed them about what was going on since Eric went off on his own. She was now aware of the show's set-up and that her apparent mentor, Michelle Snow, was formerly Michael Goode. Poppy pressed more questions on the twenty-something-year-old Lucy O'Brien, the actress playing Madeline Berkane. Lucy's childlike, youthful features, short stature, button nose, and long locks were perfect for the role. She still wore her frilly white dress. To Poppy, she seemed more like a fairy princess than a ghost.

"That was quite the punch you gave him," Lucy said, kissing Todd next to her. The actor who played Lacey the Clown had rugged good looks that only became apparent to Poppy once he'd removed his ghoulish make-up and wig. He sat next to Lucy and drank a beer as she caressed his arm. "A good punch," Lucy repeated in a dry tone.

Poppy stammered. "I ... yeah, sorry about that. I can get a little aggressive when I'm spooked." She nodded, then added. "Sorry."

"Under the bridge," Todd replied in a tone both warm and flat, almost as if it were a line he had said many a time before.

"So, you guys are a couple?" Poppy asked, digging her silver spoon deep into a tub of cookie dough ice cream as she glanced from Lucy to Todd.

"Yes. We've been together eighteen months now," Lucy said, squeezing her beloved's hand.

"Wow, that's a long time," Poppy replied with a mouthful of ice cream.

Lucy's blonde curls bounced as she replied, "Yes. We're sharing a flat here at the moment. All part of our five-year plan."

"How did you meet?"

"I trained here. Well, not *here*, in London at LADA," the actress said.

"Sorry, what's LADA?" Poppy asked, trying not to seem rude as she wiped a spot of melted ice cream from her chin.

"It's a well-respected drama school," Lucy replied, as her face seemed to stiffen, rigid.

"Oh, right, wow, you must be very talented then."

"Well, yes, but when I graduated and started looking for work, I was labelled as being too LADA." Lucy looked down sadly.

Poppy frowned. "Is that a thing then?"

"Very much so," an older man in a doctor's costume said from the corner, grey wisps of hair catching in the light. "It was easier when I trained, I won't deny, but now the business is a lot crueller. Casting directors want people already established, people who can bring in the fans from YouTube and other social media. It is no longer about talent. It's about popularity."

Lucy coughed. "Well, you get what you put in, isn't that what they say now?" she asked the room. She then doubled down, "You put the work in and eventually, with enough noise, you can get someone important to pay attention. I've always believed that you get what you deserve in the end, don't you agree?" Lucy paused once more, then jumped to her next point, filling the gaping void. "Anyway, I gave up trying to get work here, so I went out to LA, and they loved me. I was offered job after job until I met Todd on *Clocked Out*." She glanced at him and was rewarded with a kiss on her cheek.

"I think I've heard of it," Poppy said. "It stopped airing last year?"

"That's right. Did you ever watch it?" Lucy asked.

Poppy shook her head and began examining the half-empty tub for the lumps of cookie dough—to Poppy, the best bits. "How did you start acting then, Todd?"

"Child actor. An agent spotted me in LA when I was around five years old and had me cast in *Bad Boy*," he replied.

"I don't remember that?"

"It was a sitcom about a kid, me basically, playing a little shit." Todd laughed and looked at Lucy.

"Yes, but in a funny, cute way," she said.

Todd nodded and, as he raised his beer to sip, dozens of green and purple bruises were revealed, streaking his strong arms.

Poppy eyed them up and commented. "Ouch, they look painful," she said, pointing at them as the room seemed to fall silent, cringing even. All except Lucy, who watched how he would respond with a tense jaw.

Todd paused, then managed a laugh. "Yeah, I fell down some stairs the other day. I'm a -I'm a klutz." He looked away.

Poppy gave him a small smile back, knowing that he was lying.

"Anyway, after the sitcom, I did some modelling and then met Lucy on set."

"I will have to look up *Clocked Out* when I get the time," Poppy said.

"Yeah, you should. It's quite a fun show. God, it's hot in this costume; I need to take it off." Todd undressed in front of everyone, clearly not caring who was watching. He revealed a collection of bruises on his body as he transitioned from clown to man.

Lucy nodded when she caught Poppy looking at the marks on her boyfriend's body. "Things are a bit rough. Work-wise, I mean."

"But we will get through it," Todd added, putting on his top and sitting down beside Lucy.

The actress who played Lady Morsley piped up, "Todd, you know, one day you'll be a star. You've just got to hang in there."

"Aw, thanks, Joanne," he replied.

Joanne leaned forward. "Luck of the draw. That's all it is: right place at the right time."

"What about you?" Poppy asked the man in the corner.

"Me?"

Poppy nodded. "Yes, sorry. I forgot your name."

"Gregory Fitzsimmons," he replied, putting his feet up on a small stand. "I started out at LADA decades ago. Didn't get work. My career has always been ... Semper Distans." He paused, seeing blank faces, then explained, "It's Latin for always distant. Anyway, then I became a talent agent for thirty years. After that, I decided I wanted to have a go at acting again because, well, Dum Spiro, Spero." He paused to scratch his large, bulbous nose, then rolled his eyes at the blank faces once more. "It means, while I breathe, I hope."

"That's quite a journey," Poppy said. "Have you appeared in anything big?"

"Not yet, but my connections and networking are getting me places. Got some big things coming up which I can't go into now," he stated, rigidly, without making eye contact.

"And what about you ..." Poppy turned her attention to Joanne, who sat by the mirror, removing her make-up and appraising her appearance with a frown. Her black wig lay on the headstand beside her.

"Joanne Grimes." She smiled at Poppy through her reflection.

"Why does that name sound familiar?" Poppy mused aloud, not noticing Gregory warning her to stop.

"I was in the British sitcom *Nobody's Perfect*," Joanne said.

Poppy remembered. "Oh my God. I know who you are now. *Nobody's Perfect*. That was huge. It's one of the best comedies of all time."

"Well, I suppose you could say that," the actress said with a sigh.

"She's just being bashful, it won loads of awards and so did she," Lucy said.

"That's so cool!" Poppy said, then remembered the unkind headlines. About how that's all Joanne had ever done. A one-hit wonder, they called her. She had a mental breakdown and went through a severe bout of depression and alcoholism. The press caught her running through Covent Garden, screaming lines from the show, aggressively drunk, terrifying people in the process. All completely in contrast to her refined demeanour and reputation. The story was big news as a result.

"I've mainly done theatre work since the show ended," Joanne said. "It's hard to get good roles for a woman of my age, so I jumped at this role. I really think this is going to be huge. My agent thinks so, too! And Lady Morsley is such a juicy role."

"I bet she is," Poppy said. "They do say villains are the best to play."

"I don't see her as a villain, though. It's my job as an actress to create a real human being. I mean, she has motivations, fears, layers, and weaknesses just like you or me. And to play a role of true historical significance is just so exciting," Joanne said.

"Hey. I'm sorry for scaring you back at the house, by the way," Todd interjected. "It's our job."

"That's okay, let's say we're even now with the punch," Poppy said, feeling foolish. "You certainly got the both of us. The car was the worst part."

"We could certainly tell," Gregory remarked.

"Hey, this will probably be good for your career too, you know," Lucy said to Poppy.

"Probably," she said, not quite knowing where she now fit into all this.

"You seem like a nice girl, Poppy. What did you do before all this?" Joanne asked.

Poppy hummed. "Oh, not much, just college and then I started a YouTube channel that wasn't really much of anything, I couldn't decide on what I wanted it to be or who I wanted to brand myself as being. Then I worked from place to place. I don't ever really know what I'm doing."

"You're still young. You've got a lot more to come," Joanne said.

"I suppose you're right," Poppy said. "I always say to my mom that I want to be the first to do it all."

"Well, you can cross the TV ghost prank show off your list," Todd teased.

A gust of cold air blew in as the door opened, and a collection of other people entered the dressing room trailer. Eric, Michelle, Liam, and his tired assistant, Marian, who followed with a steaming drink in a paper cup. She headed over to Joanne who smiled warmly.

"Here's your latte, Ms. Grimes." Marian offered the beverage carefully.

"Thank you, dear," Joanne said.

"Poppy," Eric said, rushing over to her.

"Hey!" she replied.

"Are you okay?"

"Yes. I'm fine now. I've been talking to the cast." She indicated to the assembled group with a wave.

"As I can see," Eric said. "Hello, everyone."

"Mister Thompson, a pleasure to meet you at last. Love your work," Joanne said.

"Thank you, ah ..." Eric paused to look at Poppy, standing behind the actress. She mouthed her name. "Joanne," he answered.

"We're big fans of you and er ... Michelle here," Todd said, shaking Eric's hand.

"Thank you. You're too kind."

Lucy smiled at Eric, then looked at Michelle. "Ms. Snow, I've been looking forward to meeting you."

Michelle turned away.

"I've never watched any of your show, and I don't believe in ghosts," Gregory said to Eric. "But I've heard great things."

"You don't believe in ghosts?" Lucy stammered.

" Undecided."

"I believe in ghosts," Joanne said.

"And we both do," Lucy added hastily. "Tell everyone the story about the time you saw your dead uncle when you were a kid, Todd."

"Well, that's pretty much it? What else is there to add?"

"I've seen lots of ghosts in my time," Joanne stated.

"Really?" Poppy asked.

"Oh, yes. Theatres are full of them. There's so much history and emotion at the theatre," she said as if quoting from a script.

"That's truer than you know," Eric said, leaning against a heater.

Liam chimed impatiently. "We've just dropped in to say that now that Eric and Poppy know the truth, we can celebrate the project being halfway complete. Your jobs are mostly done, guys."

"Done?" Joanne repeated in disbelief.

"Well, yes, most likely," Liam said.

"But my agent said it was for both parts?" Joanne replied.

"Well, it might be if over the next couple days we don't get any actual paranormal stuff." Liam looked nervously around the room.

"So, we only come back if you don't get anything?" Todd asked over Lucy's shoulder.

"That's right," Liam said.

"Believe me, I think it's unlikely. I doubt you will be coming back, this place will have enough for us," Eric remarked.

Michelle smirked.

"I see," Joanne said, clutching her chest. "Please excuse me." She made her way to the door. "Liam, could I talk to you outside, please?"

"We're just about to share a toast. I know you don't drink any more, but Marian can get you something instead of the latte," Liam offered.

"No, it's fine. Thank you, Liam. I just need to get some fresh air. Please come and talk to me outside." Joanne opened the door and left.

"Yeah, sure. Hey, good work today," Liam called after her retreating figure. "I'll be out in a second."

Marian watched the actress with puffy eyes as she left.

"So, I say we celebrate with a toast. Marian, fetch a glass for everyone and the champagne," Liam ordered.

"Yes, Mr Galavan," Marian said, closing the door behind her so as not to let too much of the heat out.

"So, where were we?" Liam grinned.

"Is Joanne okay?" Poppy asked.

"She'll be fine," Michelle said, speaking up for the first time to shrug off the question.

"We should wait for her to get back," Eric added with a frown.

"Well then, while the camera and tech guys are resetting the equipment in the house, let's talk business," Michelle said.

Outside the trailer, Marian attempted to calm Joanne.

"Are you sure you're okay?" Marian asked.

"I'm fine, thank you, Marian dear, I just need some air. I get so hot wearing that wig all day."

"Okay, well, I'm here if you need anything." The assistant smiled. "I won't be a second, I just need to go over to the fridge and get the champagne and glasses. Sure, I can't get you another drink of some sort? It might help?"

"Really, I'm good. But thank you for taking care of me over the past few days. It's very kind of you," the actress said.

"It's no problem. Just doing what anyone else would." Marian walked away.

Liam opened the door. "What did you want to see me about, Joanne?"

"Well, when you pitched this job to me, you said I was to have a much larger role playing Lady Morsley, and it appears I'm nothing more than ... a glorified extra."

Liam jerked his neck as his eye twitched. "It's what you signed up for," he said.

"When you pitched this programme, you made it seem far less ... I don't know how to say this, but there's a fine line between art and trash."

Liam's face turned almost as red as his hair. "Oh, come on now, Joanne, you're doing this role because you can't deal with being out of the spotlight and you're annoyed because you believe there's not enough time being devoted to you, but that is the project. So, make the most of the screen time you have and suck it up and be grateful with what you've been given. You've had a good run." He paused, then added, "Hey, maybe after this, it's time to retire and cut your losses." Liam retreated to the caravan, shutting the door behind him. Joanne stood in stunned silence.

Tears streaked down her face. She slumped against a tree stump, alone with nothing but emptiness and memories. In life, she made many acquaintances, but never managed to make any real friends.

She moved away, closer to the woods, not wanting anyone to see her cry. A sudden humming beckoned through the trees. Her ears pricked. She no longer blinked, as the charm of the call enthralled her. A song for the desperate that wrapped around her like a snake and tethered her to it in its enchanting coils. She moved into the darkness of the woods. The sound coaxed her closer with every note. It was rhythmic like a drum or a heartbeat. Leaves meshed into the fabric of her Victorian dress, as she gave in to the mysterious pull of the forest, beginning the journey, alone, in the dark.

Inside the trailer, Eric sat in the corner watching Liam talk with the two tech guys who had just returned from checking the house. Poppy chatted easily with the others. A part of him marvelled at her acceptance of the situation and her ability to adapt to the needs of the moment. He knew that he was not that person and so sat, alone, upright, his eyes shut, calming himself. Michelle slid into a chair beside him. He hoped his frosty stare proved he still didn't trust her.

"What's up?"

"I'm trying to meditate; go away, you are ruining my chi."

"Not until you tell me what's wrong," Michelle insisted, poking him with a sharp nail.

He came out of his reverie, fully awake now. "Ow!" he said, glancing over at Poppy.

"Ah! I see. Looks like the little puppet is getting chummy with that lot. God, actors. So pretentious, the lot of them. Am I right? And the way they overdramatize everything. It's exhausting."

Eric looked at Michelle in complete bewilderment at the fact that she did not see the irony in her statement.

"What?" Michelle asked.

"Really? We're having this conversation?"

"What was that look you gave me back there with Liam?" Michelle whispered in his ear.

"Not now, later." Eric sat upright, then asked, "What are you up to?"

"You know, all has been revealed." Michelle laughed.

"Let's face it, I know you. You're up to something. Something else, I mean."

Michelle leaned in toward her old partner. "You'll just have to wait and see." She peered at him through familiar, sparkling eyes. "Well, I'll be damned. Look at that. Eric Thompson, for once in his life, is scared."

"I'm being very serious. There is something more going on here—I can sense it."

Michelle clapped her hands together. "Marvellous. This is going better than I could ever have hoped."

Eric stiffened uncomfortably at that response. "What do you ..."

"Hey Liam, where's that girl with the champagne?" someone called from across the room.

"I don't know. She should be back by now," Liam replied, scratching his forehead.

"And what about Joanne?" Poppy joined in. "Where has she gone?"

The lights went out. Everyone froze in silence for a moment before talking at the same time.

"Well, that's not good," Eric muttered under his breath.

"For fuck's sake!" Liam shouted.

"Wooooo," Todd said, imitating a ghost.

Lucy whacked his arm hard. "Stop it, Todd."

"She's probably tripped over one of the fucking cables," Liam growled. "You two, come with me." He pointed to the two tech guys who shot up upon request.

"Where are you going?" Eric asked.

"To get the power restored and to get that moron I call an assistant back with the champagne," Liam spat, grabbing a flashlight from a small drawer. "Everyone stays here until the power comes back on."

20

Reborn

Shying away from the light, Joanne moved toward the darkness. It felt within her grasp. Her mind projected a blissful blank. All feelings of shame, pain, and regret were numbed by the cleansing effect of the lullaby sung to her throughout the forest. The call of angels. Lunar light guided her path through the woods. She waltzed past a pair of discarded shoes, a laminated student ID and a smashed camera. Joanne soon stepped upon the rotting carcasses of small animals, drained of blood. Her eyes were open and entranced by the beckoning spell. A sense of calm filled her when she moved toward the sound's source.

The night grew dimmer and dimmer. Joanne continued, completely lost in the black of night with only the heavenly notes to guide her. She slipped, falling. In that moment of being mid-air, she saw her life clearly, and realized that through all the brutalities, all the rejections, and all the bad luck, she had never truly lived for herself. She only had a career that failed her.

Moments after arriving in the creatures' graveyard of bones, Joanne wished she could have one last chance to truly live. Her limbs spasmed as she hit the hard ground. Her head bounced off a piece of broken bark, leaving her body broken, but her mind alive.

Whispers took advantage of her, corrupting her. Defiling her. Blood solidified. Skin thickened.

"Kill. Kill. Kill. Everyone," the voices ordered. Insects crawled around her, drawn like filaments to a magnet. Her eyes rolled back, and her body convulsed in pain and relief. Creatures clawed across her before frantically fleeing in horror when her eyes opened. She was alive. Reborn. She rose. Back from death. *For what reason?* she thought when she climbed out wearing her Lady Morsley rags. She trudged back toward her trailer.

Joanne felt different, but not in a bad way. The world seemed grey now. Unreal. She was the only one of colour. Of clarity. Stronger and more solid, her mind wiped of pain. She entered the sanctuary of her dressing room. Grabbing her phone off the table, she stopped to access selfies with loving, loyal fans that'd usually warm her heart. Now, they sickened her. An unfamiliar viciousness came over her as she clawed at the image. She gazed down at her shaking hands, surprised at her new manner. The feeling of failure returned; fame was a drug to her. She looked at her own reflection and realized fame did not necessarily have to come to those who did good. No. She had tried to be good, but that obviously wasn't in the cards for her. *Life is cruel.*

A flicker of light picked up something glinting in the shadows: Lady Morsley's knife. A smile stretched over her face—a face that was no longer hers, she believed, but that of the former Lady of Morsley, risen and hungry for blood.

21

Be Careful What You Wish For

Three men walked through the woods, under the faint glow of the moon. Liam led the way, followed by a technician and mechanic named Matt, a dark-haired, skinny young man with a gaunt face and a cameraman named Paul.

Liam's cold hand directed the beam from the flashlight he carried in every direction. "I can't see a fucking thing," he hissed, pushing low-hanging branches out of his limited view.

"It can't be far now," Matt piped up, his voice shaking.

Liam's nose twitched. "What's that smell?"

"Sewage?" the technician suggested.

Liam's jaw clenched in frustration. "We're in the middle of goddamn nowhere. Where the hell is there going to be sewage?"

"Okay, Jesus. The poor guy was just asking," Paul snapped. "So, explain to me again what the plan is?"

"For what?" Liam snapped, walking ahead.

"This show. I mean, don't you think it's a bit ..." Paul struggled to finish his sentence.

"A bit what?"

"Risky?" Paul managed, with a wince. "Don't get me wrong, it's gonna get great ratings, but don't you think a show like this could ... I don't know ... be a little ..."

"Just say what you want to say." Liam fired back.

"Cheap? I mean, for someone like you?" Paul said.

"Ha!" Liam laughed. "Don't you get it? I haven't had a success in years. I'm stuck in a rut, and I've got the studio breathing down my neck! Yeah, you know, this could be a big success or total disaster. I can't deny it's risky but, you know what, my whole career has been based on taking risks. No sane person would risk taking a chance on two paranormal investigators, but I did and that alone made my career. So, if I need to take another damn risk to get my old self and my confidence back, then you can bet I'm going to take whatever comes my way. Besides, I'm Liam fucking Galavan. I take crap and make it credible." He boasted.

Paul smiled. "I understand but—"

"Good, that's why you're paid to hold a camera and not to think. Leave that to me," Liam barked.

"But don't you think everyone might react badly to Michael ... I mean Michelle ... for disappearing all that time?"

"No. We will make her out as a victim. The press will lap it up and love us for it."

"Surely some people won't, though?"

"They will like what I want them to like." A vein in Liam's neck pulsed. "This show will blow ratings through the roof, for good or bad."

"What do you think of Michelle then?" Matt asked, jumping in.

"She doesn't seem quite right to me," Paul murmured.

"Michael always was a nutcracker. As for Michelle, God knows?" Liam said, readjusting his glasses.

"Do you think she's up to something?" Paul asked, almost tripping over a large fallen branch.

"Oh yeah. She's counting on this show for her own needs, whatever they are. I don't care, so long as I get what I want," Liam said, stepping over a large mound of soil. "I know she wants to cook up some horror; she made that clear from the very start, back when she pitched this whole thing to me. That's good though. I need horror."

"Careful ...you might get exactly what you wished for," Paul remarked.

The leaves around them began to swirl. Matt and Paul turned, but Liam carried on.

"Did you hear something?" Matt asked.

"It's probably just a bird. Come on," Liam ordered.

"Wooooo!" Paul taunted Matt.

"Shut up, Paul!" Matt hissed back at him.

"Reckon there's any of those inbred hillbilly cannibals around here? You know, like the ones in those horror movies? Maybe the yokels of the village!" Paul said, slapping his sides in jest at his own words.

"Man, those films are bad." Matt grinned.

"Finally. We're here." Liam glanced up at the small, rectangular, grey building.

"The door's open?" Matt observed aloud.

"Well, duh. It's Marian," Liam replied.

"Or is it a ghost?" Paul joked. "Woooo."

"Quit goofing around." Liam pushed the door fully open and shone his flashlight into the pitch-black abyss, revealing several machines and a jungle of cables. "Now, where's the generator?"

"Down there. Past the fencing." Matt pointed to the left, to a tunnel-like subsection of the room behind a fenced door.

"It's open?" Paul noted.

"Fuck's sake! Marian! Why the hell would she go down there? The fridge is right here!" Liam hissed, pointing his light at the small fridge beside him. "Useless."

"Come on, this way," Matt said. The technician moved ahead through the fenced door. "Mind the cables on the floor; you don't wanna trip."

Liam's light illuminated the thick wires and cables, which he stepped over carefully. The small circle of light revealed a damaged generator, smoking and embedded with an axe.

"Shit, it's completely fried," Matt said, examining the damage.

"Fucking hell!" Liam shouted. "Who could have done something like this? Some punk kids?"

Paul spread his hands as if to say *how the fuck should I know*?

"Can you fix it?" Liam leaned closer to Matt, who was still trying to assess the damage to the inside.

"There's no way we can fix this, but we can use the backup generator," Matt said eventually.

"So where is it?" Liam asked.

"Right here." Matt smiled, and he patted a machine beside the mangled one. "I wonder why they didn't destroy this one?"

"Hold this," Liam said, passing his flashlight to Paul. "Keep watch."

Matt used the flashlight on his phone to get a better view. "It shouldn't take long to get it started," he said, getting to work.

Paul explored all around with the torch, guarding the other two from whoever or whatever destroyed the machine. The beam picked up a splattering of blood on the floor.

"Ergh, guys," Paul said urgently.

"What?" Liam spat.

Paul's shaking hands directed the light at a trail of blood across the floor. It led to Marian, who lay on the dirty floor, her throat slit ear to ear, her mouth was open wide as if frozen in shock.

"Oh my God!" Matt trembled.

Liam's face turned a shade lighter. "Shit! Christ!"

"Oh my God!" Matt repeated.

"Who could have done this?" Paul questioned.

"Oh God." The young technician began to hyperventilate.

Paul grabbed his friend by the shoulders. "Hey, Matt? Pull it together. Come on. Just breathe."

"Okay ... okay," Matt said, wheezing.

"Why would anyone want to kill Marian?" Liam asked.

Paul looked down at her, then he sprang up. "Wait a second, how do we know that this isn't just part of your dumb show?"

"What?" Liam replied defensively.

"You said you needed horror?" Paul questioned, raising a brow.

"Do you really think I would fake a murder?"

"Yes," Paul stated stiffly.

"You just checked her pulse! How the hell could I fake that?"

"I don't know, I think there's a drug or something that can do that, make someone look dead with an extremely low pulse and shit,"

"Do you idiots really think I would be able to prank Eric and my own crew?"

"I don't know, but I'm not falling for it," Paul said, stomping off.

Matt sprang at his pal to stop him, his voice frantic and unsure. "Paul, maybe Liam is telling the truth. What if someone has murdered her?"

"Nah, I'm not buying it. He can make fools out of the rest of them, but not us. Come on, we're leaving."

"Wait!" Liam said, stepping forward.

"You stay away from us. Fix your own damn generator," Paul spat.

Liam hesitated. "I promise you both this is not a joke. Don't leave me here by myself. We need to start the generator and call the police."

"Oh, you can be sure of that," Paul said, making to leave.

Matt pulled him back. "Just listen to him—how could he fake a body like that? You checked her pulse yourself."

"I don't know."

"Please just phone the police, bring them here for our own safety," Matt begged, still struggling for breath.

Paul looked at Matt and then his boss, and back to his terrified friend. "Fine," he said grudgingly, flipping out his phone. No signal.

"No signal, ah wait, got some over here," Paul said, waving his device around.

Matt shone his flashlight and caught a figure at the back of the room in the torchlight. It was a still and silent figure with their back to them, facing the wall. A woman.

"Wait. Who's that?" Matt asked.

"Hello?" Paul said, lowering his phone.

"It's Joanne," Matt said, exhaling.

He stepped forward only for Paul to halt him. "Wait, stay back—look at her hands," he said, pointing toward her. Joanne's hands were covered in blood. In one, she clutched a large knife.

"Shit!" Matt whispered.

"Joanne? Can you hear me?" Paul asked, keeping his voice kind and even.

"What's she doing?" Liam asked.

"Just stay back there," Paul instructed.

Joanne murmured something Paul couldn't make out. She stood only a few inches away from the wall, still dressed in her full costume.

"Are you hurt? Listen, we only want to make sure you're okay." Paul stepped slowly toward her.

"Don't get too close," Matt said, shining a light on her every move.

"Just leave this to me," Paul replied.

Matt's teeth chattered. "She's crazy, look at her."

"Shut up," Paul ordered. "Look, Joanne, I know you seem a little confused right now, but I need you to drop the knife. Please."

Matt stuttered. "Puh ... please, you're scaring all of us."

Paul continued towards her. "Okay, Joanne, why don't you just drop the knife and come with us, and we will get you a nice warm drink and let you sit down. I know I'd like that, wouldn't you? It's been a long day for all of us now, hasn't it? If you just give me the knife—"

Joanne jerked her head around at an unnatural speed and raised the knife, slashing Paul's neck in one movement. His eyes widened in shock and disbelief as he choked on his own blood. Clutching at the geyser spurting from his throat, Paul fell to the floor only to be met by another ruthless attack of stab wounds to his back.

Matt screamed. "Shit! Shitty! Shit!" He backed away, burying himself in a wall of thick, vine-like cables. He dropped his phone as Joanne approached, her expression dead.

Liam, who was still by the useless generator, froze and lost sight of Matt and Joanne, hearing only a painful plea. "Please, no," then a squeal as the knife did its work. He stood petrified up against the generator, holding his breath, hoping she hadn't noticed him in the dark.

A whisper sighed through the room, informing him that Joanne was moving toward him. The drumbeat of Liam's heart accelerated to a rate he hadn't known it was capable of. *She saw him.* Her irises glowed like cat eyes in the night.

In a panic, Liam felt around for something he could use to fight the woman. The axe, still wedged into the broken generator. *Perfect.* Liam grasped the wooden handle and pulled with all his might, but it was stuck fast. In the light of Matt's dropped phone, Joanne moved closer and closer, her stride strong and steps loud as she marched faster and faster. Liam used his adrenaline, huffing and puffing, to muster enough strength to release the axe.

It was too late. He released the axe as Joanne plunged her blade deep into his chest. Liam whimpered.

Liam Galavan wanted horror. He got what he wished for.

22

The Frog and the Scorpion

Pain swelled in Eric's lower abdomen. He groaned as the room swirled in a drunken mist. Letting out a brief sigh, knowing it was his senses flaring up upon something nearby. Michelle dragged her chair over to his.

"Are you okay?" she asked.

Eric clutched his stomach. "Listen: I don't know what's going on here, but we need to leave." He winced, pinching what felt like a bad stitch.

"Why?" Michelle's earrings jangled as she spoke.

"It's not safe," Eric breathed, recovering.

"Ha. It's never been safe for either of us, has it?" She nudged Eric with her elbow.

"I'm serious." Eric frowned. "This time it's different. Something about this place isn't right. My senses are...clouded. Can't you feel it?"

Michelle's eyes narrowed to slits. "No, but then again, I never have. I always relied on you for that, but that's why this place is so perfect."

"My dreams—I think they've been leading me here," Eric said. "To this place."

"Your dreams? You only used to have them every now and again."

"They've been getting more frequent."

"How frequent?" Michelle asked.

"Constant."

"Have you seen Tamara about them?"

Eric paused, then answered. "Yes."

"And?"

"She said the dreams were foreshadowing something that would cause my life to change in a big way. Forever."

"And here I am, baby," Michelle said with a cackle.

"No. It's not just you," Eric continued. "It's this place. I'm sure of it. It's more ... alive than anywhere else we've ever been too. I can feel it even now. And it's like the longer we're here, the faster we're waking it up."

"Interesting. Is it really that much more haunted than any of the others?"

"Let's say the average haunted house is a three ... this is a ten. It's a lot more potent, stronger, darker."

Michelle blinked. "Oh, my."

"Even taking away all the stuff you've been doing, there's much more going on."

"What do you mean?"

"Well, like I said earlier, I followed a little girl into the woods yesterday, and it wasn't your actress friend over there. Liam said the cameras malfunctioned. I think it was the real Madeline, the one who's been stuck here all these years, along with the Morsley's old occupants."

"What happened to you in the woods?" Michelle asked.

"I heard voices calling out to me. That wasn't part of the show?"

"That's weird. No."

"I've seen shadows, shapes in the corner of my eye constantly."

"Paranoia?"

"No. It isn't me, don't you get it?" Eric's forehead creased. He turned to look out the blinds, then back, his expression became serious. "Listen. I have a feeling something bigger is going on here, bigger than your TV show, bigger than your tricks, bigger than any of us. Something is coming—"

"Okay. Calm down. I'm worried about you."

"You? Worried about me?" Eric snickered. "Sure."

Michelle's cheeks reddened. Her tone dropped in pitch. "No matter what you're feeling or think you're feeling, we have to finish this for both our sakes. We need this to get the world back on our side—to rebuild what we have lost. Together."

"Keep telling yourself that."

Michelle's brow furrowed.

"I need the toilet. Is it okay if I take one of the flashlights?" Gregory said from the other side of the room.

"Sure," Michelle said. "There should be a spare in the drawer."

The actor moved over to the drawer and rustled through the contents. Finally, his hand emerged wielding a torch. "Gratias tibi."

Gregory's heavy footsteps shook the large trailer, and everyone jumped as the door banged shut behind him.

Michelle watched him as he headed in the direction of his own caravan, which had a toilet. She noticed her pale reflection in the window. "It's creepy out there tonight, isn't it? Full moon. Reminds me of that time we investigated the beast of Dartmoor over here. Do you remember?" she asked Eric.

"Of course," Eric replied.

"If I recall correctly, that night was a code brown for the cameraman?" Her eyes lit up.

"Yes," Eric said, unimpressed.

"And he never turned up to another day on set after that." Michelle chuckled.

"Nope."

She paused, biting her lip, then added, "Listen: I realize that this is a change, but you'll get used to it. I'm still your best friend."

"I'm not so sure anymore," Eric said.

"Look me in the eyes and tell me I'm not." Her blue eyes were wide open, like Venus flytraps.

"We'll see," Eric said, avoiding her gaze.

Michelle's expression twitched while she stared out the thin glass window.

Gregory had always kept to himself. He planned on the new year being different, however, and pushed himself forward, a skill that'd make him more sociable. He hoped every night before bed, the next day would bring him new opportunities; he just needed to reach out and take them. He learned that from a motivational book. He pondered as he reached his trailer, thinking about how he should try and socialize with the others when he got back. Maybe it would bring him some happiness—something even more productive than just shooting the show. Yes. He would try. *Ex Nihilo Nihil Fit. Carpe Noctem,* he pounded into himself as he left his toilet with his head high, opening the trailer door, stepping out.

Joanne, still in costume, stood before him, with her back turned. Gregory nearly jumped out of his skin. Leaning back on the door as he stepped out, he rattled it against the metallic trailer.

"Oh, Joanne. It's just you." He clutched his heart. "You gave me quite a scare. What are you doing here?" He rubbed his eyes, only to see that she remained silent and still. "Out for a stroll in the moonlight?"

Gregory rotated round to her side and gasped at the blood dripping down her dress. "Is that...is that blood on you? God, what's happened? Are you hurt?" He froze—she held a blood-soaked knife in her right hand. "Why do you have a knife? What happened? What have you done?" *This cannot be part of the show.*

Joanne's make-up-streaked face looked ravaged from distress and madness. "Doctor, we must cleanse our land of these filthy trespassers," she said, staring straight ahead in a voice not her own.

Gregory recalled Joanne discussing her attempts at method acting. He knew actors who had become slaves to the form, driven slowly insane. *Is that what this is?*

"Joanne? Listen to me. You're confused."

"There is no Joanne. I am the lady of this land. Elizabeth Morsley. I have been reborn through this new vessel." Her head turned toward him.

Gregory chose to play along. "Of course, but before we cleanse this land, please tell me what it is you've done?" he asked, clasping his sweaty hands together and attempting to retain his doctor persona.

"I executed the vermin that brought these boxes here, and I destroyed their machines of noise and light," she rasped, her tone dripping with anger and disgust.

"Liam?" Gregory asked, his throat dry. He struggled to remain in character.

"The redheaded man, his two wards, and his servant girl." Her mask cracked as remorse seeped through, a twitch.

"Marian?" Gregory asked.

"Yes."

Joanne had clearly gone off the rails. She lived a disappointing life, but she wasn't a monster. She developed the Lady Morsley persona from nowhere, it seemed. A vestige of herself remained behind the madness, though Gregory sensed it.

Gregory tried to reach out to Joanne as himself. "Listen, Joanne. I know part of you is still in there: the good woman I know. That we all know. The talented actress. You've just delved too deep. Gone method. I know you don't want to do this."

Joanne stood shivering and then stopped, turning rigid. Her expression scrunched up into something venomous.

"No. I need to do this," she said in an emotionless voice. She turned quickly, stabbing her blade deep into Gregory's neck. His eyes bulged, and he clutched her sleeve as he dropped to the floor.

"I'm sorry," she muttered. She stepped over Gregory, leaving him to exhale on the floor, with only one thought on his mind. One that had always been on his mind, one that he had always run from, one that had always haunted him: *Memento Mori*. With that, death rattled his lungs, and he died, alone, always alone.

Eric sat isolated for some time with an open magazine on his knee, which he pretended to read in the dim moonlight. His attempt at ignoring Michelle seemed to have worked as she sat in the opposite corner, watching him, also pretending to read a magazine. They knew one another too well, aware that the other was not reading but thinking, planning, plotting. Eric could neither tell what Michelle's plans were nor decipher her true intentions, but he knew they couldn't be good.

"Hey," Poppy said, jumping from behind onto a chair next to Eric.

"Hey?" he said, caught off guard.

"You okay?" Poppy asked.

"Yeah, I'm just tired. It's been a long day." The magazine slid from his knees as he rubbed his eyes. "A long, crazy day."

"You can say that again. So, what's up?" Poppy asked.

"Nothing's up," he said.

"I haven't known you that long, Eric, but I can tell when something's wrong with someone. So, tell me." She dropped her voice to a whisper. "Is it something to do with Michelle?"

"Maybe I'm just not in the mood for talking."

"You're a lousy actor."

He chuckled. "I'll give you that."

"I think it's something to do with your friend." Her eyes travelled over to Michelle, still seemingly engrossed in a magazine.

"I wouldn't exactly say that we were on friendly terms right now."

"It's true she has screwed you over big time, both of us. Things must have changed between you?"

"Yes and no."

"How do you mean?" Poppy asked, leaning over to reach a packet of biscuits which she riffled through and took one out to eat.

"Yes, things have changed. How could they not? But we've still got the history. We know each other too well. We've spent so much time together. Too much time. I know how crafty he ... she is. And this has been quite a shock. I need time to take it all in. I thought ... she was gone from my life, forever. I'm angry but relieved all at the same time. It's confusing. The change isn't really the problem, it's everything else."

"Is she still the same person? Has she changed at all?" Poppy asked through a mouthful of crumbs.

"People don't change, they evolve. They add layers on to their old skin while the original person is tucked away beneath it all, clawing to get out."

"Really, that's what you think? A leopard can't change its spots?"

"It's what I've learned from life. You're surprised?"

"I am. It's just for someone who's so open to things, to the wonders of the world, I'm surprised how close-minded you are about people," Poppy said.

"It's not that I'm close-minded, more like the vast majority of the time I don't think people can be trusted."

"Do you trust me?" She raised a quizzical eyebrow.

"Course I do."

"But not her?" Poppy nodded toward Michelle.

"I don't know. Have you heard the story of the frog and the scorpion?"

Poppy dug her hand into the packet for another biscuit. "No? What's it about?"

"It's an old bedtime story we were told at the orphanage. A fable." He tapped his foot on the floor repeatedly as he recalled the sights and smells of his youth. "One day, a friendly frog asked a scorpion why he was crying. He said, 'I need to eat, and all my food is across the other side of the river, and I can't swim, without food, I will die.' The frog offered to give the scorpion a lift across on his back if he promised not to sting him. The scorpion agreed, and the frog believed him, knowing that if the scorpion did sting him, they would both drown. So anyway, the scorpion jumped onto the back of the silly frog, who began to swim, but halfway across, the scorpion stung the poor frog. As they both began to sink and drown in the water, the frog asked, 'Why did you do that?' The scorpion simply replied, 'Because I'm a scorpion.' And they both died because the scorpion wouldn't, couldn't, stop being who he was; it was his nature."

Eric ceased tapping his foot as he let go of the memory of the orphanage.

"Is that how you see Michelle?" Poppy frowned.

Eric looked at her. "That's how I see the world; we've all got our own nature. Some are just deadlier than others."

"I still think people can change."

"Maybe a few, but most fool themselves for a while and, in the end, they always end up being who they are. Just got to accept them for who they are, I guess, strengths and weaknesses." His eyes drifted over to Michelle and back to Poppy. "But I'm a frog, I know that you know that, and she knows that. Given time, I won't be able to help myself but give her a chance. Besides, she's my oldest friend."

"You can make other friends, better ones."

"The trouble is she's not like anyone else."

"In what way?" Poppy asked.

Eric looked directly into Poppy's eyes. "I don't know."

"But you do, really."

He shrugged his shoulders. "She's the only person I've ever known who's like me."

"You just said you are opposites?"

"Well ... opposites both attract and repel, but can also influence one another. I know that, with time, I can forgive her, and I can influence her to be decent, to do the right thing."

"So, wait, more than anything, you want ... her to be good, is that why you chose that name. Goode? Michael Goode?" Her brows narrowed.

"Maybe." Eric glanced down.

"And you think she might change if you can convince her to?"

"Maybe," he said quietly. Then, upon reflection, "Yes. I'm certain she would. She just needs a chance. I know it."

Poppy laughed.

"Yeah, I know, I'm an idiot," Eric said, "but that's the problem with hope, it's hard to resist."

Poppy's gaze met his. "Just promise me one thing," she said.

"And what's that?" he asked.

"Just promise you won't let me get killed." Her tone was an equal mix of joking and seriousness.

Eric laughed. "You're not going to get killed. It's a television show!"

Poppy paused. "Is that what you said to those guys in Japan?"

A heart string snapped within him, seizing Eric's muscles. Flashes of the lost souls' faces ran through his mind. He lowered his head, batting away a tear as he sniffed.

"I'm sorry," She whispered.

"It's fine."

"Please, just promise."

Eric lifted his neck and leaned in toward her. "I promise."

"Good ... want a Hobnob?" Poppy asked, waving the packet at Eric.

Eric looked confused. "What is it? A cookie?"

"Yeah, well, they're called biscuits over here, but they're amazing. Try one." She pressed the packet to his face.

Eric took one and bit into it. "Hmm ... not bad." He took another bite.

"Shouldn't the others be back by now?" Todd called from across the room.

"What, Liam and the other two? It must be taking longer than they thought," Michelle mused.

"I don't like it," Eric said, rising and putting on his coat.

"Where are you off to?" Michelle hissed.

"To find them. I can't just stay here twiddling my thumbs all night. Anyone want to come with me? Stretch their legs?"

"I will." Poppy sprang. Michelle rolled her eyes.

"Anyone else?" Eric asked.

"Well, of course I am, if anyone's going to be kicking Liam's ass it's going to be me, after all." Michelle rose, flicking stray hairs off her face. "I'm done with sitting in the cold anyhow."

"We'll come too. Could be good to get some fresh air." Todd jumped up.

"What about Greg? Won't he wonder where we've all gone when he gets back?" Lucy asked. "I guess we can leave him a note." She grabbed a pen and scribbled something on a piece of paper. "Done."

"Good. Now, everyone, follow me. I know the way," Michelle instructed, marching over to the door.

"After you then ... Mikey," Eric said, allowing himself a hint of a smile.

Michelle smiled back, thanking him in her head, Eric knew. They did not need words to communicate with one another.

The pair led the group out of the trailer into the night to find the rest of their group.

23

To Even Exist

Joanne paced her trailer. A small light from a flashlight lying on the table lit up her mirror, reflecting her madness back at her. Her hair was completely wild. Her eyes drooped heavy. Her dress was scarlet, soaked with blood and sweat. Her hands were clammy, and her skin itched with a fever that could now never leave her, mutating into something new.

"Treacherous, despicable, wretched ingrates! They should not have cast me aside." Joanne padded around in circles in the confined space. "They deserve to roast for an eternity in the flaming depths of hell with all this ... blood." Her derangement ceased, anger morphing into something else. "She had a baby." The actress's face froze. "Marian had a baby. She was a mother. Oh God, what have I done? I robbed that baby of her mother. And what about those other two lads, what about their families, their friends?" Joanne collapsed against the mirror, holding herself up against it, and she gazed upon her reflection in the dwindling light, seeing the monster she had become in such a short time. She clasped her slippery hands tightly together. "I'm sorry. I'm so sorry. What have I done? Please forgive me." She sniffled.

A switch flipped; synapses sparked. "Though they robbed me of my land, my dignity." Her throat constricted, turning her tears into spiteful words. "I was once the nation's most beloved treasure, and it was never enough. And now I am nothing. I will always have that stain on me. I could have proved them wrong, but life won't let me. This entire production has been an elaborate way for them to humiliate me. I won't be made a joke of, no, not anymore. Never again. All these vermin are the same; they should all die. Their worthless carcasses will warn others not to come forth. My actions will secure my legacy." Joanne rose up, standing proud.

"It is my destiny," she whispered, having gone too far down the rabbit hole, full method actor. "I was chosen because I could do what no one else could. All my life, people have underestimated me. I was destined to be a one-hit wonder, and now look at me. No longer a failure. I am so much more now. The Lady of Morsley, reborn."

"I will purify this land with blood and fire. And once my deed is done, I shall never stop, no, I shall never rest. I shall give this land the lady it deserves," she growled.

Joanne grasped her bloodied blade. She breathed out hate-filled mania and reached clumsily for her torch, knocking it off the table and onto the floor. Joanne felt around on the floor for its plastic handle and picked it up. Upon standing, she stared at the reflection in the mirror. A demented face with grubby blue hair and two button eyes stood behind her. His evil grin showed yellow teeth. In his hand, he held a yellow balloon. Lacey the Clown—the real Lacey.

Joanne recoiled in horror, dropping the flashlight again. Hysteria hastened her reflexes, and she stooped to pick it up once more. The demonic entity had vanished. Joanne looked around shakily. But there was nothing. What was it? Joanne thought quickly. A warning? A message? A tease? A savior? Her angel? Yes. He had come to warn her of something. Coming to serve the new Lady of Morsley. Her minion. But warn her of what?

Joanne wasted no time finding out, leaving the door wide open behind her.

24

The Long Road Back

The crunch of leaves beneath Eric's boots, as he made his way along the winding wood path, put him at ease. Woodland, nature, always had this effect. The infinite loop of life and death, growth and decay, always settled his buzzing nerves, which vibrated harder and harder every moment, traipsing upon that cursed land. His veins pulsated, strong. It was as if he were a battery being charged.

Michelle leant into Eric's ear and whispered, "Boo." She sneered.

Taking a deep breath, Eric turned, quietly and sternly stated: "No." Drawing a line in the sand as he walked ahead of her, feeling her eyes linger on him. Pain suddenly hit Eric like a strong drumbeat to his very core. He winced, trying to keep it to himself as much as possible as he fell to the back of the line. The group walked ahead through the woods with their torches, looking out for anything malevolent lurking in the dark. Michelle turned as if sensing Eric's discomfort herself. No one else did.

"Cramp?" she asked. Eric gritted his teeth. "You know what it is."

"Course I do. What do you think is causing it?" She clasped his shoulder. He paused, uncertain. "I'm not sure."

"Come on then, keep up." She slapped his back and waltzed ahead.

"Still as mean-spirited as ever, I see."

"Not mean-spirited." She turned around to face him. "It's just not easy being the smartest person around all the time."

"Still as narcissistic as ever, I see."

"Of course. Do you remember when we used to run through Central Park in the summer? The hot summer sun. The crap we'd eat and drink," Michelle said, perhaps to distract him from the obvious discomfort he felt.

"Every day," he replied, smelling the freshly cut grass even now, then let his expression mellow. "I remember taking the fall for you a lot also."

"The things we did, the trouble we would get into. They are my happiest memories."

"So, how happy would you say you are now?"

"Not very." She smiled, paused, then asked, "When you realized it was me earlier, were *you* happy?"

"Yes," Eric struggled to admit, even to himself, but he realized it was the truth. "Does that make you feel any better?"

Michelle nodded as they continued to walk together through the dark wood.

Eric glared at her, still suspicious, then his expression melted with a sigh. "Why did it take me so long to see you?"

"You refused to."

"That's not fair."

Michelle scoffed. "How many times did you catch me trying on dresses? Wearing make-up? Putting on women's wigs or walking around in high heels?" she asked as Eric's head tilted downward. "Why didn't you ask me about it?"

"Why would I? You were just being you," he said softly. "And I didn't care if you were gay, trans, or whatever. You knew that."

A loud gulp escaped Michelle. "I tried to tell you; I did but ... I just never quite could."

"It's okay. It's okay."

"You must have known, I just wish you had asked, then I could have—"

"There was no guidebook for me, for either of us! We were just two lost boys—kids, raising each other."

"We still are." Michelle smiled at him, and he did the same. "But yeah, this is me, Eric. Always has been, in truth."

"I see that. The outside may be different, but at the end of the day, all I see is you." He said, then added. "My family. I ... I ... have missed you."

Chin trembling, Michelle lifted her open palm and husked, "I've missed you, too."

Eric bit his lip, stepping away from the palm, refusing to mirror their united gesture of friendship. "W-we're not *there* yet, I'm still hurt, I am—"

"I know." Michelle lowered her hand.

"It's gonna take time, but we're still *us*." He clarified, then continued. "Let's survive tonight and see where we can go next."

"Okay, okay." Michelle nodded. "Thank you."

Eric bobbed his head ever so slightly, then called ahead. "Hey, you guys okay?"

Poppy fell back, following the leaders and just listening in, absorbing what she could in the moment, as she so loved to people-watch. She found others fascinating.

"Yes, thanks, it's just a bit spooky out here and cold," Lucy replied, hugging her arms. She was sticking close to Todd as they stepped over dead branches.

"It's all part of the fun though, isn't it, babe?" Todd said.

"And my ankle hurts." Lucy stopped to rub it.

Poppy recalled the time she twisted her ankle on a trampoline as a child. Her father told her to apply ice to stop the swelling, but then her mother told her to make it warm, to ease the nerves. They often contradicted one another, so it was hard for Poppy to ever make a choice because of it, to pick a lane. She had been raised by two good choices, so she tended to overthink and thus not even come to a decision at all. Thinking of her mother and father, she longed to see their faces in the coming week. "I miss my parents," Poppy said.

"I don't have any," Todd turned to reply.

"Oh, I'm sorry, are they dead?"

"No, we just don't talk anymore." He put his hand against his mouth and whispered, "They don't get on with Luce."

"Oh, why's that?" Poppy asked quietly, so as not to be heard by Lucy, who was still lagging behind.

"They told me she was no good for me...said she was too controlling and manipulative."

"Do you think that?" Poppy asked.

"No, of course not," he said, reaching into his pocket for his phone.

"Then do what makes you happy."

"I will," Todd said, turning to Lucy as Poppy continued to listen from behind. "I've just got an email saying they want me to go to London for a screen test for a big-budget movie," Todd said. He looked like a kid on Christmas morning.

"That's fantastic," Lucy said. "Which one?" She wrapped her arms around his middle like a boa constrictor.

"I'm not sure. It's untitled." He waved his phone around, clearly ecstatic.

"Who's the director?" Lucy asked, seemingly happy for him.

"I don't know. But if I get it, it could be my comeback. My big break." He spun round. "It's a leading role."

"That's great. Where is it?" Lucy's tone became hollow.

"Filming would be in … Scotland," Todd said, glancing at his phone.

"For how long?"

"Six months."

"So where would that leave me?" Lucy's jaw stiffened.

"Well, I suppose you'd stay in London and keep auditioning, I'd go there for shooting. Anyway, I haven't got it yet, so nothing's set."

Lucy walked ahead, alone, leaving a huge gap between herself, Eric and Michelle ahead, and Poppy and Todd behind her. Todd ran ahead to catch up, as Poppy increased her pace slightly, still hoping to eavesdrop.

"Luce!" Todd called out to her. "Hey, don't get all upset with me. What's up?" "Nothing's up," Lucy said, waiting for him to catch up.

"Well, when you're ready to talk, just say."

"We're supposed to be a team. We're engaged," Lucy reminded him, waggling the ring on her finger. "We're meant to do everything together, and I don't think you get that."

"But, Luce, this could get us a lot of money and lead to a lot more afterwards. Think about it," Todd begged her.

"I have," she said. "I've done everything I can for you, and what do I get for it? Nothing. I thought we were meant to rise up, together? We had a five-year plan but if you want to throw that all away for...*this* wasn't part of the plan! If your career means more to you than me then go for it, just don't expect me to be waiting for you when you get back."

Poppy bit her tongue, still listening and watching as Todd's shoulders slumped. *Jesus, his parents were right about this crazy bitch,* she noted to herself.

"Lucy," Todd said, grabbing her thin waist. "You're the best thing that's ever happened to me. Nothing means more to me than you. If you don't want me to do it, I won't."

Poppy's insides bubbled and boiled as she watched Lucy smirk slyly.

"But that's the thing, I don't want it to be me who's stopping you, it has to be your decision." Lucy stated.

"I don't want the part if it means losing you."

Lucy smiled. "Thank you." She patted him on the nose like a loyal pet, then held his cheeks, pulling him in as she whispered, "We stick to the plan, and we can—*will*—have it all. I promise you." She added, "We will get what we deserve in the end, baby, we will, I know it." She kissed him on the forehead. "We will get what we deserve, in the end."

"I'll call Will and tell him it's not for me," Todd said, pulling away. "Be back in a sec." He whipped out his phone again and walked ahead to call his agent.

Poppy frowned. She was beginning to see the young actress as she really was. Her puppetry of Todd was masterful.

The group approached the trailer that housed the generator, the metallic, grey building that Eric had previously ventured through.

"We're here," Michelle said as she gestured.

All was silent beyond the open door of the trailer.

"It doesn't sound like anyone is here," Poppy noted.

"They've got to be," Michelle scoffed. "Liam!" she shouted, entering only to be stopped by Eric's firm grasp.

"Wait. Be careful," he said, clutching his onyx amulet and sensing something bad within.

Michelle licked her lips. "What is it?"

He gave her a look that signalled he didn't quite know, but whatever it was, it was bad. "Everyone, be careful," Eric said again, stepping inside and shining his flashlight ahead.

"Is that blood?" Poppy pointed to the floor. There were drops of it everywhere, illuminated like rubies upon the dirt-riden floor.

Eric aimed the beam from his flashlight at the ceiling and moved it around the room, checking where the blood could have come from. He had no clue. He knelt and sniffed. He could smell iron. "Yes, it's blood," he confirmed, looking back at the group.

Lucy remained just outside the door, burying herself in her boyfriend's arms.

"Are you sure it's not fake?" Todd asked. "Some prank by Liam?"

"There's more down here, loads of it." Poppy inspected the room with her torch. She stepped slowly forward.

"Blood with no bodies?" Eric mused.

"That's creepy as shit," Michelle exclaimed.

Poppy gasped. "Look at the generator!" She shone her light on the machine, revealing the damage to it.

Michelle peered down. "Is that an axe?"

"Yes, I think it is."

"Well, that explains why the power is out," Michelle muttered.

"It's covered in blood too," Poppy stammered.

"Oh, this has got to be a prank!" Todd shouted from outside.

"That sick bastard. We're not falling for it. Liam!" Lucy screamed through the trees.

"Eric?" Michelle looked at him.

Eric stared down at the blood, feeling the pain that had transpired there earlier. "This is real. We need to leave," he said, pushing the two women out the door ahead of him.

"What, why?" Poppy asked as they now stood outside, crunching their boots upon the leaves. "Why are we leaving?"

"Just do what the man says. Go!" Michelle ordered.

The group diverted off to the side, toward something apparently none of them had seen upon walking past, something displayed beneath a tall tree. It was a bloodied circle, a collection of white, ripped-out teeth in a shallow pool of crimson dirt.

"What the ...?" Michelle winced.

"Teeth?" Eric asked, frowning.

"Not just any teeth," Lucy added, pointing toward them with a shaky hand. "They're Greg's teeth. I recognize his silver filling."

"How do you know that's his?" Poppy questioned.

"He mentioned it." Lucy trembled.

"There are enough teeth here for about four people," Michelle pointed out.

Eric breathed hard. "And five are missing. So, who's the one still alive?"

"Wait, what? You're saying this is real? That someone is killing everyone?" Lucy demanded.

"I'm not sure. It could be something else, maybe there is just one survivor," Eric stated. "We don't know."

"Wait a second, I mean, how do we know those teeth are even real?" Lucy asked.

"Because, like it or not, they are," he replied.

"But how do you know?" Todd persisted.

"Because I just do."

Michelle pointed at Todd. "Phone the police, now. I'm not prepared to take any more risks."

Todd checked his phone. "There's no signal."

"How is that possible?" Lucy said. "You just phoned your agent."

Todd began waving the device around in an attempt to get a signal. "I don't know, it was fine a minute ago."

Poppy checked her phone. "Mine too! No signal."

"And me," Lucy said. Michelle also checked. "Same."

Eric even pulled out his also—no signal. "I think we're being blocked intentionally."

Suddenly, all the phone screens fuzzed and crackled, then went black. The group eyed each other in amazement.

"No," Lucy cried, her hands rushing to her face. "This has Liam written all over it. This has got to be a joke."

"Don't count on it. This is real, and whoever did that in there wasn't any kind of spirit." Eric's necklace vibrated against his moist skin.

"He's right," Michelle said. "Spirits like to torment their victims or watch them. Very rarely do they do any actual harm. Then again, this is Morsley."

"It's definitely not out of the question," Eric added. "We need to get back to the house." "What about our trailers?" Lucy's voice squeaked.

"No. Whatever it is hunting us knows that's the first place we'd go. It's too predictable."

"And the house isn't?" Lucy sniffed loudly.

"I don't think they would expect us to head there. Besides, if it's just a prank, or there's been an accident, then we would have already passed them on the way here. The house is our best bet," Eric said.

"And the house is like a fortress. If we all stick together, it's our best shot," Michelle pitched in. "And there's a car there, remember, which we can use to get out of here. Failing that, we can wait it out for the pickup crew. They are coming in the morning for you actors."

Todd raised his arm as if in class. "Umm ... problem with that. The car battery was drained, so Poppy couldn't leave." He looked in her direction as he spoke, "You know, when we jumped you in the car? We made the radio and lights work with some other tech stuff but the engine didn't work."

"Oh shit, that's right!" Michelle said. "That was my call, too. Why am I always my own worst enemy?"

"Whatever's going on, it doesn't matter. We need to stick together, whether this is a prank or not," Eric cut in, attempting to neutralize the rising tension with a calmness mustered by previous paranormal situations.

Lucy placed her hands on her hips. "Why don't we just walk to the village?"

"These woods go on for miles," Eric said.

"But we walked it earlier," Poppy said.

"Yes, and it took us an hour and a half." He spun round to face her. "It's too far, we might get lost in the dark, and God knows what else is in these woods with us. Best to get to safety and try to get our phones working again or any form of contact. If it comes to it, we will walk to the village in the morning daylight. It's our only chance."

Eric stood beside Michelle and faced the group. "Now, you see this mad woman beside me? She knows me. And she knows what I'm capable of, and how honest I am being when I say that I will get us all out of here alive! But you must trust me. I know what I am doing."

"I'm not sure." Lucy shook her head. "Maybe it would be better if we split up. Todd and I will go to the trailers, you guys can go to the house and—"

"No," Michelle interrupted. "We need to stick together and go to the house."

"I'm not being funny, but if you're saying all this weird ghost stuff is true and this blood and teeth shit is real, then why are we going to a haunted house?" Todd questioned.

"To the spookiest place here," Lucy added.

"It makes no sense, unless ... you're in on it." Todd pointed at Michelle and Eric.

"Don't be ridiculous, this is not some kind of joke," Michelle snapped.

"Oh, isn't it?" Lucy asked.

Eric breathed hard. "Listen, we really need to go—"

"To the house," Michelle cut in. "Enough said. There is an emergency first aid kit under the kitchen sink. If Liam is the survivor, then he knows that and would have headed there if anyone is injured. Let's go."

Lucy whined like a child. "But what if—"

"I'm still a producer on this project which, at this moment, makes me in charge. I am your employer, the person paying you. We are going to the house. Do you understand?" Michelle said, her patience tested.

The young actress nodded in submission. "We'll sue you if anything happens to us, anything."

"You can try," Michelle replied, leaning over with a sneer before beginning to walk onward. "Let's go."

The five of them trekked toward the mansion under the glow of the moon. Lucy and Todd trailed, whispering quietly to each other. Poppy walked in silence.

Eric walked beside his old friend, who hummed a little tune, nonchalant. This was always the way of Michael, well, now Michelle. Fear and adrenaline seemed to slick off her back like water off a duck's feathers, and he couldn't help but be comforted by her swagger in the face of danger. It was something he had always admired about her. He scratched his neck. "Thank you for backing me up. Is it true what you said about the first aid kit?" he asked.

"Yes, but you and I both know we won't be finding any of the others at the house." Michelle exhaled, staring forward.

Eric nodded. "You trust my instincts?"

"No, but I trust *you*. I always have, haven't I?"

"Not enough back when you decided to take off without an explanation."

She nodded. "Okay, okay, I deserve that. But I do think it's time you and I started trusting one another again, especially if we're going to get through this night."

"You're right," Eric said. His lips formed a half smile. "Why did you lie to them? Just to get them to follow us?"

"That, and so as not to scare them."

Eric let out a genuine laugh. It was strange being back with Mikey—but also comforting. He reflected on how he'd acted toward Michelle. "Listen, I know it seems as if I've been keeping my distance from you, but it's just ... a lot to take in."

Michelle raised a hand to silence him. "I know, I understand. But we're talking now, and that's good."

25

Descent

A reborn Lady of Morsley walked through the trailers. It was Joanne's new favourite role, the best of her career, one she couldn't now let go of. She felt powerful walking upon that soil. It was a feeling she hadn't felt in many years.

Blood coated Joanne's skin and seeped into her pores. Faces of the dead, of those she had killed, flashed through her mind ... Liam, the producer; the tech boy, Matt; cameraman, Paul; and the assistant, Marian. Poor souls she had passed judgment on. Their screams hurt deep inside of her, burning into her soul. Every muscle in her body ached. Whatever had come over her had truly driven her, unlike anything she had experienced before, an energy that maimed, murdered, and butchered others. It was a monstrous power she wielded, and she was not willing to be weak ever again.

Joanne was about to pass Greg's trailer, where she had killed him a short while earlier. She fluttered away with remorse and disgust, and a sickening pleasure. Her shoulders tensed. There was nothing but splatter marks. Where could his body have gone? She hadn't moved it. A chirp sounded behind her. Her gaze darted in every direction, her knife ready. Silence.

A song called through the darkness. The same song that had lured her earlier. Her eyes widened. Her muscles relaxed. A smile spread. It was like a drug she could never be rid of. She marched into the depths of madness towards her only escape.

26

Siren Song

Wind chimes jangled in the autumn night breeze. Unforgettable tunes. Chilling. The mangy black feline watched the survivors return with its illuminated eyes. It sprang away into the bushes as they approached the mansion.

Lunar rays dimly lit the exterior of Morsley. Shadows crept through the cracks and crevices, watching. Eric's pain spiked upon his return. The onyx stone dug into his chest.

"We're here," Michelle said with relief, stomping toward the entrance.

Lucy looked around. "Where's the car?"

"It should be there," Todd replied.

Poppy rubbed her eyes. "Yep, that's where I left it when you guys got me."

"Yeah, but we killed the battery, then took out the controlled one we were using to scare Poppy with the radio and headlights," Todd stated.

Eric scrambled around, wind blowing his coat behind him like a cloak. His flashlight soon revealed the car lying on its side, down in a ditch, inoperable. "Found it."

"Now, who the hell ...?" Michelle began.

Eric's eyes darted around, fixing on Morsley's grim exterior. "Let's not question it. Just get inside."

Michelle burst through the door and into the manor's dark interior. "Finally, back in hell," she said.

Poppy entered behind Michelle, jumping at the sight of Rosie the doll seated on the steps to the landing as if waiting for them. "Ergh! I hate that doll!"

The floorboards squeaked as the group gathered in the living room. Eric flashed his flashlight around the room.

"Where are they then?" Lucy threw her arms in the air.

"Umm ... not here by the looks of it?" Michelle responded, sitting down on the sofa in a heap.

"You said they'd be here," Lucy muttered through gritted teeth.

"I said Liam knew the first aid kit was here and would most likely head here; clearly, whatever has happened has meant that's not possible."

"How do we even know if Liam was the one to survive?" the young actress snapped at Michelle, who was adjusting her hair.

"Please, that man's a turd that has never been able to flush."

"You don't know it was him who survived though, you can't."

Michelle's lips puckered. "No, I guess that is true. But comparing him to the others, my money would be on Liam; the man's a cockroach."

"You're so full of shit," Lucy spat. "I don't care if you're paying us or not, we're leaving."

Todd and Lucy walked toward the front door, Todd trailing his fiancée like a reluctant child.

"What? You're going out there alone?" Michelle said.

Lucy stopped and turned. "We're not alone. We have each other."

"Ha. You two together? A pretty boy and a snooty little bitch. I'm sure you'll manage just fine when you meet whatever is out there. Good luck to you."

"Enough," Eric said. "Both of you should stay," he said to the couple. "If there is something out there, you two won't last a second."

Todd and Lucy stood silently, without moving, and considered his words.

"Listen: just humour me and stay until morning for your own safety as well as ours," Eric said. "I know you're scared and there's nothing wrong with that, scared is smart. But you also need to be rational because that's the only thing that's going to keep you alive. So, let's stay and be safe together. Okay?"

Todd looked to his girlfriend as if for permission.

She nodded.

"Fine," Lucy said. "We'll stay. But at sunrise we're leaving." She walked toward the kitchen with Todd following.

"Where are you going?" Eric demanded.

"I need to visit the little girl's room. Come on, Todd."

Eric looked at the pair. "Just stay together."

Todd moved himself and Lucy away from the rest of the group, and several pairs of eyes watched them. Lucy walked quickly through the kitchen to the downstairs toilet. Todd followed as they both did not notice, or seem to care, that all the knives that had been used as a prank for the show had vanished. All except one: it glimmered menacingly on its own, left out on the side. Lucy hurried.

Todd moved faster to keep up, knowing Lucy's bad mood would rub off on him. "Hey, don't let them get to you." He grabbed her by the waist.

Lucy swung round and slapped him hard. "Are you out of your mind? We are most likely going to die here, and you didn't even stand up for me back there!" She glared at Todd, who was rubbing his cheek.

Lucy put her hand to her mouth. "I'm sorry, really I am," she said, caressing his cheek and kissing his forehead.

"You promised you would stop with the hitting," Todd said.

"I know. I know. I'm sorry. It's just this place, it ... it wasn't part of the plan." She sniffed. "You know I have control issues—"

"I know, baby—"

"This place it's just, it's out of my control and ... I'm scared."

"Hey? You've got me." Todd smiled and looked into her eyes lovingly. "And I've got you."

"I'm so sorry," she said. "I ... I know I've been a bitch tonight—"

"No—"

"Don't, just, please, I ... I ..." Lucy cleared her throat, stepping back, then began. "The whole control thing—I'm realizing it's not right. I shouldn't be taking out my aggression on you, and I shouldn't be making you my meat puppet. I just, I'm realizing ... I just don't think I know how to love very well. I wasn't capable of it for a very long time but I ...

read, that if you hold onto someone too hard, that doesn't make them love you. I'm sorry."

"Shhh ... the hitting, it was just a moment of weakness. That's all."

Her voice croaked. "I think we should get help, once we are out of this hellhole, I think we should see someone."

"Yeah, maybe we should, baby, maybe we should." Todd's eyes widened as if he were driving a car onto an icy road, committing to the skid. "We're going to be fine." He stooped down to kiss his fiancée, who quivered a smile with a nod.

"I've got to wee," she said, moving toward the toilet beside the back door.

Todd grinned. "I'll be right here waiting."

Poppy sat, watching Michelle lounging out on the sofa, evaluating the room by torchlight. "I've got to say, given a bit of decorating and DIY, this place could be quite nice, setting aside the murder and suicides," she said, more to herself than the others.

Poppy gazed at Eric, who paced up and down, deep in thought.

"Yes, slap a bit of paint on the walls, get some decent furniture, flowers, liven it up a bit, would be very fancy."

A buzzing came from the dining room where he had previously attempted to perform a séance. The door was shut. Poppy observed Eric creep slowly, and Michelle rose from the sofa upon seeing him approach the door.

"Hey! Eric! Why are you going in there?" she called.

THE HAUNTING AT MORSLEY MANOR

Eric did not reply. Inside, a light flickered on the floor, across the wood. His EMF device. It picked up something powerful. He knelt to grasp the device to switch it off.

"What is it?" Michelle asked, entering the room behind Eric. "Is the EMF giving us a warning?"

"It's not a warning," Eric said. "It's a message. They're here."

A warm glow hit Todd's belly, knowing he was his beloved's anchor. He looked forward to marrying Lucy when they got out of there. Engrossed in his thoughts, he didn't see the shadows gathering as he sat alone in the dark. He checked his phone. It was still dead.

Todd had never been a fan of the dark since he was a little boy, always having his mother check under his bed for monsters before he went to sleep. The dark meant uncertainty, something Todd feared more than anything. He thought of his mother, and a part of him missed her. If she couldn't love Lucy, he'd always pick his Juliet over anyone, including family. Lucy pushed him, made him better. Yes, life was finally looking up. Love blossomed along with his career. He experienced regret at having passed up the opportunity his agent contacted him about, but there was plenty of time. He could fulfil all his dreams. He recalled what his beloved drummed into him: "It's not part of the plan." He trusted her mantra and would follow it and her until the bitter end.

A strange humming sensation coursed through him, bringing a new sense of pleasure he'd never experienced. A song. His eyes widened, his brain slowed, and a reassuring feeling entered, tightening like a serpent. It took control over him completely, the source of the rhythm summoning Todd.

"You still out there, Todd?" Lucy called from the toilet. "I'll be out in a moment."

"I'm still here, Luce," he assured her.

"Alright, good. Won't be long."

Todd crept closer to the kitchen back door that led outside. He turned the knob, pulling the door to peer out into the black wilderness. A pale shadow flickered in the trees, drawing him nearer, forcing him to let go of his senses and give in to the enchantment. His feet stepped down to the ground, and he strode off to follow his caller. His siren.

A brisk flush accompanied by the creak of the door revealed Lucy, looking for her Romeo. "Todd? Where are you? Todd?" Her eyes wandered around the kitchen, then, feeling the draught at the back of her neck, she turned to see the open door. She approached cautiously and looked out. A figure walked away in the distance.

"Todd!" she screamed.

Footsteps followed. The others ran in, torches in hand.

"What happened?" Eric shouted. "Where's Todd?"

"Out there." Lucy pointed to his disappearing shape, now engulfed by the forest. "He just went into the woods."

"But why would he do that?" Poppy questioned with a shaky voice. "And on his own?"

"I don't know!" Lucy wailed. "I'm going after him." She headed towards the door.

"Not on your own, you're not," Eric said.

"Then come with me," she replied, not looking back, knowing they'd come.

Eric turned to Poppy and Michelle, who both furrowed their brows.

"We need to stick together," Eric said. "For real this time."

"Oh, can't we just let her get on with it?" Michelle asked.

"No, we can't," Eric snapped, walking after Lucy.

"Why not?"

"Because it's the right thing to do, and I'm not letting another person get hurt," Eric said, recalling all the times he had not been strong enough to protect others; young Alice Hickford's mutilated face reminded him that he would not allow it to happen again.

"Their well-being is not your responsibility. We told them not to run off. One simple task, and the idiots can't even do that!" Michelle said, the veins in her neck bulging.

"She has a point," Poppy said.

Eric huffed and began to walk off into the woods.

Poppy looked at Michelle, waiting to see what she would do. Michelle sighed, then stepped outside and headed after Eric.

"Hey, wait for me," Poppy said, briskly walking toward them with her flashlight.

27

The Thing You Fear Most

The group walked a long way, gathering speed without finding any trace of Todd. They entered a different, darker part of the woods where the tree branches loomed over in a sharper, clawing nature, and everything else seemed to be dead brambles, thistles, and leaves. Sinister trees loomed over them, brown and dry, displaying an overwhelming need for water. Anticipation turned to exhaustion and fear. The night had drained each of them. All except Michelle.

Lucy walked ahead, calling out for Todd.

"So, how long do we give it before we give up?" Michelle groaned.

"We're not giving up until we find him," Lucy snapped.

"This is stupid. I'm heading back," Michelle began.

Eric grasped her thin wrist. "No, not yet. We will search for another twenty minutes, but then we are all turning around. If we go too far, we may never find the way back. Agreed?" He looked at Lucy.

"Fine."

Eric caught up with Lucy. "I know this must be hard for you, but remember to stay strong," he whispered.

"I am strong. That's why I need to find him. Todd!"

"Keep your voice down, we still don't know what happened to the others," Eric warned.

Michelle approached Eric. "Why are we out here, putting ourselves in danger, looking for that idiot? He's gone."

"Listen, we said twenty minutes," Eric said. "After that, she can't argue."

"Maybe we should lower it to ten," Poppy added quietly.

Eric turned to face her, massaging his jaw as he frowned. "What's with you all of a sudden?"

"And who put you in charge?" Poppy snapped back as her hands fidgeted. "I'm scared as fuck, and we don't know if everyone else is already dead. Maybe we should head back to the house sooner."

Eric looked from one woman to the other and sighed, feeling exhaustion overcome him. *They're right,* he knew. "Fine," he exclaimed. "Lucy. Where's she gone? Lucy!"

"Ah, that stupid bitch," Michelle hissed. "Well, that settles it, let's go." She turned to march back to the house.

"No," Eric insisted. "She can't have gone too far. Come on." He pointed his flashlight forward.

"I can't see her," Poppy said, squinting.

The three checked from all angles, facing opposite ways for a split second, time melting away without them noticing. Their search revealed nothing.

No Todd. No Lucy.

"Lucy?" Poppy loudly whispered, then stopped, not wanting to draw the attention of whatever was out there. There was no sign of life until something snarled close to her. Then something moved behind a tree in view of her light. "Lucy, is that you?" she called. "Hey guys, I think I've found the—" Poppy spun round to find herself completely alone. There was no sign of anyone. Not Eric. Not Michelle. No one. Just whatever it was that moved behind the tree.

How could that have happened? She stepped back from the tree. Initially, she had wanted to be like Michelle and Eric, courageous. But now she was alone. A slither sound circled her. From the corner of her eye, she saw the "something" move out of sight to God knows where. Its pale skin was just visible in the nightmarish dark. It possessed long limbs that appeared skeletal and made cracking sounds when moved. The noise it made was harsh, gnashing its teeth like a wild beast. It hid. But where?

Poppy almost forgot to breathe. She kept her voice steady and tried to refrain from panicking. Then there was more movement, multiple ones. Circling her like sharks. Growling. Rabid. Poppy looked in all directions but couldn't catch a full image of the creatures, just their scuttling, pale bone-like bodies and glimpses of teeth and glowing eyes. Eyes that seemed oddly familiar, as if she'd seen them somewhere before. Four of them.

With no way out.

Michelle muttered, unable to see the girl anywhere, although she wasn't looking very hard. "I can't see her," she called. "She must have wandered off after lover boy—" She halted, realizing she was alone. "Sorry, am I boring you?" Her question hung in the air.

No one answered.

A rustling of leaves sounded behind her. Michelle froze as a chill seeped into her. Using a coping mechanism from past cases, she said, "I am the worst thing in this wood, and I am not afraid."

She rotated to find a small, black cat in the torchlight, hissing. "Stupid cat, get out of here," she said and ushered it away. She walked a few feet, stopped abruptly at a huge tree. A large knife stabbed a broken pig mask into the wood and had a red spray-painted message that read, *Get out of here.*

Michelle's second coping mechanism sprang into action—her sense of humour. She laughed out loud. "Well, that's not at all creepy."

She caught sight of a glimmer of light in the distance ahead and struggled to make it out. "What is that now?"

Eric panted, finding himself alone. "Poppy? Michelle?" he called. A crunch issued from below his boot. He pointed his flashlight at the ground. A spider. No, a trail of spiders, hundreds of them marching along in a line. *Disgusting,* he thought, gazing down to make sure none had climbed on him. Wait, *spiders don't usually like to socialize.* Eric recalled his dreams—the spiders that crawled there. Swallowing his fears, he followed the line, knowing that this could lead him where his dreams had called him the whole time. Eric gritted his teeth.

Walking for a few minutes, he arrived at a lake, undisturbed and still. The moon danced in ringlets over its depths. Stars shone like angels. The arachnids had crawled up an old tree beside the lake. They scurried up the trunk and into a large hole cut into the side. All of them scuttled loudly inside and disappeared. *For what? Sanctuary?* Eric backed up and took a deep breath. He shined his flashlighth into the heart of the ancient tree, only to have the light reflected, blinding him. He shielded his eyes with his hands, hoping to make something out. No, the light was too much. Then he thought he saw something else within the hole of gleaming white feathers and two large eyes staring deeply and directly into his soul. Muscles melted all of a sudden, Eric's energy sapped. His legs gave way. He fell to the soft floor, asleep, to dream another dream: the one to which his whole life had led him.

The watchers circled Poppy. "Eric? Michelle? Lucy? Todd? Anybody? Oh, my God!" She tried to think what Eric might do under such circumstances. He'd not panic and stay strong. "Never give up and never give in," she whispered, breathing deeply. "Stay back. I'm warning you. Stay back," she threatened, only to be answered by cruel, tormented snarls. As quickly as they began, the noises stopped. Ghoulish eyes faded away into the night.

Why? Who the hell cared? They left—that's all that mattered.

A familiar voice in the distance called, "Todd?"

"Thank God! It's only you, Lucy," she said, exhaling the pent-up air she had been holding in her chest.

A blonde head loomed into view from out of the darkness. "I wondered what happened to you all. I turned my back for a moment, and you disappeared," Lucy said.

"The same thing happened to me."

A branch snapped, and the two women turned to see someone else through from the trees. "Todd! Todd!" Lucy yelled, smiling and waving. He didn't respond. Lucy's smile dropped. As he continued to walk, it became evident that he was not alone. He held hands with someone. A naked woman with long, dark hair escorted him through the woods.

"Oh my God! That son of a bitch!" Lucy seethed, charging at them.

"Lucy, no!" Poppy pulled her back with a steady arm.

"What? My fiancé is running off with some slut."

"Just keep it down," Poppy whispered urgently. "Something's not right."

"Well, I've seen enough," Lucy spat, shaking free of Poppy's grip. She ran after Todd, screaming his name repeatedly.

"Lucy, come back!" Poppy called.

Suddenly, the mysterious figure disappeared. Todd stood alone, still as a statue.

"Where'd she go? I'm going to rip her hair out! Todd!" Lucy yelled.

Todd turned to face his fiancée as she approached. His eyes were open wide, and he swayed slightly, as if he were drug-induced. "Lucy?" he murmured, still somewhat entranced.

Just before Lucy reached Todd, Joanne suddenly stepped out from behind a tree, knife in hand, and slashed Todd across the chest. Blood spurted down his body as he fell to the ground, cushioned by a carpet of leaves.

Lucy screamed.

Poppy couldn't form words, sick to her core, but too petrified to vomit.

Strangely, Todd felt no pain, just a struggle to breathe, his eyes wide open. He craned his neck to look up at the stars shrouded by trees. He eyed the new murderess of Morsley: Joanne Grimes. He looked relieved to see her, his angel of death.

"You said I was going to be a star," he rasped, feeling all the bruises and scars he had acquired from his "love" melt away. Todd let out one last breath. Then there was nothing. He was finally free.

Joanne felt numb behind her new mask, this role of Lady Morsley, as she gazed at her handiwork: Todd's corpse. She then shifted her eyes to Poppy and Lucy.

Poppy stared at Joanne in shock—the gentle lady she respected and admired—was the same, fast-approaching woman wielding a knife. "We have to go now!" she said.

Lucy sobbed.

"Run, Lucy!" Poppy insisted, backing away.

Lucy ran after Poppy as Joanne roared behind, chasing them both.

Adrenaline fuelled the young women's flight. They approached a huge fallen tree and climbed over its branches. Poppy slickly contorted her way through, but Lucy's sloppy footwork made her slip and fall, twisting her ankle. The branches of the tree formed a barrier around her like a prison cell.

"Help me!" Lucy shouted to Poppy, thrashing.

Poppy reached through the tree's wooden bars, her fingers unable to reach the young actress.

Joanne continued hustling toward her helpless prey. Lucy scurried back onto the thickest wood pole for support.

Poppy couldn't free Lucy and stepped back, so she was obscured by the thick branches. All she could do now was watch and hope not to be seen.

Lucy blubbered, "Oh, please, thi ... this wasn't part of the plan, it wasn't part of the ... Joanne—"

"In this life, we all wind up getting what we deserve in the end, isn't that what you declared earlier, girl?" The broken woman spat with venom as Lucy raised her hands in surrender.

"Don't, please. I will do anything you want, anything, just please ... please!" she begged, bringing her hands together in a sign of prayer.

"You wish to be granted mercy?" Joanne's head twitched.

"Please, yes. Oh, please."

Joanne smiled. "Then mercy ... you shall have."

Lucy shrieked as Joanne raised her blade, sending it crashing down on Lucy's head, cracking her skull. Her vindictive smile made Poppy wince. The young actress's blood soaked the soil before being absorbed. Feeding the land.

"Sleep now, child, for eternity," Joanne hummed. She looked through the branches to her next victim, Poppy, who was standing frozen in horror. She backed away to be met with a sharp claw of a hand. Michelle.

"Come on this way," Michelle ordered, digging her nails deep into the woman's arm, dragging her along, as Joanne began to hack through the branches.

Michelle ran faster, guiding Poppy. They approached a familiar sight: the building housing the generator. Michelle sprinted up the narrow steps. Poppy trailed, shutting the metal door and sealing it.

"That should do it," Michelle gasped, shining her flashlight onto the lock.

The door shook violently with a succession of bangs. Again, and again. "We need to get away from here." Michelle moved to the other side of the room, sidestepping the puddles of blood.

"To where?" Poppy asked, following her.

"Through the tunnel and back to the house," she replied, opening the door and beginning her descent.

"What about Eric?"

Michelle paused. "Believe me, he can look after himself," she said. The banging continued. "Let's go."

Michelle closed the door behind them, and they began their journey down into the deep underground depths of Morsley. Neither spoke, Poppy wondered and worried about what might have happened to Eric.

28

Destiny Calling

Eric opened his eyes. A coldness seeped into his bones. The mist settled clear, the air still. He seemed to be in the same place he had fallen unconscious moments before, but something was different. It was grey. *What was that thing in the tree?* But whatever *it* was, along with the tree itself, had vanished. The moon was large and lifeless. The sky twinkled a sapphire shade of dark, gleaming, fiery stars.

Eric turned to find the lake still beside him. Still on the ground, he winched himself up and took a step toward the water, only to be met by dozens of pale faces that peered up through the black depths below. They cast no reflection on the water's surface. The creatures' hair was dark and flat. An army of sinister entities faced him. Eric retracted his step, and the bobbing heads sank down to the shallows. He shuddered, rattling his spine all the way down to his base. His gaze stretched to the trees, but everything beyond drowned itself in grey fog. Eric went to clutch his amulet, only to find it must have fallen off. He dropped to the floor and began looking for it in a rising panic. Nothing but twigs, rocks, and dirt. No leaves. No amulet.

"I have been waiting for you," a distinct female voice echoed through his mind. Her accent was unlike anything Eric had heard before, both guttural and elegant at the same time. He sprang up, looking in all directions.

"Who's there? Show yourself."

"Do not fear me, my child," the voice soothed.

Eric's mind stopped spinning. "What do you mean 'child?'"

"You are all my children," the voice purred through the tall, dead trees.

"You know me?" Eric asked.

"I know you ... all of you. All of my children," she rasped. "You are late."

Eric grew ever more suspicious. "How did you know I was coming?"

"I watch all as they are led. I brought you here," she whispered.

Eric blinked. "I don't understand."

"Your gift, your curse, your dreams."

"You led me here through my dreams?"

"You carry a great sadness in your heart."

"Are you a spirit? Or a witch?" he asked.

"I am more, much more. And so are you."

"What are you? Tell me," Eric insisted.

"I am the beginning. I am the end. I am chaos. I am order. I am everything. I am eternal, child."

"Is this a dream?"

"Yes."

"So, this isn't real?"

"Yes and no."

Eric gulped. "Am I dead?"

"In a way."

Eric gazed down. It was obvious where he was. As Tamara said, the netherworld, the astral plane. The space between worlds—the place he had been travelling to in his dreams.

"Why am I here?"

"You are here because I am here," the voice answered through the deepening mist.

"I don't understand. Why bring me here, to Morsley?"

"Fate. Destiny. You have been brought here as I have, to help you understand yourself, the meaning of your existence."

"Show yourself," Eric cried out into the vast emptiness surrounding him.

The voice giggled. "You will never see me, not truly. You'll only ever see what you want to see."

"Please. I have to see. I have to know," Eric said, desperation creeping into his tone.

A clawed hand grasped his shoulder from behind. "You are strong and wise, just as I had envisioned." Cool hands now ran over him as if he were an animal at a fair. Eric shivered in anticipation as the spectre wandered into his sight.

A feral goddess of beauty and nature whose gaze was enough to smother her prey into submission. She was organic, free-flowing.

She had decorated her minimal clothing with polished shells and rocks. Mud, feathers, and dust somehow complemented her strange beauty. Her cloak had a seaweed or vine-like quality, draping along the floor like a net, with lacy tendrils through which were woven many other strips of tangled and knotted fabrics. It moved as if in flowing deep water, guided from a current she controlled.

The light glowed behind her.

Eric resisted the urge to kneel. "Are you a god?"

"I am not such a limited idea."

"Are you ... human?" he pressed.

"I was."

"Do you even exist, or is this all just in my head?"

"I exist where there is no future or past; I come when I am called." Her deep green eyes glowed.

"Okay, so what do you want with me?"

Her pupils darkened. "I bring a message. The prophecy is coming true. You are the one who will save this night, and in doing so, you shall be led down a path. Your intended path. Dark times are ahead, monsters will rise, but remnants of light must remain. This is the path of only a few. Events will occur that you cannot stop. The flames of sin shall burn this world, cleansing it, and a dark hero will rise from the ashes. You will have to make a choice. The ultimate choice."

"The flames of sin shall burn this world ... Firebird," Eric whispered in realization.

"Yes. It was a message to lead you here and beyond. You have always been able to see." Her veil flapped. "That is why it must be you, my child. You can see what others cannot. The light and the dark. The balance."

"You have been leading me to this moment, haven't you?" Eric asked.

"Yes." Her body contorted unnaturally.

"When will this happen?" he asked.

"Not this night, not tomorrow, but soon, the hour approaches. Knowing that, will you stand, or will you run from your fate?" she whispered, her voice echoing.

Eric breathed deeply. "I'm really not sure. What do I have to do?"

"Follow the road laid down for you. Trust your instincts, they will guide you."

"I still don't understand!"

"You will, in time. Be patient." She smiled down at him.

"But what if I die tonight?!" he yelled.

"You won't. There are more important days ahead for you. Death can wait," she said, a lunar glow beginning to swallow her shadowy outline.

Eric gazed up at her in the large, shining mass. "But ..."

Her voice rose above his, her body disappearing into the light, smothering all around. "Always remember the light, the dark, the balance. There is always ... another way."

"There is always ... another ... way," Eric repeated, burning the message into his subconscious. Energy wrapped around him and carried him away. Everything was engulfed in the light.

And then darkness.

Eric gasped into waking. He lay on the Morsley forest floor, taken aback by what he had just experienced. He grabbed his onyx necklace, which was now back against his chest. The lake beside him was still present. The tree with its now obviously empty hole remained rooted there. He rose, gathering his thoughts. But he realized where he was. Joanne was still out there. Michelle and Poppy were alive—he felt it. Time for him to do his work, to end the night as was foretold. A flicker of light amongst the trees in the distance caught his attention. Eric struggled to his feet as he began his journey.

29

In Two Minds

Emotion was a tool Joanne Grimes had used to pave a steady career. She had the ability to draw on her own pain to bring forth a character, complex and real, but also not. She fooled her audiences with each role she'd accepted. She always understood a character's psyche. Their loves, their fears, their pain, their very being. Joanne learned to create a suit for herself, a fleshy costume she could put on when needed. The perfect mask. Her commitment to her craft was true, her talent aging like a fine wine. Knowledge and instinct spilled into her own story. It was a defence mechanism to shield her true thoughts and feelings in this cruel world. Donning the perfect smile to block all attempts to read her often worked in her younger days. However, as the years drifted by, people stop noticing her and she found herself redundant, unwanted.

Cracks grew on the carefully crafted shell Joanne had created over the years. Not having anything left to hope for, she found herself restless and lost within her mind, not quite knowing who or what she had become.

"No more. No more. I can't do this anymore," she sobbed, seated in her trailer, gazing upward to a higher power. "Please. Please. Kill me now. I don't want to go on, not like this. Not even before this. I'm a failure and a murderer. My life has been meaningless; I've never accomplished anything. Not one good thing. Not one." Her whimpering made the table shake. "It's not fair. That little fame and glory—what has it got me? Shame and loneliness. I am left with nothing but myself and blood on my hands. And it's all my fault. I'm sorry, I'm so sorry. I'm so pathetic, so weak. I'm nothing. Nothing but alone."

She wept, torchlight dazzled her sore eyes.

Glancing in the mirror, her tears turned sour. She forced herself to wipe them away through sheer willpower. Her voice became deep and harsh. "No. No more. They cannot stop me!" Joanne sniffed. "I've lived too many lives. I've been imbued with power that they cannot even imagine. This land and everything in it shall be consumed by my fire," she hissed. "Only ashes shall remain by the end of this night. I shall be a curse upon Morsley. They will scream at the thought of me, and my legacy shall be death, guardian of this land."

30

Ready or Not

Centipedes ran like veins through the tunnels of the land, scuttling across beetles, worms, and other insects. They clambered over each other. Damp, muddy walls ran with moisture, like leaking sewage pipes.

Michelle and Poppy continued their long journey back to the house and to safety. They went through the tunnels with their torches, the bugs scurrying away at the brightness. Each squelch beneath her shoes made Poppy's chest tighten and her muscles clench as she thought about Eric and where he could possibly be. Flashes of his bashful expression phased in and out of her mind's eye. *I hope he's okay.* She watched Michelle strut ahead. Poppy sighed, dragging her feet through the thick molasses mud of the tunnel. *I know where I'm going, I know the path ahead.* It was a fiction she told herself, a mantra, day in and out. It gave her a numbing sense of control. She could feel twinges of doubt trickle across the cracking lines on her face. *All those failed videos I did on YouTube,*

I doubt anyone remembers them. I doubt anyone will remember me after Michelle and Eric's reunion takes the spotlight. Past, present, and future, I'm forgotten. But right here, right now, she needed to see the lighthouse in the fog of night. She needed to survive; she needed to remember herself. Clenching her fist, she pounded a new mantra deep within her core. *I'm not Eric, I'm not Michelle. I'm not the adventurer or the thrill seeker. Not the fearful, or the feared. I'm my own brand. I'm the protector. It's not my job to control, but to feel and to learn and to fight.* She made the executive decision: *I won't let a single other person die tonight, I won't, I can't.*

Then two other warm faces illuminated the dark recesses of her thought, their glowing expressions like two blooming flames in a mist of black.

"It's a bit of a mess down here, isn't it?" Michelle said, breaking the long silence.

Poppy did not respond, still deep in thought.

"Oh, you're not going all silent on me, are you? Showing emotion! Oh no, that is very boring." Michelle rolled her eyes. "I do hate it when people shut down on me."

Poppy licked her lips before speaking. "I was just thinking ... the last thing I said to my parents was how excited I was about this opportunity. How it was my big break, a fresh start, and the beginning of my life, finally. Now they're sitting at home thinking I'm having a great time when, in fact, they could find out tomorrow that I died to kick-start a dumb career. It will destroy them." She looked at Michelle. "And it's all your fault."

"Excuse me?" Michelle's face turned gaunt.

"It's your fault," Poppy repeated. "You got us all into this, and for what? To prove a point. Now, I don't care what that is or why you've done it, but I do know that you started this, so you must find a way to end it. People have died."

"People die. It's what they do," Michelle said. "They pop like balloons."

"Do you not feel at all responsible?" Poppy persisted, clearly shocked by Michelle's casual attitude. "Everyone's dead because of you and you feel nothing?"

"What's done is done," Michelle replied. "There's no point in mourning the dead. I should know, I've spent my life investigating them." She paused to step over a large puddle.

"If Eric dies tonight and the two of us survive, I swear I will do all I can to make your life a living hell. Do we understand one another?"

"Wow, jeez. Look at you. Finally growing a spine. Good for you! I have to admit that I kind of like you better for saying that." She prodded Poppy's arm with a long, sharp fingernail.

Poppy shook her head and let out a little laugh of astonishment. "You're a piece of work, you know that? You need help."

Michelle swung round. "I am what I am. You are what you are ... which doesn't mean much, but so be it. If we're going to survive tonight, we're going to need to work together as a team, my little protégée."

"We're not a team," Poppy replied.

"Course we are. Every cat needs a canary."

"I don't need you," Poppy said, scurrying ahead by herself.

"You won't survive down here on your own," Michelle shouted out after her.

Poppy stopped. "You think?"

"Well, do you have a genius plan to stop that old Cracker Jack and save Eric?" Michelle asked, approaching cautiously.

"You have a plan?"

"Of course, I do."

"Not with Eric," Poppy asked quickly.

Michelle sighed. "No, not with Eric, but a way to end this madness."

"What kind of a plan?"

"Wait till we get to the house," said Michelle, nudging her way past Poppy and taking the lead, just as a pained shriek came from behind them. The pair jerked their heads in the direction they had come, shining their torches in the dark. Their spotlights revealed nothing.

"Fuck off!" She yelled with force. "What was that?" Poppy's eyes darted around.

Michelle looked up with a pause, then spoke. "It's nothing, just keep walking." She quickly changed the subject as they moved forward at a faster pace. "You don't get scared, you get angry! I like that about you."

"Who says I'm not both?"

"Ooooh!" Michelle teased, then asked, "So, what do I call you now? A sidekick? A pet?"

Poppy knew Michelle was merely playing with her, or rather, taking her frustrations out on her. Biting her tongue, she followed closely behind, glancing back. "How can you and Eric be friends?" she asked, trying to take her mind off what might be following.

"Why shouldn't we be?"

"You're the opposite of one another," Poppy stated. "He's a bit weird, but he's kind and brave and always puts everyone else first. You are thoughtless and hide your fear behind this tough façade!"

"Exactly. I'm the yin to his yang. I understand him. I'm his friend, and you're just a ... complication."

Poppy scoffed. "Maybe what you really feel is love."

Michelle let out a sickening noise. "Oh, don't be disgusting. There is nothing quite so simple or primitive as that between us."

"Whatever you say. So, what makes you so certain he's still alive?"

"I just know. That man has no finesse, but he is a survivor. We'll make it out of this, as we've made it out of a lot worse." A warm face fell upon Michelle. "Just like the time he saved me from ..."

A shrill sound came from behind. They sprang against the wall, peering back through the pitch-black dark.

"That was definitely something," Poppy said.

"Stay back," Michelle ordered quietly, pushing the younger woman back. "Who's there?" she called out.

Nothing but silence answered. The air smelled dank. Michelle's torchlight only reached the end of the tunnel wall. In the shaking beam of her torch, a figure appeared around the corner, dressed in a bloodied doctor's coat. The spirit stood still, regarding them behind circular spectacles. Then he let out a horrific, hollow scream that vibrated off the walls; the insects skittered.

Michelle grabbed Poppy's hand and ran. Every step hit her hard like a heartbeat and made her breathing uncontrollable.

"This way. Quickly," Michelle instructed, heading toward the broken, two-way mirror that Eric had previously used to escape the cellar. Michelle leapt through the glass first and Poppy soon followed. They ran fast through the cellar, ignoring the macabre scene. They went up the rickety stairs and slammed the door, locking it behind them. Poppy leaned over the kitchen sink.

"Still want to be alone here?" Michelle chuckled to Poppy, breathing hard.

"No way," she answered.

"Marvellous." Michelle smiled. "Now, shall we?" She gestured toward the landing.

"So, what's your plan?" Poppy asked, walking past the cobwebs.

Michelle picked up a black umbrella by the coat rack and did a little dance with it. "Well, I thought I'd start with this," she said, smashing one of the windows loudly beside the front door.

"What the hell are you doing?!" Poppy shouted.

"Luring the looney here ... and Eric." She smashed again. "Curiosity is a powerful thing."

"But she'll come for us," Poppy squeaked.

"Yup, and we'll be here waiting to spring on her. Now, I suggest you go and find something to knock her out with and be ready to use that fiery anger of yours. Go to the kitchen and get a knife or two, just in case." Michelle waved her hand in the direction of the kitchen.

"Okay," Poppy breathed.

Poppy headed through to the kitchen once again as Michelle continued to smash windows, making as much noise as possible. Poppy grabbed the one knife left on the kitchen sideboard before kneeling in front of the sink. She looked upward to the moon outside the window and began to pray. "Oh, please, whatever is out there. Don't let me die here tonight. Please. I will do whatever you want me to, just please don't let me die. I have so much more to do, so much more to offer, give me a sign and I will take it. Whatever it is. Just please give me a chance."

A vibration hit Poppy's pocket. Her phone. It had switched itself back on somehow ... and it was fully charged. Poppy smiled. With hope in her heart, she immediately phoned 999, and they answered.

"999, what is your emergency?"

"Hello? Yes! Please come to Morsley Mansion. It's an emergency; people are dead. Joanne Grimes has gone insane and is attacking us, please come quickly—" The signal gave out. Poppy gazed up at the full moon once again. "Thank you," she said.

"I've phoned the police," Poppy announced, running back to Michelle. Michelle was now guarding the windows.

"How did you manage that?"

"I don't know, I briefly got a signal, and it seemed to work. I'm not sure if they got the message, though."

Michelle's pale eyes widened. "Well, don't just stand there. Try again."

Poppy fumbled with the mobile as she also carried the knife.

"Urgh ... give it here," Michelle said, snatching the phone and waving it around above her head.

The two women began to squabble, face to face over the phone, muffling out the quiet footsteps that approached from the back door, through the kitchen.

"You're doing it wrong. Here." Poppy grasped the phone back and went over by the large window behind the sofa as Michelle followed, to grab it back as the figure slowly crept closer.

Michelle then looked outside and spotted a figure approaching. She tightened her grip on the umbrella, but then noticed they were wearing a navy and white ombré coat jacket. Her face lit up.

"Eric." She smiled as he waved to her. Then another figure came into focus, reflected in the glass behind her. A crazed, feral person wielded a knife poised to plunge into Michelle's back. *Joanne.*

Michelle turned and gasped as she saw her life flash in the gleam of the blades moonlit shine. All her past regrets, her shame, her poor decisions haunted her, drowning her until there was Eric, the only bright light in an ocean of darkness. Her breath escaped her lungs as Joanne's knife came down to her chest, that is, until Poppy released a powerful kick, knocking the deranged actress back against the couch. Poppy gripped her knife, placing the phone in her pocket.

"Leave her alone you crazy bitch." Poppy grunted.

There's that anger, there's my little protective pet, Michelle thought with a sigh of relief. Poppy proceeded to scuffle with the feral murderess, avoiding her blade with bouncing jumps, pushing back with two slashes of her own, causing Joanne to retreat and then to snarl and growl. The crazed killer began to thrust her blade at Poppy, who fell back onto Michelle, who held her up. *Get off me and fight!* Michelle thought frantically as she pushed Poppy forward, just as Joanne lunged, blade in hand. The knife slid straight into Poppy's stomach. The young woman yelped as the blade cut through her, and she dropped her knife

Viewing all this through the dim window, Eric also felt as if he had been stabbed. Both Poppy's fatal blow but also Michelle's betrayal. Eric ran as fast as he could. Michelle used Poppy as a human shield with one arm, whacking the murderess with the umbrella with the other. She hit her hard, multiple times, knocking her down to the floorboards. But not for long.

Joanne sprang up with her knife and ran upstairs. Eric rushed through the door, pushed Michelle aside, and approached Poppy, who bent over as jets of blood spurted out of her back. He helped her onto the sofa. Rosie the doll had moved and now seemed to watch from the other sofa. Eric supported Poppy as best he could.

"Poppy!" he rasped, trying to remain calm. "Let me see."

He rolled her over, and she winced. Blood poured from her wound. "Alright. Just keep pressure here. We can get you some help," he said, trying to make out that it was not as bad as it was.

"I managed to phone the police," she wheezed, grimacing in pain.

"Good. You did good." He caressed her cheek gently. "You're going to be okay. They'll get here. We've just got to patch you up a bit until then, okay?" Eric placed a cushion behind her back to try and ease the flow of blood.

"I'll be fine," she managed.

"Just take it easy. Try not to talk," Eric said, directing her hand against the pillow. "Where are the other two? Where are Todd and Lucy?"

"Both dead," Michelle said, not looking at him. "There was nothing we could do. Nothing I could do."

"Liar. I just saw what you did!" Eric hissed, then caught a whiff of egg. "What's that smell?"

"I don't know?" Michelle said, her voice shaky. "I'll go and look."

"No! I'll go. You stay here and look after Poppy. Make yourself useful for once," Eric snapped, heading through to the kitchen. The gas burners had been switched on. Eric quickly turned them off before returning to Michelle.

"It was gas. She was obviously planning to blow the house up."

"But why?" Michelle asked.

"I don't know. And you're not exactly one to judge a crazy person's logic," Eric said, clasping the knife that Poppy had dropped and heading up the stairs with a look of steely determination.

"Where are you going?" Michelle shouted after him.

"To end this. Someone has to. You just look after her. And remember, if she dies, you'll be next," Eric said.

Joanne waited for him; he could sense her bitter hum. Eric had to answer the call to meet the new monster of Morsley Mansion and put an end to her madness.

31

An Act of Mercy

Shadows lurked around every moonlit doorway. Eric's heart thumped manically. He pointed his knife forward, ready for anything. Beyond any doubt, Joanne lay in wait in one of the rooms, ready to pounce on him. The black stone dangling against Eric's chest pulsed, icy cold. It seemed to radiate a signal, protecting him, may it shield him now.

In the corner of his eye, he caught movement. A blonde girl skipped past the nursery door, giggling. Then, she was gone. Two Victorian teenagers, one in a finely tailored dark wool suit and the other in a flowing silk gown complete with a delicate bonnet, darted past the end of the corridor. Eric headed after them, but not to investigate. Again, in his peripheral vision, a doctor watched him from one hallway, then disappeared. Two children, their eyes stabbed with crayons, ran past. His head swam. He turned to see Lacey the Clown grinning and peering at him with his button eyes from around the bedroom door. Then, in a blink, he was gone. Eric spiralled into confusion. The memories of the house flashed before him.

"I'm not afraid," he said as he hobbled past the nursery. Eerie doll eyes followed him. A young woman appeared at the end of the hallway, a teenager in modern clothing, pointing to a bedroom door. *That's the girl from the missing posters in the village. Shannon.* The young deceased student grimaced, lowering her hand, turning to enter the room she was pointing at. A cry beckoned from the bedroom. Eric slowly stepped in to see that it was where a sobbing Joanne sat in the near dark, alone. Eric approached her with caution, in that room where it all began, where the fate of the Morsleys changed forever.

"Don't run away. I know you're afraid and confused. I can help you," Eric called out, entering the room to find the tormented actress standing in front of the window, her head low, as her hand shook, holding a knife.

Eric touched the doorframe for support, and his brain flashed to Mrs. Morsley finding out her husband had butchered their children. She sobbed while her husband looked on completely unmoved. Her heartbreaking screams pierced Eric's thoughts as Mrs. Morsley lashed out and bashed her husband's head with the fire poker, knocking him unconscious, then continued to beat him to death. Eric snapped out of his trance. "Please, Joanne. I can help you."

Another flash hit him. He travelled, in his head, to another room. He watched Lady Morsley cradling her children's dead bodies, rinsing them with jugs of water, to wash them clean. Then she ascended to the attic, gazing out upon the world one last time, restraining her pain and grief for as long as she could. Finally, she took a deep breath before slitting her own throat and collapsing dead to the floor. Eric truly understood the purpose of the visions as he gazed upon Joanne Grimes' madness. Lady Morsley's truth.

"She wasn't a monster," he murmured.

"What?" Joanne said, still looking away.

Eric understood. Like Lady Morsley, Joanne was not a bad person. Maybe she needed to know as much. "She wasn't a monster," Eric continued. "Lady Morsley. Neither are you." He attempted to reach out to the woman, breaking through the fog to her.

She remained still as if paused in thought. Then her expression changed as something seemed to click inside her. Her eyes swelled with hate. "No! That's what they all say. That's what they've always said. It's too late for me—and for you."

Joanne approached, and Eric backed away. His muscles froze in sheer horror as her shadow loomed over him with the knife. Suddenly, a dark figure jumped ahead of Eric, hissing. It was the black cat, leaping up to scratch and tear Joanne's dress and leaping towards her neck. The actress screamed, aiming her blade for the furry devil, but missed with every thrust. Jumping to the windowsill, the small mammal's glowing eyes hit Eric with a look that made him feel as if it were buying him time. Eric nodded at it and did as he was seemingly instructed: to leave. Stumbling away, he heard Joanne yell and scuffle some more with the cat.

"That's it, run, run you foul, wretched feline!" she ordered as Eric felt her thumping footsteps soon follow him through the floorboards.

He ran, with his knife, up the stairs to the attic where all the mirrors from the house were kept. Eric crawled behind them, big and small, hoping she wouldn't find him in the maze of mirrors. The room was illuminated only by the round circular window resembling the full moon itself.

Joanne hobbled into the room, stopped as if confused by the mirrors' reflections. She peered through, searching, then gasping. Eric peeked out from behind an antique frame to see her staring at her own image in the mirror. Bloodied, cut, frazzled, teary, broken, tired, and hate-filled. Everything she was not.

"That's me?" she whispered.

"Yes," Eric's voice boomed through the mirrors, seeing his opportunity to catch her off guard. "Just look at yourself, at what you've done." Eric lowered his tone. "I'm sorry, Joanne, but look at what you've become." He spoke softly, watching the broken murderess.

A shred of Joanne's soul glistened in the moonlight, teetering from her eyelids. She wiped it away, falling to her knees.

"No. It's all make-believe—just like my family, my friends, my life," she choked, her eyes darting around as she saw Eric's reflection in a mirror, ready to jump on her. "Why couldn't you just play along?" Joanne screamed as she began to smash every mirror, chasing Eric's image that seemed to dance around, dodging each shard of glass.

Joanne used every fibre of her strength and mania to destroy every image of the man until he disappeared. Only one mirror remained. She looked at herself as she held the blade high, gazing deep into her own self, trapped in a new persona. Trickles streamed down her face. Her hand shook. Pain swelled within her now. She couldn't bear to look at herself, so she stabbed the mirror with vigorous thrusts, obliterating her former self for the new, cold-hearted self she had become. As the glass broke, Eric toppled out from behind it. The shards cut into his arm, causing him to lose his knife somewhere amongst them. He scurried into the corner of the room like a rat, as Joanne stepped toward him.

"Take comfort in knowing that your death shall be a warning to others. A message to the world. My legacy shall endure."

Eric breathed hard in anticipation and acceptance of his fate. His visions, his fate, must have been in his head. He had been like Joanne all the time, lost in his own mind. His hope of escape was snuffed out. Then, behind the dark shape of Joanne Grimes, something loomed.

The onyx burned deep into him.

Joanne followed his gaze, turning to look behind her. Her eyes widened and she dropped her knife. Her face contracted in terror at who stood before her.

"You're Lady Morsley," she muttered, falling to the floor in submission.

Joanne knelt, almost kissing the floor where her idol stood. She wept in the cold, cruel light, pleading. "I'm sorry. I didn't mean to. I didn't mean to..." She looked upward for mercy but was instead stunned by something unnatural and unnerving. A frozen, skeletal hand reached out to caress her face. Joanne felt the mother's mercy. She wiped away her tears with her thin finger, her other hand resting on her other cheek, kindly.

Joanne's fear dissolved as she felt kinship with another tormented, damaged woman. She gazed into Lady Morsley's soul, and thus into her own, into the heart of Morsley itself, evaluating the one mirror she could not destroy. For now, she finally understood the lesson she had never learned. *In life, we merely play the parts we're cast in.*

"Thank you," she said.

Joanne's head twisted with a snap, releasing her. Her limp body dropped to the floor in a heap. Eric trembled to his core. The shadow spirit turned her attention to him. Even with the fogginess, he could not miss the empty eyes. His amulet beat back and forth with his heart. His fingers tingled, and his pulse raced

Each second felt like a lifetime. She moved slowly, with her head downwards, as if in a sign of respect. Eric blinked. His onyx went still, and the dark lady dissolved into the night.

He rubbed his eyes, glancing around. There was nothing except the lingering trace of death and despair. The wind chimes played in the breeze on the porch outside. Eric breathed deeply, knowing that something had saved him.

32

An Eternal Sleep

Eric rushed down the stairs, almost falling over his feet, adrenaline still pumping through him. He clambered down to see a struggling Poppy gasping for life. Michelle rather gently patted and winced as she tended to Poppy. Michelle turned and tiptoed over to Eric. The pillow behind Poppy was soaked with blood, draining her like a sponge. Eric threw the knife on the table and briskly walked past Michelle, hanging metres away from Poppy.

"How is she?" he asked, out of breath.

Michelle buffered a quiet response at his side. "I don't think she's going to make it; she's lost a lot of blood. She's dying. I'm sorry." She cast her eyes down to the floor.

Poppy overheard. "We can fix this, can't we? You always fix it." She smiled weakly at Eric.

"No, I can't," he said, turning to Michelle. "But you can."

"Me?" she replied, stunned.

"Yes, you. You *will* fix this."

"I can't."

"Oh, yes, you can and will, because otherwise? It will be over," Eric said. "I'll tell the police this was all you. I'll tell the press, and you'll be a hated public figure. How's that for your comeback? You will save Poppy with whatever kind of trick you have up your sleeve, or I will make your life a living hell until the day you die."

"You can't," Michelle said, her gaze hardening.

"Oh, I can. You know who I am better than anyone."

"Eric, this isn't you."

"No. It's not. Look what you've made me into. Right now, you're stuck with *this,* Eric! And he will end you if you don't somehow manage to fix this."

"Eric ... stop," Poppy intervened, clutching her stomach.

"No," he replied.

Poppy breathed through the blood. "Please ... just stop."

Eric was suddenly haunted by the words of his former companion, Megan, *Find that person who can stop you from going too far. Because I think sometimes you need to be told stop.* His lip trembled in realization. "We can get you some help, find a way."

"Listen to me," Poppy whispered. "It's okay. But if this is the last I ever see of you, don't make it like this. Not like this." Her head shook. "Is there anything you can do?" Poppy asked Michelle directly.

"No. I'm sorry."

"But the police will be here soon." Eric attempted to assure her.

"Not in time."

Eric exhaled and gently edged his way beside Poppy on the couch, whimpering. "I was meant to protect you. I promised you. This is all my fault." Eric turned away.

Poppy grabbed his face with the little strength she had. "This ... was my choice. I chose to come ... here."

"Poppy... hold on just a little while longer," Eric said quietly.

"I can't." Poppy coughed.

"Don't be scared."

"Never. Just do ... one thing for me. Bring ... me back to my parents."

"You did. And I will," he agreed, squeezing her hand.

"And destroy this house." Her voice sounded faint.

He nodded. "I will."

Poppy and her peaceful smile stiffened as she drifted away. Eric felt her soul leave her body as a gust of wind filled the room, a fraction of light leaving the world to be at peace forevermore. Eric gazed down, wracked with guilt, filled with sorrow—so much so he felt he might drown. Eric cried as he shut her eyelids and let go of her limp body.

Turning, he gazed through the lobby, over to see the kitchen door wide open. Michelle had escaped. No, Eric wouldn't let her get away. Spotting the knife he had dropped earlier, he picked it up and ran out to hunt his oldest friend.

He intended to settle things once and for all.

33

Web Unwinding

The night suffocated the light as Michelle frantically scurried through the woods. Her head turned constantly to all sides, afraid of what other cruel creatures could be lurking, ready to pounce on her. She certainly felt a strong presence watching her. Her boot heels kept sticking in the cracked terrain. A crunching of leaves came ahead, and she almost jumped at the figure standing in front of her. Michelle came to a halt, smirking. Ahead of her, Eric stood, pointing a large knife toward her, his eyes flaring with intensity, a mixture of anger and sorrow. Sweat glistened on his forehead.

Eric's conflicted emotions showed on his face—likely weighing whether he should hand his friend over to the police, kill her, or let her go?

Michelle breathed heavily and flicked her fingers. "So, is this how it ends?"

"Yes," Eric replied, pointing the knife at her chest as he stepped closer, now inches away.

Michelle's gaze lowered to his quivering hand, then back up to meet his eyes. She let out a hysterical laugh she couldn't seem to control. She attempted to hold it back but simply couldn't.

Eric appeared confused by her reaction.

"I suppose this is where we've always been heading; this is our perfect ending!" Michelle said.

Eric winced. "I guess it is?"

"What are you waiting for then? Do it. Get it over with."

"You said you were my friend."

"Do it," she repeated, her eye twitching.

Eric glanced down at his weapon, gleaming in the moonlight. "Something's been nagging at me. Why? What was it for? Why have you done this? Not just for your career? For revenge?"

Michelle looked down in shame. "Because ... you're mine." She gazed up at him through long lashes. "Because you're the only friend I've ever had. Everything I've done was to get back the only person I care about. The one person who cared for me. You. That's all I ever wanted. I want my ... friend back. I need you back in my life."

Eric froze, taking a moment to process her words. "Everything you've ever done has been for yourself, and you've never seen that, you've never understood. Seeing the world was not enough for you. People have lost their lives. Poppy, that poor, sweet girl. You used her to get to me, along with everyone else. Everyone here is dead because of you. And the worst part is you don't even care. You don't understand why that is wrong. I don't think you've ever understood."

Michelle shrugged. "What can I say? It's my nature."

"You're never going to change because you don't know how to."

Michelle saw her reflection in the silver blade. "Then show me," she whimpered. "Help me. Teach me how to be like you."

"What's the point? You won't change. Never have, never will."

"I will. Please, just give me a chance. I-I'll make this right, I-I promise."

Eric shook his head. "Why didn't you just find me? Why didn't you do what any normal-minded person would do?" he asked in frustration.

"Because ... I don't know," Michelle cried. "I knew you'd be angry. I was scared you'd reject me. I needed to make sure you would take me back, that I had control."

"Oh yeah, and how's that turning out for you?" Eric swallowed; his chin held high.

Her chin trembled. "I'm sorry. I just need you to know that we're not so different. I want my friend back by my side. For good. Please," Michelle pleaded.

The pair really looked at one another. Eric's face tightened and turned sour as if he was about to finally muster the courage to put Michelle out of her misery.

"You know the best thing that happened to me was being friends with Eric Thompson. With you," said Michelle. "Everything I've done in my life, possibly the best thing, was turning you into...the great Eric Thompson. How could I let something like that go?" she said, choking on her words. "I know I'm crazy, and no one loves me. But ... I had hope, you. You know it's true. You know me. Face it, Eric, we'd be lost without one another, whether you like it or not. You're a part of me, and I'm a part of you. Forever."

Eric's muscles loosened as he felt himself become disarmed by Michelle's speech, by his friends' words. Her heart, her motives, her intentions were all revealed. Her web now finally unwound. It was true. Everything she said. He shook uncertainly as he held back bitter tears. He lowered his aching arm and dropped the metal blade to the ground. Michelle recoiled in surprise.

"Goodbye, Michelle. This time ... don't come back," Eric ordered.

Michelle registered his unexpected act of kindness, but also the finality. Eric did not like goodbyes, and she knew that all too well. She glared at him, uncertain whether it was a trick. It was not.

She ran as fast as she could, thankful for Eric's gift, another chance at life. She knew there was no better gift than a future, no matter how uncertain.

She disappeared into the wilderness, to wherever fate would next take her. Perhaps, never to see Eric again.

Eric knew she wasn't escaping. Not really. He would never hurt his friend, but could let her go. Eric stood alone in the glow of the moon, trying to hold on to what remained of his shattered soul, remembering his greatest enemy and his greatest friend.

34

A Peaceful Hell

Morsley Mansion stood empty as Eric walked through its wretched doors, but he could no longer hear the creaks and whispers that had called to him before. He went through to the kitchen with the knife and slashed at the gas line from behind the stove; it soon snapped and hissed. The place had to be destroyed. He had made a promise. Eric rummaged through the kitchen drawers for matches, a lighter, anything that might trigger a spark and ignite the gas.

"Please, just help me out here. Give me something to work with!" Eric pleaded.

He pulled open the final drawer and found a half-empty box of matches.

"Thank you," Eric whispered.

Taking some pillows from the couch, he set fire to each with a match and tossed one in each downstairs room. He moved quickly, knowing it wouldn't take long to trigger a hellfire of an explosion, but he couldn't go without fulfilling his final promise to Poppy.

As he approached her body, he saw she was watched over by another, Rosie the doll. The doll sat beside Poppy on the sofa with one hand on her lifeless body. The image was strange and unexpected but comforting nonetheless. Eric approached cautiously, anticipating more activity, but the doll merely tipped over, lifeless. *Rosie, no, Madeline, all this time, she's been trying to help through that doll,* he realized.

A feeling of shame enveloped Eric. He sat opposite Poppy's body and, just for a second, considered burning himself with her in the house. But something inside of him kicked in. *No! I need to return Poppy's body to her parents.* That and he had things to do. He realized more was planned for him. He was still breathing and alive, however lonely and regretful, he still had a life after all.

Sirens broke through the night, and flashes of red and blue light appeared outside. The police—belated hope. They had obviously received the call Poppy had made. Eric looked down at his remarkable assistant, her face at peace, glowing in the police lights. The smell of gas wafted through the air. The clock was ticking. Morsley knew its time was over. Its reign of terror was about to end, and, for most that dwelled within it, that was all they had ever wanted—peace from the meddlesome world.

Smoothing a stray strand of hair from Poppy's face, Eric lifted her limp body up off the sofa. Carefully and respectfully, he carried her outside. Five police cars rolled up, the occupants within stepped out and watched with shocked and horrified expressions as Eric stepped down the porch toward them, a lifeless body in his arms, his coat flapping in the wind.

The house became ablaze. The fire ripped through Morsley, cleansing all within. A sudden weight lifted from Eric as he felt the warmth behind him. The sins of Morsley were finally being erased. *No one would ever have to suffer the horrors of this place again,* he thought.

The police tried to talk to Eric, but everything was a haze as he placed Poppy's body down gently on the ground. Her face bore a pale expression of serenity he had never seen on her in life. Someone quickly wrapped a blanket over Eric and escorted him to a nearby ambulance to tend to his forgotten wounds. He watched as they took Poppy's body away in a bag. Embers cascaded down to the floor. Eric knew, in his heart, that everything was going to be okay. He sat in the back of a police car, still shrouded in his blanket, as they drove him away. As the wheels steadily turned, Eric thought, for a moment, he caught sight of a shape, a person in the shadows of the woods, watching him leave. He checked again. *No.* Most people would have thought it nothing, but Eric knew who it was: Poppy. He smiled. The nightmare was finally over.

35

Worry, and You Suffer Twice

Six Months Later ...

They say time can heal all wounds. Eric wished that were true. Bright lights cast away all his creases and wrinkles, helped by excessive make-up that had been crudely applied. Microphones caught every movement and sound. The crew watched in anticipation of what was about to happen next. Eric sat in a chair opposite Cedric Marion, his exclusive interviewer, personally recommended by his confidant, Tamara Alzin. Cedric had moved up in the world in the six months since Eric's last interview. From panels to talk shows. Since the step up, he had clearly invested in plastic surgery, and his face had a strange, unmoving quality.

Eric sat beside him on the colourful, early morning set, decked out with a fake city background. Garish props sat on a table between the two of them. The feeling of panic was swelling in him now; he needed to rectify all the gossip and rumours that had been spread about what happened that dreadful night. In a few seconds' time, they would be on the air. Cedric licked his lips with his cue cards in hand, one leg crossed casually over the other.

Eric breathed deeply. He could do this.

Three, two, one. Action.

"Oh, good morning, America. I am here live with the world-famous paranormal investigator, Eric Thompson. Hello, Eric, how are you?" Cedric asked warmly.

"I'm good, thank you, Cedric," Eric replied, coming across calmer than he could have hoped.

Cedric looked Eric up and down as he squirmed. "So, tell me what's been happening and what have you been up to?" The interviewer asked.

Eric exhaled. "Not a lot, really. You know, just keeping it chill right now."

"Sorry to throw a wrench into that plan because right now, we have to talk about what happened at Morsley Mansion."

"Yes," Eric said, ready to face any questions that were fired at him.

"That's why you're here, after all, to set the record straight after the police report was released and GMD released the footage from the estate." The presenter read off his card with rehearsed ease. "As we all know, no charges were pressed against you but like you've said to the press, you've received many horrible accusations."

"Yes. That's true: many from my fans, which is quite disheartening." Eric clutched his chest.

"So, Eric, this is your chance. Please tell the world what you want to say. In your own words." Cedric waited in anticipation, along with the cameras that loomed over Eric, and the millions watching on TV at home. All eyes were on Eric.

"I would like to begin by saying that all the ridiculous rumours about the entire thing being a giant hoax by Liam Galavan and everyone else involved are not true."

"Except the footage of the actors pranking yourself and poor Poppy Dearly," Cedric butted in.

"Yes, that. But everything else was real."

"Speaking as an observer, of course, you have to admit that aspect of the case certainly seemed somewhat ... fishy." His hands shook a little.

"Are you referring to the missing bodies?" Eric sighed.

"Well, yes, the bodies of Liam Galavan, Lucy O'Brian, Todd Phillips, Joanne Grimes, Gregory Fitzsimmons, Marian Franklin, Matthew Harper, and Paul Salt. Their bodies were never recovered. You told police that they had all died, or you suspected they had. How do you explain that, Eric?"

"Police found their blood and DNA everywhere around the estate and grounds."

"Yes, but no bodies," Cedric retorted. "You have to admit that it's more than a little strange."

Eric looked directly into the camera for a moment before lowering his head. "Morsley Mansion was a strange place. Throughout history, people have gone missing, from the Bermuda Triangle, the Aztecs, to the Roanoke Colony. People go missing, Michael proved that."

Cedric leaned back and smiled. "People have theorized that the whole show was fake, a charade to revive, and I quote here from *The Times*, "failing careers." A way to have one last attempt at success?"

"That's utter nonsense," Eric said.

"Many people have backed up your story ... what you told the police about the supernatural events that occurred there, Joanne Grimes's sanity breaking and her killing everyone. They have even supported what you say about Michelle Snow, who also appears to have gone missing. You say she was your former partner and best friend, Michael Goode, who disappeared years ago." Cedric sat up straight.

"Yes," Eric said.

"You say he transitioned and became Michelle Snow. It's all a little farfetched, don't you think?"

"Yup. That's exactly what it was. I admit it, but I didn't write the story that night, I just ... had to live it," Eric replied quickly, having prepped the quote beforehand.

"Do you know where Michelle Snow has gone?"

"No."

"I see. It's also funny how the power seemed to go out, rendering all the cameras in the house completely inactive, and not able to record these apparent murders you claim to have witnessed at the hands of Joanne Grimes."

Eric fidgeted anxiously. "That's true, but you should watch the show GMD studios released on the case, and the events that happened beforehand."

"Yes, but everything that did happen was hoaxed, a prank."

"Not all of it. Some things didn't happen on film," Eric pointed out.

"Like what?"

Eric looked around at the smirking producers and crew. "Voices in the woods, shadows moving in corridors, things like that."

"Right ... so who killed the apparent murderer, Joanne Grimes? I know you've explained before, but can you tell us again how she died?"

Eric's shirt felt tight as his chest constricted. "The spirit of Elizabeth Morsley killed Joanne." He heard a few crew members snicker.

"Can you explain how something like that can happen?" Cedric continued.

"Joanne Grimes lost her mind. I don't know what caused her to snap," Eric said. "Whether delving too deep into her role, that place got to her, or she just got lost in her own head, I don't know. She killed everyone. I tried to stop her, but I failed. She was about to kill me, but was stopped by the spirit of the real Lady Morsley, who snapped her neck. I think it was a mercy killing to put Joanne out of her misery, give her a release."

"And now, like everyone else, her body is missing." Cedric eyed him in disbelief.

"Yes."

"It's also suspicious that you burned down the house, maybe to cover up any evidence left behind?"

"I did it to stop anyone else from making the same mistake we had, along with others from the past."

"It's true that the house does have a dark past, a correlation with what happened to you all," Cedric agreed.

"Yes, I don't know how to explain it, but the place itself had a way of getting into your head ... of making your emotions feel heightened," Eric said, beginning to doubt himself.

"Some have said that you are the real killer and are trying to cover it up. After all, you are the sole survivor."

"Along with Michelle," Eric added.

"Who, strangely, has not been seen since. You left the building carrying the one body that remained, Poppy Dearly." Cedric took a sip of water.

Regret and pain consumed Eric at the mention of Poppy's name. "She was sweet and smart and funny; I couldn't save her she died protecting someone, Michelle, and she deserved better." He felt as though he was about to cry, but held back.

"Quite," said Cedric. His shoulders seemed to tense, then mellowed as he soon added: "Now let's talk about something else. The future. What's next, Eric?"

Eric looked up again, suppressing his emotions. "Not much, I'm doing a bit of investigating on a few projects and might start a new channel. I don't know, I am keeping it very flexible right now." His cheeks flushed hot.

"Oh, that's great. It's good to see yourself pushing through it all." Cedric made a gesture in the air with his fist.

"Thank you," Eric responded.

"Now, I will ask you this only one time, just the once." Cedric leaned in for dramatic tension. "Just to finish up this interview, is there anything else you wish to confess to the audience?"

Eric looked at the camera directly. "No."

"Good, good," Cedric said, clearly disappointed. "Oh, it appears that's all we've got time for. It's been an honour, as always, talking to you, Eric. Thank you for coming to speak with me today to set this whole matter straight."

"No problem, thank you for having me. It's been a pleasure, as always." He glared at Cedric.

"Next, we will be catching up with a new band who recently hit the charts …" Cedric continued to talk as Eric left the set. He walked past all the now-silent, crewmembers and producers, who parted like the Red Sea.

Eric's heart swelled as he left the studio, exiting to his changing room to pick up his personal effects and leave this dreaded place for good, knowing now there was nothing more he could do to save his public image. His career might be broken, but his sense of purpose had never been stronger.

36

When Two Worlds Meet

Checking that all his belongings remained untouched in his navy duffle bag and sliding on his patched-up ombré coat, Eric prepared to leave his dressing room as quickly as he could. Zipping up his bag, he felt a presence behind him, cold, calculated. Selfish. His eyes widened in realization.

"Well, well, well. What do we have here?" noted a familiar voice.

Eric chuckled, turning to see the slim woman lurking in the doorway of his dressing room. She wore a chic, designer black dress topped off with a collection of statement jewellery. She had long, platinum blonde locks. A lavish silver and ruby ring sat on one of her fingers. The gem was hypnotic, like a snake's gaze. It seemed to be a part of her, and she was never seen without it.

"Hello, Lydia," Eric said to the famous author of books about the mind. Lydia was followed by an arctic chill as her meticulous eyes darted around, no doubt analyzing. Usually, Eric would stop and chat, but he was in no mood.

"My goodness, I haven't seen you since ..." she said through glossy lips. "Oh, yes, that's right, that dreary New York honours dinner. It must have been around two years ago now. You look awful," she said bluntly, looking him up and down.

She fully entered the room, shutting the door behind her.

Eric laughed a little. "Thanks, you're about the only person who's said it."

Lydia click-clacked toward him in stiletto-clad feet. "You know I don't want something from you when I don't mince my words. I heard you were here. Thought I'd pop in to say hi."

Eric rolled his eyes, swinging his bag into his left hand. "Well, you've said it, so how come you're here then?"

"I've got an interview with that sap Cedric Marion about my latest book. I heard you've just come off with him." Her gaze frosted over.

"I have," Eric replied.

"Any tips?"

"Not really, just smile and nod. Try to be humble, I guess." He looked at his watch, drifting past her.

"I watched your interview. Loved the use of body language and direct eye contact you used, very trusting."

Eric took a little bow. "I just do those things, I guess."

"No one just does anything," she replied. "I don't suppose you would consider being a part of one of my future works, focusing on why people have faith. You know religion, fate, ghosts, and monsters, and all that?"

"Me? I don't know, Lydia. A lot of people still think I murdered those people or was part of a much larger hoax."

The blonde rested her arm on the wall and tilted her head. "True." Her eyes met his. "The way I see it, your funny, little, happy-go-lucky life leaves death and chaos in its wake. Anyone who stands too close to you seems to get burned, or worse. Perhaps you should retire."

"No. Never," he said.

Lydia's scarlet lips parted for a moment, and she smiled. "You're a hard man to read, Eric, you always have been but now ... you have a flicker of madness in your eyes. I wonder what you'll do with that?"

Eric smiled. "I guess you'll have to wait and see."

Lydia tutted. "Oh, you know I'm not one for surprises."

Eric exhaled and said, "See you next time, then," and went to leave.

"Have you ever heard of Mortem Asylum?" Lydia asked, moving in closer.

Eric stopped and recalled the name. "Yes. It's an asylum, very old and supposedly haunted."

"If you believe in the supernatural, that is," she mocked.

"I believe it's still in use as a home for the criminally insane."

"I suppose it would have been a fitting place for Joanne Grimes, had she survived Morsley," Lydia said.

"Indeed. I was going to do a special there with Michael years ago, until we decided on another case." He gazed down in memory, scratching his neck. "Never been there myself. Why are you asking about it?"

Lydia hesitated. "No reason. Curiosity, that's all."

Bullshit. Nothing Lydia said was asked out of curiosity. "Right then, if there's nothing else ..." Eric said, brushing past her.

Suddenly, the room seemed to spin. Eric felt his muscles seize up as the colour red flashed everywhere. He saw a grey wolf, a locket, blood, and an infant screaming. A symphony of death and pain hurled itself through

Eric as he passed Lydia. And then the vision was gone, as quickly as it had come.

Lydia eyed him up and down and frowned. "Something wrong?" she asked.

He paused to get his breath, looking at her ring once again, then rubbed his head as he caressed the amulet hanging still from his neck. "No, no it's nothing." Eric opened the door, with a shaking hand, not quite knowing what it was he had just sensed or what it meant. "Just...take care, Lydia, with whatever it is you are up to."

"Well, where's the fun in that?" Lydia joked with a smirk as she left.

Eric tried to smile back but couldn't, knowing something bad was coming for her. *Fate must play its hand,* he knew.

Eric sat at a bus stop in the rain, watching people. He noticed that others had tried to keep a distance from him since Morsley. He was evidently seen as a freak or worse. Despite everything, Eric couldn't deny the fact that it was humans who made life interesting, even when they despised him or didn't understand him anymore.

In the months since Morsley, he accepted his fate to be a lonely one. He spent his time absorbed in hobbies, creating things: painting, drawing, and writing. He had even taken up photography. He read countless books and reviewed them, and binge-watched endless TV series, anything to take his mind off things. He spent hours at the gym each day. Nothing could penetrate the loneliness he felt.

Eric sat at home, drying himself from the rain on his couch. He turned on his television, flicking through endless, pointless channels, stopping abruptly to listen when he heard an extremely intriguing item on the news.

"Breaking News. Michelle Snow has come out of hiding and has confessed to murdering actress Joanne Grimes in self-defence on the night of the Morsley massacre."

Eric looked at the screen and saw Michelle's broken and tearful face as she was escorted into custody. After all the terrible things she had done, she had done a good thing. Saved her friend, Eric, from all accusations, she had taken the blame for everything. Eric couldn't quite believe it. The phone rang, and he dashed for it.

"Hello?"

"Eric? It's me. I'm guessing you've seen the news?"

He hesitated. "I have."

"I need to see you ... please," Michelle pleaded.

Eric stood, phone in hand, without answering, knowing he would have to see her one last time.

37

Old Wounds

Eric's fingertips tingled. Inside, he was a swirling cocktail of emotion. He had no idea what would happen next or how he would react. He sat awaiting the arrival of the lead detective on the Morsley case. He tapped his foot on the chair leg. A tall, stocky man approached with a hard, New York accent.

"Thank you for coming in, Mr. Thompson. I'm Detective Morgan. I am glad you've come. You were her one phone call," the detective said.

"What kind of person would I be if I hadn't come." Eric rose from his chair. "What has she said?"

Detective Morgan's eyes grew cold. "That she murdered Joanne Grimes out of self-defence. She broke her neck and buried the body, along with the others, somewhere in the woods, all in different places. She hasn't given a reason, but this seems to exonerate you of any blame." The stern line of his brow seemed to emphasize his last remark.

"Yeah, it does." Eric's chin dropped. "Have they managed to find the bodies?"

Morgan beckoned for Eric to stand and directed him through a pair of double doors that swung through to a seemingly endless corridor. "Police there are searching while we speak, but as of right now, we have nothing."

"So, the hunt continues," Eric said glumly.

"Yes," he replied, leading Eric to the visitors' waiting room. "She has been missing for a long time. She could have run away, scot-free. Why do you think she decided to confess now?"

"I have no idea, detective. I can only imagine she confessed for one reason." Eric paused. "To appease her guilty conscience."

Moments later, Eric sat alone, arms folded, in a cold room with a glass wall. A metallic table cooled Eric's sweaty palms, the barriers on both sides protruded from the edge of his gaze, for privacy, he assumed. It felt claustrophobic, like a coffin. A red light shone above the door to the right, on the other side of the thick glass. The door opened, revealing a police guard who politely held it for the orange jump-suited prisoner, Michelle.

Her eyes hit Eric immediately, seeming puffy but sharp as ever, two steely, sapphire ice picks. Her face was washed out, and she did not look as glamorous as when he had previously seen her months before. Yet, she still retained a sense of grace and beauty. Her hair was a tight bundle of knots, with strands dangling down like legs, as if she wore an arachnid on her head. She sat down on the hard seat in front of Eric. The guard left the room, and the red glow disappeared with a simple click of the door.

Michelle smiled as if surprised. She picked up the cream-coloured phone, her action mirrored by Eric on the other side. His breathing could be heard on the other end. "Hello, Eric, thank you for coming to see me. I'm surprised you came after all I've done, but I'm glad you did."

Eric blinked slowly. "I came here because you're in trouble and you asked me. Now tell me what you want?"

"I wanted to see you again. I needed to talk to you. Even if this is the last time."

Eric took a deep breath, glancing up and down at her with a measured expression. "You look like crap," he said.

She grinned. "I've had to turn my eyebrow pencil into a shank."

"I can see that." Eric visualized it in his head.

"You can only imagine the number of questions I've got from other prisoners in here. Is it a hot dog or a bun? Are you gay or straight? Such tedious questions." She rolled her eyes.

"Spoke to your lawyer," Eric said, changing the subject and uncrossing his arms, and placing them on his lap like a disappointed father. "For what you've confessed, he believes you'll be in here for life, mainly because they suspect that you also murdered all the others. Anyway, they need someone to blame it all on. They're talking about extraditing you to the UK, but I don't know. Best case scenario is a few decades."

"Good," she snapped. "It serves me right. I need to pay for what I've done." Her gaze looked beyond his shoulder, guilty. "But aren't you going to ask me why?"

"Why what?" Eric rubbed his eyes, growing tired of his friend's mind games.

"Why I confessed to moving those bodies we both know I didn't move, why I confessed to a crime I didn't commit." The vein in her forehead pulsated in time with her escalating heartbeat.

Eric shook his head. "I don't care. Not anymore."

"To protect you."

"I don't need your protection."

"No. That's something I'm sure of. You don't need protecting from me or anyone ... or anything for that matter." Her lashes fluttered. "You're stronger than I could ever be. All those years, when we were kids, teens, adults, you took the blame for so much of my crap and it's funny, really funny now. Poetic justice." She sniffed, then added, "When I saw your interview with that louse Cedric Marion and realized how badly the accusations were affecting you, I knew I had to help you. You see, the past six months in hiding gave me time to reflect. We all have our uses, our purposes, our own destinies. Mine is to save you. You saved my life at Aokigahara. You saved me through everything, and now I am saving you. It's what ... friends do. And don't you dare take that away from me." She pointed at him through the glass with her now blunt nail.

Eric's heart softened slightly. "You're going to die in here, you know that?" he said with regret.

"I know, and it's fine." She smiled despite the pain in her eyes. "I can live with that so long as you can do one thing."

"And what's that?" Eric asked.

"Forgive me," she pleaded. "Forgive me for all the mistakes I've made."

The sentiment hit Eric like a stormy sea. He looked away but then back up as cold realization hit him. "It's a horrible world we live in ... because of monsters like you. You," Eric insisted, "were the real monster of Morsley that night." He scalded her with his own rare brand of cruelty. "We all make our choices, and now you have to pay for yours." Eric waited for some witty comeback only to witness further displays of grief.

"I don't sleep well anymore," she stated. "I keep remembering all of them, their names; the people I got killed. I hear their screams in the night. Every day it gets worse. Memories are so much worse in the dark." Michelle gulped in shame. "I ... I don't even know why I keep crying; tell me why I keep doing that? What's the point? It won't bring them back!"

"I don't know," Eric said.

"There has always been collateral damage with us, hasn't there?" Michelle smiled. "It doesn't matter, not anymore. At the end of the day, you are my friend, my family. And that's all that really matters." She rested her hands on the cold desk.

"You're right," Eric agreed, surprised.

"So, can you forgive me?" Michelle leaned forward, struggling to hold back her tears. "Say it, and I can endure anything in here. I can take it. Please just say it. Forgive me, Eric, please and I can face my judgement, whatever that may be." Her eyes pleaded with him. She rested her open palm against the clear glass as a way of reaching out to touch and be touched by her only friend in this world. She awaited his hand to reach out to hers and meet on the opposite side. Hand to hand, as they had always done.

Could Eric put aside his rage and sorrow and make amends with her, despite all the wrongs she had done? Eric winched a smile back, looking at her weak hand shaking on the other side as his rose, moving up to meet hers.

Michelle's pupils dilated; her face flickered with hope for a moment, then diminished as Eric retracted his hand. He sank back into himself and gazed back at her. He slammed the phone back on its holster and rose, feeling her grasp over him fading, the webs of lies and deceit snapping from him.

As he left the room and Michelle behind him, he felt free.

THE HAUNTING AT MORSLEY MANOR

Michelle's face dropped, but her hand remained pressed up against the cold glass even as he shut the door on her, seemingly for good. And so, the spider was left, alone, to drown in her own tears ...

38

You'll Never Walk Alone

Whistling winds blew past the thin glass Eric stood behind, high in the sky, as he looked out, contemplating life.

"Still having the dreams?" Tamara asked.

Eric closed his eyes, seeing only emptiness beneath his lids. "No. Not anymore."

"Hmm ... when did they stop? Six months ago? After Morsley?" she asked, seated on her comfortable throne behind her authoritative desk.

"Yes," Eric said. "You knew they would."

"I suspected they would. None of us ever truly knows anything, Eric. We guess and hope for the best. Even me. I don't pretend to know everything." She shook her head.

"True," he replied, still gazing out on the city. "I said I would get them all out," he whispered in shame.

"Get who out of where?"

"All of them, I promised, and I failed them," Eric said.

"You had the best intentions—you didn't fail. You only fail if you don't try. So, why the sudden urge to speak to me now?" Tamara pondered, leaning back, examining him closely. "What have you been up to all these months, Eric?"

"Thinking and revaluating," he answered, locking his fingers together behind his back.

"Have you heard about the reported cult sightings being spotted at the ruins of Morsley over the past few months? Seems like your little adventure may have inspired more than a few freaks."

"Yeah, I've heard," Eric responded. "People are doomed to never learn from their mistakes, it would seem."

"So, I believe. I suppose it's just part of their charm ... your charm."

Eric gave Tamara a harsh look.

"Have you spoken to Michelle?" she asked.

"Yes. I have," he replied.

Her eyes widened in surprise at his response. "And?" she pressed.

"I'm not in the mood to talk about ... about her."

"A lie with a heart of truth is a powerful thing." She said, then asked: "So, why have you come?"

Eric turned to face her, his hands still laced behind his back. "For your opinion."

"On ...? She stood and smoothed the creases from her black designer pantsuit.

His voice cracked with uncertainty. "What should I do? Where should I go next?" he murmured, stepping closer to her, as if she were his mother.

"I expect there's more to the Morsley story than the news is revealing. More than you're revealing. So, tell me, and we'll go from there."

"A witch, a goddess of sorts, relayed a prophecy." He hesitated, his brain freezing like a computer buffering. "It's a little hazy. Like a dream." A hypnotic look came into his eyes at the recollection. "But I do remember being told that dark days were coming, that the flames of hell would cleanse this world."

Tamara gazed down, fiddling with her glittery, clear gemstone clutched close to her chest. "The firebird?"

"Yes," he confirmed. "But there was one other thing. I was told that I had a destiny, one that fate would guide me to. That one day I would have to make a choice."

"What kind of choice?"

"I don't know, but whatever it is, it can't be good." Eric folded his arms, feeling a shiver drift down the nape of his neck.

Tamara hummed. "What will you do now?" she asked.

"Move forward," Eric stated.

"Where to?"

"I don't know, Tammy. Isn't that the point of life?" His brows came together.

She paused in thought for a moment. "Follow your instincts."

"That's what ... *it* told me to do too," Eric said, remembering.

Tamara clasped his hands in hers. "Then do it."

"I'll certainly try."

"Hmm ... you know if you need my help, Eric, I am here."

"Thank you," he lifted a smile at her.

"You're more than welcome." Tamara stroked his cheek with her fingers, as if he were her pet. "And if you ever want to go on an adventure, give me a call," she said with a wink.

"I travel alone now. It's best that way."

"Suit yourself." Tamara brushed off the comment. "I do hope the gift I gave you helped you at Morsley?"

"The amulet? Yes and no." He blinked, recalling the pain it brought along with the warnings and protection it offered him. "Is this the part where you try to convince me to join your coven?"

"No. Not anymore," she said with a sad smile. "You will always be linked to us, but you have your own path to follow now. That much is clear."

Eric nodded in agreement. "Still a know-it-all, aren't you?" He nudged her playfully.

"Always." She escorted him out, linking her arm through his. "So, Eric Thompson, tell me: where are your instincts telling you to go right now?"

Eric's eyes twinkled at the question. "Well, I've thought about it a lot, and as of right now, I only know I need to do one thing before I can move on."

"And what's that?"

"Get closure."

They locked on to each other in a warm embrace. They didn't let go for some time. Her sharp, diamond amulet dug into his chest. "Thank you, Tamara," he said, finally releasing her.

"One thing before you go, Eric," Tamara called out as he moved toward the door.

He turned. "Yes?"

Her black silhouette stood proudly. "Remember ... there is always another way." Her words echoed through Eric, piercing him like a knife. Recalling the message, rooted deep in his subconscious, but not remembering where he had heard the words before. He left without parting words.

39

Goodnight

Sometime Later ...

S pring arrived. The sun was setting through the newly green trees. The grass grew tall and wild, and flowers were blooming. Life crept back to the land of Morsley. The burnt-down ruin was now blooming with nature. What was once hell's waiting room saw a fresh start.

Eric's taxi drove him to the wreckage of Morsley. As he stepped out, a sensation hit, a kind of freedom. The burnt remnants of the house were scorched and untouched. Marble gravestones had been set beside the house in memory of all who had died that horrific night. Actual poppies grew around Poppy's memorial. Eric thought their smell would perhaps help ease her soul to a blissful, eternal sleep. He tried to block the sight of them away with his batting eyelids as best he could, shame swelling inside him.

He stopped as he saw a familiar face. The black cat sat on the stump of a tree, gazing at Eric. The feline bowed her head to Eric, who mirrored the gesture. They shared the briefest of moments before the animal jumped off and disappeared into the forest.

Eric walked toward the burnt porch and entered through what remained of the door. He wondered if anything would be left of the house, whether the village officials would have condemned the ruins and tore it all down but, clearly, they still didn't want to touch the haunted debris or disturb the soil, not even now. The mansion still creaked and moaned, but not in a bloodthirsty, menacing way as it did before. Eric saw the shattered chandelier that used to hang in the centre of the landing at the bottom of the stairs. The scorched walls had been sprayed with satanic messages and symbols in a foul, metallic red paint. To his left was the lounge and the remnants of the couch that Poppy had died on, reminding him again of his failures. A feeling of self-loathing seeped back inside him. He tensed his fists and whispered, "Let it go, Eric. Let it go."

He unclenched his muscles, and his tension eased. The effect Morsley had over him had waned, but only a little. Upon inspection of the stairs, he found the melted Rosie doll still guarding the house, now positioned on the bottom step. Always watching, always waiting. Eric smiled in thanks. He would have to take the next step. Looking behind him to see the taxi driver lighting up a cigarette, he knew he had time. Time to finally wash his hands of the stain that Morsley had left upon him.

Every step Eric took around each room of the house, he took with caution. Every room was hollow. Very little remained. Some floors were destroyed in places, the boards giving way underfoot to the rooms below, and Eric narrowly avoided falling through. Eric felt a great deal of sorrow at the pain that was soaked into the ground at Morsley. What was once a breeding ground for chaos, madness and death was now nothing but ashes. The house itself was a ghost, a pile of desolation. Although remnants of malevolence remained, most had been washed away. Cleansed. Eric felt it through his senses, knowing also that few would come back to this place for a very long time. If ever. Saving more lives than had already been taken in the process of his actions that night.

Some of the upstairs walls had also been stained with bright red graffiti messages: "666", "Evil Within", "Hell", "She lives". Foreboding scrawl of all kinds now coated the house. Eric still felt as if he kept catching glimpses of shadows, figures darting past his line of vision from the narrow walls. Not in a cruel way, more mischievous and curious. Eric swore he could hear a childish giggle coming from somewhere. He peered around, knowing he was in no danger.

Eric began his rickety ascent to the attic. Most of its floors had gaping holes. Looking out the window to the vast green woods, Eric felt a tingle down his nerves. There was something behind him, something with a knife; he spun round, hearing the slash of the blade in his mind. No vision came. It was just unsettled air, an echo, or a memory. *No rest for the wicked,* Eric thought. *Or the mad, it would seem.* Deep down, he knew evil could never be destroyed.

Eric caressed the ash-coated banister as he made his descent down the stairs, feeling nothing, no visions of the doctor hanging, nothing. He looked at his charcoal-tainted hand and smiled. At the door, he turned to take one last glance around the empty ruin. He smiled when he noticed Rosie had vanished.

"I understand now. I want you to know that," said Eric. "I understand why this had to happen. I had to come here to stop the suffering, the madness, the death. I had to come here to receive that message. I ... er, I don't remember it all, but I know when the time is right, it will come to me. I believe that. I believe this all had a purpose. That it always had to happen, and it's still happening right now. It's time to follow my path. This place made me change, evolve. I understand, and I'm sorry. If it was up to me no one would die or have to suffer the way this place has made you all suffer. But it's not up to me. If I had the choice, if anyone had the choice to decide who lived and who died, well that would make them a monster. It would make me a monster." Eric hesitated. "I just hope you have managed to find some kind of peace."

Eric kissed his hand and pressed it against the wall, smiling with relief as the weight of guilt lifted from his soul and shut the door one final time.

As he walked back to the taxi, a sudden gust of wind flapped his coat all around. Wind chimes called out. Eric turned back to the house, accepting the call. Nothing. Everything sat still, even the thick, black dust that armoured the surroundings.

As Eric sat in the back seat of the car, he felt an urge, an instinct to look back and up. Eric gazed up at the silhouette of a figure holding their palm up to the top left broken window of the house as if waving goodbye. Eric held his hand up, mirroring the gesture, knowing who the watcher was and happy to see her one last time.

"Everything has its time, and everything ends," he murmured, looking out to the setting sun, knowing her fire would protect both the living and dead of Morsley for eternity.

"So, did you find what you were looking for?" asked the taxi driver.

"You could say that."

The radio played the soothing notes of Doris Day's "Dream a Little Dream of Me." As the wheels rolled over on the soft ground and Eric left Morsley through the treacherous wild woods toward his destiny, he had a feeling that he was being watched.

THE HAUNTING AT MORSLEY MANOR

The inhabitants of the land gazed upon him through the trees as he left. They watched him as they had always watched everyone and always would. Watching and hoping the living would put aside their feelings of bitterness, envy, regret and hate and embrace all life had to offer—what the living take for granted every second of every day. The spirits wanted the living to realize and remember that even the most damaged and broken life was still a life worth living.

Epilogue

A Secret Admirer

Classical music echoed through an old attic on the dark outskirts of Decanten City. Mementos of victims were scattered all around, as the night sky trickled in through the window. A shadow loomed over a table, one with many newspaper articles. The centre displayed a photo of Michelle Snow being arrested for her crimes. The man smirked at her image, outlining it with a red pen, drawing a heart around it. A spider scurried over the newspaper. Two long fingers playfully followed the arachnid before pausing and smushing it into the fine print of the paper.

Reading the headline and admiring Michelle's beauty, this face of evil thought he had maybe, finally, found his twisted equal ...

Acknowledgements

I'd like to thank my publishers and wonderful editors: Tina Beier and Marthese French for seeing the book's haunting potential in the first place and helping me tell it in the best way possible.

And my agent, Erik McManus at Breakeven Books, for believing in me and my work.

I'd also like to thank Nat Mack for her amazing cover of the book! Thank you so much to Doaly, who allowed us to borrow his concept design for the cover, it is truly meant a lot to me.

I truly couldn't have written this book without these amazing people.

About the Author

George Morris De'Ath is a British author who writes thriller and horror books that explore the darker aspects of the human psyche. He is a London West End playwright, actor, and model, as well as a gin drinker. He lives in London where he allows his creative flare to shine. *The Haunting at Morsley Manor* is his third book. His next novel, thriller *Something on Your Mind* will be releasing Spring 2026.

Looking for more chills? Check out Rising Action's other horror stories on the next page!

And don't forget to follow us on our socials for cover reveals, giveaways, and announcements:
X: @RAPubCollective
Instagram: @risingactionpublishingco
TikTok: @risingactionpublishingco
Website: http://www.risingactionpublishingco.com

Anita Walsh, still reeling from her husband's sudden death, finds herself haunted not only by grief, but his Negative Image, a new phenomenon where the deceased prey on those they loved in life, turning intimate memories into nightmares. This spectral figure uses their shared past as a weapon, systematically dismantling her friendships, career, and self-worth. Desperate for escape, Anita plunges into a quest to sever the ghostly bonds that tie her to her tormentor.

As society grapples with the rising terror of NIs, a charismatic extremist proposes a radical solution to isolate the haunted from the unafflicted, gaining dangerous followers. Anita, alongside another victim of this spectral affliction, must navigate their personal hauntings and societal threats to prevent the breakdown of their community.

With its gripping narrative and eerie exploration of love and betrayal, Negative Images marks Rebecca Schier-Akamelu as a powerful new voice in horror. This novel delves deep into the psychological horrors of grief and the supernatural, making it a must-read for fans of horror and ghost stories alike.

In this haunting psychological horror, Willow's life has become a fever dream, her days lost in a twisted loop where time no longer flows as it should. Is she held captive by her husband Liam's iron rules—or by the insidious darkness of her own mind?

Her only connection to the world beyond her walls is a young girl named Sarah, whose unexpected visits to Willow's garden spark a glimmer of hope. But as cracks form in her carefully controlled existence, horrifying truths seep through, twisting the familiar into something sinister. The floral wallpaper peels back to reveal haunting messages carved into the walls, and the house itself pulses with malevolent life. When Sarah suddenly vanishes, Willow is forced to confront the dark shadows of her past and the horrors lurking within her fractured psyche. The question remains: is Willow truly a prisoner of her home, or of her own mind?

Some doors, once opened, can never be closed. And some truths are better left buried in the garden.

NAMELESS THINGS

ERNEST JENSEN

In the aftermath of a painful breakup, Mike and his friend Wade seek solace in the remote beauty of Devil's Cup State Park, Colorado. Their quest for peace is abruptly ended when a meteor strike causes a rock to fall, trapping them and a diverse group of campers within the ancient volcanic caldera. As they grapple with their new reality, a far more sinister challenge emerges from the depths of the earth.

The sanctuary they sought becomes a hunting ground as the group discovers the ground infested with lethal, flesh-piercing worms. The situation turns dire when they realize these predators are merely the heralds of something far more terrifying: the NAMELESS THINGS. With no way to call for help, survival hinges on their ability to outsmart the unseen terror lurking beneath their feet. As alliances form and fray under the weight of fear, Mike is propelled into a desperate bid for freedom. Facing treacherous terrain, dwindling supplies, and the psychological toll of their predicament, the campers must confront the true nature of the horror they face. In a thrilling fight for survival, Mike's journey to escape and reveal the nightmare within Devil's Cup becomes a testament to the human spirit's resilience against the unknown.

Something is wrong in Bunker, Illinois.

Nora Grace Moon thought her toughest challenge this semester would be managing her OCD, but when her deceased roommate turns up as a reanimated corpse, her world starts to collapse.

When her uncle sends her a cryptic message, Nora realizes it must be a call for help. She reaches out to fellow gamer Wesley for advice, a US Marshal with real-life skills for tactical survival, not just in-game. They venture out into a world that is growing more and more deadly by the moment—not only are the undead spreading, but other humans are taking advantage of the societal breakdown. And unknown to Nora and Wesley, they have been targeted by an ancient archeological society who will stop at nothing until they have what Nora has: an artifact that will unleash a new world order of the undead.

IRL is a paranormal thriller about leaving the online world and dealing with things "In Real Life."